AIR

THE ELEMENTALS BOOK TWO

L.B. GILBERT

PUBLISHED BY: L.B. Gilbert
Copyright © 2016, L.B. Gilbert
http://www.elementalauthor.com/
ISBN: 978-1-942336-14-3

First Edition.
All rights reserved.

❀ Created with Vellum

CREDITS

Cover Design: Rebecca Hamilton,
   http://qualitybookworks.wordpress.com/

Logo Design: Juan Fernando Garcia,
   http://www.elblackbat.com/

Editor: Cynthia Shepp
   http://www.cynthiashepp.com/

Readers: Thank you to all of my readers, especially Priti Patel and Jennifer Bundesen Bergans for their feedback and editorial comments.

TITLES BY L.B. GILBERT

Discordia, A Free Elementals Prequel Short,
Available Now
Fire: The Elementals Book One
Available Now
Air: The Elementals Book Two
Available Now
Water: The Elementals Book Three
Available Now
Earth: The Elementals Book Four
Available April 2020

Kin Selection, Shifter's Claim, Book One
Available now
Eat You Up, A Shifter's Claim, Book Two
Available now
Tooth and Nail, A Shifter's Claim, Book Three
Coming Soon

Forsaken, A Cursed Angel Novel
Available now

Writing As Lucy Leroux

Making Her His, A Singular Obsession, Book One
Available Now
Confiscating Charlie, A Free Singular Obsession Novelette
Book 1.5
Available Now
Calen's Captive, A Singular Obsession, Book Two
Available Now
Stolen Angel, A Singular Obsession, Book Three
Available Now
The Roman's Woman, A Singular Obsession,
Book Four
Available Now
Save Me, A Singular Obsession Novella, Book 4.5
Coming Soon
Take Me, A Singular Obsession Prequel Novella
Available Now
Trick's Trap, A Singular Obsession,
Book Five
Available Now
Peyton's Price, A Singular Obsession,
Book Six
Available Now

Codename Romeo, Rogues and Rescuers, Book One
Available Now
The Mercenary Next Door, Rogues and Rescuers, Book Two
Coming Soon

The Hex, A Free Spellbound Regency Short
Available Now
Cursed, A Spellbound Regency Novel

Available Now
Black Widow, A Spellbound Regency Novel, Book Two
Available Now
Haunted, A Spellbound Regency Novel, Book Three
Coming Soon

PROLOGUE

TWO MONTHS AGO

L ogan hummed softly, trying to distract herself from the unpleasant task she had to perform tonight. Her voice blended with the winds as they whipped around her on the way to the Burgess estate.

A few days ago, she had left her sister Diana with the intention of taking care of this particular errand right away. But the Burgess family hadn't gathered with the sitting patriarch, Gerald, until now. And he, most of all, needed to hear what she had to say. Hillard too, but mostly Gerald.

She let the wind carry her to the Georgian mansion the Burgess clan called home in the English countryside near Somerset. Normally, the trip would have taken hours, but up here in the currents, it was a matter of minutes. She paused when she sighted the house, counting the number of cars outside. Judging from the crowded state of the drive, both Gerald and Hillard were inside. The winds confirmed her hunch, so she looked around for an opening. Spotting an unlit chimney, she plunged inside.

Logan materialized on top of a formal dining room table laden with crystal and fine china. Her high-heeled boots rested on a silky-looking tablecloth.

Glad I opted for leather pants instead of that miniskirt I was going to wear.

Pants had been the better choice, considering how many pairs of eyes were on her now. Each expression ranged from shock to startled discontent. One young man sat with a spoon frozen halfway to his mouth.

They were only on the soup course, which was good. It would have been far less intimidating if she'd materialized over a roast or leg of lamb.

"Hello, Gerald," Logan said, addressing the austere, grey-haired man at the head of the table.

Gerald Burgess slowly lowered his spoon. He met her eyes with a steadfast composure she reluctantly found impressive. As far as she knew, he'd never met any of her kind before, but his steady grey eyes didn't betray a hint of surprise. He didn't know why she was here, but as the head of one of the seven families, Gerald had seen a lot in his day. Enough that he was able to school the shock he must have felt at having a six-course meal interrupted by an Elemental.

"Hello," he said in a cultured British accent. He leaned back in his chair. "To what do I owe this pleasure?"

The other family members didn't move. Diana was right about the head of the clan. He had seen to their education. They knew when they were outmatched.

"I've come about your granddaughter," Logan said.

She almost felt bad about it. Unlike some of the other family heads, Gerald cared about all of his grandchildren and great-grand-children, even the illegitimate ones. Why Hillard hadn't chosen to inform his father about the product of his affair was a mystery. But it wasn't her problem.

The youngest girl at the table made a whimpering, choking sound when Gerald turned to her with a surprised expression.

"Not *that* granddaughter. And it's not the one in the States either. You haven't met this one. And you never will. Her name was Sage. She became...a problem. One you don't have anymore."

Gerald swallowed. His expression grew cold and remote. Power crackled in the air, surging forward in her direction, but Logan chose not to take offense. The old man was agitated, and she hadn't pulled the punch.

"I see. And was it *necessary* to rid me of this problem?"

"She broke the covenant and killed a child. She was going to take the life of a second one when she was stopped." Logan's voice was implacable, her usual exuberance subdued—buried under the coldness of the Air Elemental.

There was a smattering of gasps as a little shockwave swept over the small group. Logan studied the expressions on the ring of faces surrounding her. Diana's guess was right. One of those shocked expressions was fake. But Gerald's was genuine. He lifted a weathered hand to his head. The tremor that ran through it was almost imperceptible.

"It's not our fault! Whatever this child did, we can't be held responsible," Hillard shouted.

Logan turned to him. Hillard's thin aristocratic face was contorted in indignation and fear.

"That's where you're wrong. *Your* child was *your* responsibility. You knew that. You knew, and you let her make her own way in the world without you. Well, she did. Left quite an impression too."

All heads turned to Hillard. Gerald shot him a dark look filled with disgust. Though this situation was news to him, Logan guessed this wasn't the first time his son had been a disappointment. She turned to the woman seated next to him. Hillard's wife was sitting there with a fixed, frozen expression. Logan almost understood why she had done it. *Almost...*

Logan knelt down in front of her. *Stephanie*, the wind whispered.

Yes, that was the name Diana had mentioned. "You know the consequences of what you've done, Stephanie. I'm here to render judgment."

"What is going on here? What has she done? It's Hillard who should be punished," Gerald said in surprise.

Hillard sputtered incoherently in his own defense, but Logan ignored him and answered Gerald.

"He will be. But so will she," Logan answered. "Stephanie knew about her husband's mistress and the child. She fed Sage secrets. Things that should only be passed down to those worthy of keeping them. Both Hillard and Stephanie broke the covenant, one through neglect, and the other for revenge. I'm here to strip them of their magic. By rights, Hillard's entire line should be treated to the same, but I'm willing to be lenient in this case."

Hillard found his voice. "You call that lenient? I'm to be punished because I didn't know I had another child?"

His voice didn't fit what she knew of him. It was rich and deep, the voice of a politician—one meant to be a great statesman.

"Don't bother. I know you're lying," Logan said. "It's useless to even try. It was your duty to take *all* of your children in hand. Even those whose existence you wanted to bury. You'll be stripped of your magic, but I'm leaving your line intact. Your other children get to keep their talent, so count your blessings. It's more than you deserve."

Logan turned to Stephanie. The elegant blonde met her eyes and said nothing. But apparently, Gerald was fond of his daughter-in-law.

"Stephanie wouldn't have done what you're accusing her of," he protested. "She knows better."

Logan sighed. "That's sort of the point. She did know better. But her anger over her husband's affair got the best of her."

She knelt on the table. "Stephanie, give me your hand."

Stephanie adjusted the sleeve of her fine cashmere sweater and rose gracefully to her feet. She put a fine-boned manicured hand in Logan's. "My children are innocent in this. They didn't know about their sister."

This one definitely has class. It was a pity she'd let her rage and disappointment in her husband overcome her good sense.

"I know," Logan said in a low voice as Stephanie's son and daughter exchanged a quick, startled look.

Reaching deep, she called the wind and silently invoked the Mother's name in the language known only to her kind. Other ancient words followed. The wind picked up as if someone had opened a window during a storm. It passed over Stephanie and

Hillard in a sweeping rush. In her mind's eye, she could see the undefinable little something she associated with magical talent disappearing from their auras like sand being blown off a hill.

It was over quickly.

"You can't hold me responsible for the actions of a child I didn't know was mine!" Hillard shouted, unaware Logan had already finished carrying out his sentence.

She was tempted not to answer him. She had met his type before. Men like him, born into privilege and power, expected the world to bend around them. Most of the time, it did—at least in the human world. But among Supernaturals, when push came to shove, a legacy would only get one so far. A person had to have intelligence and talent, a lot of it, to rise to the top. And Hillard was not Gerald.

"But I do hold you responsible," Logan answered. "And so does the Mother, or I wouldn't be here. There are rules to this world, and a price to pay for the ability to use magic," she added, irritated by his refusal to accept responsibility.

"I didn't know about her," he hissed.

The winds whipped around him, calling him a liar.

"Don't you know better than to try to deceive me?" Logan asked, raising an ebony eyebrow.

She decided he didn't when Hillard drew himself up for a moment before launching himself at her. He hit the wall with a resounding crash, slumping to the floor in a graceless slide. No one seemed surprised but him, although most of the others flinched at the noise.

Hillard groaned loudly, but he stayed prone on the floor as she hopped off the table, studying Stephanie carefully. The woman hadn't moved in all this time. She looked like a statue, a brittle one that might fall apart in a strong breeze.

Logan sympathized, but she remembered what the winds had told her. Stephanie watched Sage for a while. Long enough to learn that the young witch was well on her way in a downward slide. Faced with the concrete proof of her husband's infidelity—again—she decided to help Sage along to the black. Stephanie had fed her husband's bastard spells and information—dangerous things an inexperienced witch shouldn't have had access to.

The pain and shock on the faces of Stephanie's children was hard to see. But it was part of the job. She turned away to face the fireplace that had been her entrance.

Above it was a weapon she didn't recognize. It was an odd, silver-black matte color. It had a hilt like a sword that curved up into a wicked curved blade with three sharp points—except the points met on the interior of the curve. The exterior looked dull.

Not a very effective weapon...but, like the thing that had been used to stab her sister Diana, it wasn't of this earth.

Jesus, how many extraterrestrial weapons were lying around waiting to be discovered? Where exactly did the Burgess family come from?

Logan frowned. The family's origins were not her mystery to solve. She and her sisters had enough to deal with right now.

The young woman at the table stirred. "It no longer responds to any family member," she said in a small voice.

Logan narrowed her eyes. The girl flinched and looked down. *Truth*, the wind whispered. *And lie.*

She hesitated, tempted to filch the thing and make a break for it. But the covenant was clear on these matters. Practitioners got to keep their objects of power and their tomes of magic so long as they didn't use them to harm others.

She tore her gaze away from the piece and turned to give Gerald a nod of acknowledgment. It was to his credit that he was able to give her one back, although his gaze was still on his daughter-in-law. Logan dematerialized and whipped out of the room.

In the air currents, her conscious mind processed what she'd done. She had never stripped anyone of their magic before. It was why Gia had agreed that she should do it, so she could gain firsthand experience. They hadn't done a stripping for a long time. But that wasn't because it wasn't deserved in a lot of cases.

It had been a lot easier than she thought. Physically, anyway. The act itself was simple. But the reality of it had been damn depressing.

At least, it had been in Stephanie's case. She didn't feel that bad about Hillard. The winds had some nasty things to say about him.

Logan coasted the currents a few minutes longer before deciding to hit a club. Maybe she would find a little company.

There was that young actor she'd been hanging out with. Michel had asked her to meet him tonight. Of course, he did that every night. But after the scene at the mansion, she was suddenly up for companionship. Michel was always ready to drop everything when she called. And Logan was pretty sure he could distract her from tonight's unpleasantness. A little mindless dancing with a cute guy would do wonders. Maybe more...

She was still trying to decide whether to allow Michel to take her to bed. And unlike the other offers she'd gotten lately, she was giving this one serious thought. The actor was good looking, amusing, and basically harmless. Most importantly, her heart was not involved, which was exactly what she was looking for in a man right now.

Logan didn't need any emotional entanglements. Her position as the junior elemental was still relatively new, and it required her full attention. However, there was no rule that said she couldn't have a fling. In fact, the actual rules were few and far between. She just wasn't sure Michel was the right man to fling with.

Well, staying away from him wasn't the way to figure it out. Besides, he was a good kisser and she wanted to dance.

Much later, when Logan had abandoned herself to the beat while dancing with her actor, she became aware of a new sensation. It was the feeling of being watched.

Whipping her head around, she scanned the other dancers. But no one paid her any attention—no more than usual. She shook off the feeling when Michel wrapped his arms around her, pulling her in closer.

1

The heavy bass of the music vibrated through Connell's body as he made his way through the shifting crowd. Instinct told him his prey was here, though he hadn't laid eyes on her yet.

He'd wasted the better part of a month hunting her in the expected places—the Underlife clubs of the U.S. and Europe. But there had been no sign there. He would have known if she'd been in disguise, something she was fond of doing when she moved among the Supernaturals.

He'd done his homework when it came to the Air Elemental. *Know thy enemy* had been an internal mantra since this whole mess had started.

The crowd shifted and swayed in time to the music in the dark club. He was pretty surprised that she chose to spend time in places like this, among so many humans. The rich and spoiled elite of the human world were here to drink, dance, and do drugs before indulging in whatever sexual thrills their kind could afford. In his experience, those weren't much.

He dismissed a beautiful girl who sidled up to him invitingly with a dark glance. She took one look at his forbidding features, the cold set of his lips and eyes, and wisely retreated.

His enhanced hearing and sense of smell, still blessedly intact, were threatening to shut down against the onslaught of music combined with the scent of so many sweaty people. Under normal circumstances, he would have avoided this place like the plague, but where his quarry went, he followed.

He threaded through the dancers on instinct, letting his senses guide him to the girl who had almost destroyed him.

A tingling at the base of his spine guided him to the left of the bar. From there, he could get a clear view of the balcony that ran along three sides of the room. His skittering senses told him she was there. He didn't know what she looked like, only that she appeared quite young. But that was the case for all of her kind. They took up the Mother's mantle while in their teens or twenties, and then they stopped aging.

He dismissed one woman after another until his eyes locked onto a figure moving high above. A thrill of recognition coursed through him, as well as surprise.

She's tiny, he thought, taken aback.

He'd been expecting someone more physically imposing. But the Asian girl dancing in the corner of the catwalk was petite, barely five feet tall. And she was completely unaware of his intense scrutiny.

Grateful she couldn't sense the danger she was in, he leaned against the wall, intent on his prey. The Elemental was wearing dark pants and a red corset tank with a black design on it.

He watched her, transfixed, aware with some disgust that he was getting hard. His hatred was still a fire in his blood, but some of that warmth was swiftly being channeled in another direction. It made him angry, mostly with himself, but his enemy wasn't what he'd expected.

Shifting uncomfortably, he continued to stare, hyperaware there was something wrong with him.

The problem was the way she moved. He'd never seen anything quite like it. She'd completely given herself over to the music, her fluid, rhythmic movements abandoned and free. She moved like the element she was supposed to embody—like wind whipping over a field of wheat.

He hadn't realized she would be so...sensual. She was keeping perfect time with the primal beat of the music. For a second, he forgot himself and pictured taking a fistful of her sleek, black hair, using it to force her mouth toward him.

For fuck's sake. He couldn't even see her features clearly, and he was struggling for control.

He recovered more slowly than he liked, but he was able to push the erotic image away. He had a plan and couldn't afford to be distracted by inconvenient lust. The creature might be graceful, but she was also dangerous and possibly corrupt.

The music changed, pausing between tracks. The momentary reprieve made him aware of how long he'd been staring at the sprite. By rights, he should be trying to rip out her throat. Reminding himself of his mission, he started up the stairs to the balcony with large, purposeful strides, his tunnel vision trained on his target. He skirted the shifting dancers, pushing them carefully out of his way as he went.

His control was straining, the instincts of the wolf still alive inside him, but he didn't want to alert his prey to the danger. Not until it was too late for her to escape. And now that he'd finally found her, there was no way she could get away from him. *Not again.*

The crowd was thinner on the balcony, but there were still enough people to block his view of the Elemental as he prowled closer. He wanted to push them away and leap on the girl. Tamping down his impatience, he forced himself to move with normal human speed. In a few moments, he would have her.

He spared a second's thought for how he would get her out of there, but he dismissed it just as quickly. His black-ops training had already helped him spot three viable exits where he could carry an unconscious woman out without too many prying eyes. It would be a simple matter to convince anyone who tried to stop him that his woman had simply had too much to drink. The fact that he was six-foot-five and built like a brick wall would be enough to discourage anyone who thought to argue with him.

With another step, he reached the darkened corner where the sprite was dancing. A light breeze ruffled his hair. The platform was empty. He swore viciously, spinning around. He couldn't see her anymore. With a growl of frustration, he looked up and realized there were skylights on the distant ceiling. And one was open.

LOGAN LET the weird sense of being watched fade away as she took to the air. Of course someone had been watching her. The club had been full, and people were always checking each other out.

It had felt a little different tonight, though. For a split second, she felt hunted, which was ridiculous. No one hunted an Elemental unless they had a death wish. She'd scanned for threats but found none. Shaking off her uncertainty, Logan paused to savor the night air.

She was high above the ground, her physical form gone. Logan enjoyed the sense of weightlessness that came with drifting high above the earth. Not all her predecessors had enjoyed this the way she did. A few had disliked the sensation of being formless so much that they chose not to travel in the winds unless they had to. But she had loved it from day one. It was one of the reasons she'd been able to take to the air almost as soon as she'd inherited her power.

Unlike Diana and Gia, Logan hadn't had Elemental abilities from birth. Her gifts had been run of the mill...for her family. Then she had been given dominion over Air at seventeen—old enough to have accepted the fact she was not going to be an Elemental like her great-grandmother and other distant ancestors.

The Mother had turned to her after all, and everything had changed.

Her life had altered dramatically over the past few years. Logan no longer sat and read about the great deeds of Elementals. Now she was living the life she had always dreamed of. She worked and played hard, trying to make the most of each new experience. She had to. At any moment, the Mother might change Her mind and choose someone else.

Gia assured her it wasn't likely, but Logan still felt like she was on probation. After all, it had only been a little over a year since she was allowed to work solo. She was devoted to her job. She'd taken a break for a few hours to decompress, and she was good now.

It was time to get back to work.

2

TWO WEEKS LATER

"I'm fine," Logan repeated for the fourteenth time. And it had been fourteen times. She was counting.

"You need to be more careful," Serin said. "You were seriously hurt, and it would have been far worse if you'd not taken out those witches beforehand. They might have killed you."

Her sisters, Serin and Gia, were communing with their elements, water and earth. When they did, their voices carried to her along the aether, the fifth element, which bound all magic to the world. They sounded different from the spirits Logan had heard since she was a child. Though those voices could be annoyingly loud at times, they didn't resonate with the vibrancy of magic and life she associated with the living. And unlike those others, her sisters never lied to her...

As the Air Elemental, Logan technically communed with her element at all times. She had to breathe after all. And she was usually grateful she could keep in touch with her sisters so easily, but not when one of them wanted to lecture her.

"I wouldn't go that far," Gia said eventually, coming to her defense. "They weren't a match for our Logan. Even crippled, she's a force to be reckoned with. Not that I don't agree about being more careful. But I have faith you can handle most anything anyone throws at you, including those newbie grey witches. But a little discretion in whipping objects heavier than yourself might be in order."

Logan sighed, a long, drawn-out sound of suffering. She'd been getting the riot act from all three of her sisters since she'd returned from Quebec. Even Diana had lectured her on keeping things simple when she'd contacted her yesterday.

Logan had been hurt while giving some witches a much-needed set down. The witches had dabbled a little too close to the dark, enough to shift the balance in their vicinity. They hadn't done anything worth stripping them over, and they weren't black yet. Instead, the girls referred to them as grey. As a group, the Elementals had decided to send a message before the witches did something that would shift them all the way to the black.

And Logan had delivered it with style, as she always did.

But it was her flair for drama that had gotten her in trouble. She had been showing off—although that wasn't something her sisters frowned on. Making a lasting impression was a big part of her job. In this case, she had decided to huff and puff to blow the witches' house down.

Unfortunately, it had been more than a dark shack in the woods belonging to some old crone. The substantial log cabin had been difficult to destroy, and Logan had whipped a heavy log a little too carelessly. It had hit another log embedded in the dirt, causing it to rebound on her. It struck her back with considerable force.

The log would have broken her spine if she'd been human. As it was, she had a couple of cracked ribs. Fortunately, the witches were rolling around the ground, too busy groaning and praying for death to notice what she now called "the little mishap". Despite her injury, she'd managed to dematerialize and make her way out of there.

"The little mishap" was why she was currently rusticating in Provence, enjoying the mistral's soothing touch in the south of France. They had a cozy safe house there, one passed down from earlier generations of their kind. The Air Elementals had always loved it there, especially when the wind blew so hard it shrieked.

"I'm almost as good as new," Logan assured them. "And I've

learned my lesson. No more playing the big bad wolf without knowing where each log is going to land."

"How about no more whipping around huge logs instead?" Serin persisted.

"Well, how about a compromise? No more than one log at a time anymore," Logan said, feeling rather generous.

She loved the Water Elemental, despite the older woman's need to mother her to death.

Serin sighed. "I'll take what I can get."

"That's the spirit." Gia laughed before her voice became serious. "Has anyone heard from Diana lately?"

Logan smiled. Gia was still suspicious of Alec Broussard, Diana's new mate. It *was* an unusual choice for a Fire Elemental. Vampires were the most flammable of all the Supernaturals, with the possible exception of very old wood nymphs. But Logan had met the man in person and thought he was worthy. Alec was certainly less annoying than Serin's pompous and conceited mate, Jordan.

But comparing the two was not fair. Serin and Jordan had been together since before Logan was born. Just because she'd never liked him didn't mean he was a bad guy. He was simply irritating to be around.

"I heard from her yesterday," Logan replied. "She and Alec are in Adelaide, wrapping up a case. They're good. They're heading to the North Coast afterward. Alec wants to take Diana to dive the Great Barrier Reef for a little vacay. And before you ask, she already lectured me too."

"Well, that's good. About the vacation, I mean. She doesn't take enough downtime," Gia said.

The Earth Elemental sounded upset, but Logan suspected it was more complicated than that. Gia was happy for her sister; they all were. She just didn't approve of her choice. Gia had issues with vampires, but they seemed small compared to the giant chip Diana used to have on her shoulder before she met Alec.

Once upon a time, there wasn't a species Diana had detested more than vampires. But now, she was practically married to one.

"Yes, well, she has been a little quiet," Serin added, but her voice held no judgement.

"She and Alec are still in the honeymoon phase," Logan explained. "And Di deserves a break. She's always worked too hard."

Before Alec came along, they had all taken turns trying to talk Diana into relaxing more. Unlike the rest of them, Diana had no family—no obligations to stop and check in with anyone. Until she met her vampire, Diana had avoided any relationships outside of their small circle. As a result, she had never learned to rest in between missions. She went from town to town, doing her job and not much else. Alec had forced Diana to slow down and learn to enjoy herself a little. They were probably sexing it up and down all over the Australian continent right around now.

Logan sighed, a little envious.

"No one is disputing that the relationship has been good for Diana. She deserves to be happy. And I am glad she has someone... supportive," Serin said, a very noticeable edge in her voice.

Was there trouble in paradise? *Maybe she'll break up with Jordan*, Logan thought gleefully.

For half a minute, she let her hope rise before the guilt set in. After, she started hoping whatever was bothering her sister wasn't related to her mate. Serin loved the man, and on paper, there was nothing wrong with him. He was simply a bit selfish. The biggest problem was that he seemed to make Serin's job harder instead of easier, like Alec did for Diana.

"In any case, I'm glad she's happy," Serin continued without acknowledging her lapse. "No doubt she'll check in more often once she and Alec settle into a routine."

Of the four of them, Serin was the most concerned with appearances. She wouldn't want to discuss anything wrong with her personal relationship with her sisters until the issue had been resolved. Serin was tight-lipped about family issues too.

That last part was understandable. If Logan had been saddled with Serin's parents, she'd spend a heck of a lot more time whining.

"I'm sure that's true," Gia said carefully.

Gia had obviously also heard the unusual note of frustration in Serin's voice, but she'd known the Water Elemental for almost a century, long enough to know not to bring it up.

"It is true," Serin continued in a determinedly upbeat tone. "I have to go. I'm meeting Jordan for dinner before heading out to Cancun again. Not a cartel this time. A shifter is acting up. Feel better, Logan. Don't move too far from the mistral until you feel like your old self."

"I don't intend to," Logan assured her. "I'm sitting on my favorite rock. The wind really picked up today. It's great."

"The wind always picks up wherever you are," Serin said with genuine humor this time before saying goodbye.

"Rest up and be more careful next time, sweetie," Gia said.

"I'll be fine. Practically one hundred percent now. Already back in dance form," Logan said, opening her eyes to check how long she had till darkness fell.

She was basking in the sun on a windswept hill close to their safe house. The two-story dwelling was nestled between some trees at the bottom of the hill.

"All right," Gia said. "Try not to break anything else. Like your bones or anyone else's unless it's absolutely necessary."

"I did not break any of my bones. I only cracked 'em a bit," Logan said, knowing better than to promise not to break anyone else's bones, despite her forced vacation.

You just never knew.

3

It was dark by the time Logan finished prepping her dinner. It was a quiche in homage to her current location. She couldn't cook much, certainly not any of the elaborate Chinese meals her aunt had tried to teach her to make. Cooking wasn't a high priority, unlike her training and missions.

She reminded herself to make time to go see her family before she went back out again. Hope, her mom, lived in San Diego with her sister. Aunt Mai was almost ten years older than her sibling, but she was every bit as youthful and energetic. Both women had emigrated to the U.S. in their teens with their globetrotting parents, who had lived all over Europe. The Air Elemental was the only one in the current generation born in the U.S., although Diana had ended up there after her mom died.

Logan had lost a parent too. Her dad had been killed shortly after her seventh birthday, but between Hope and Mai, she had a rich, supportive family life. She was close to her mom and aunt. And even though they hadn't dreamed she would inherit, they'd taught her about her legacy as soon as she could walk.

Though Mai and Hope were gifted, neither had demonstrated Elemental-level talent. But they knew their place in history and what they owed to future generations. They had told her about the Elementals because it was a part of who they were—the legend in their blood.

Unlike Diana, Logan had grown up with full awareness of her lineage—her ancient forebears Feng-Po-Po, the Goddess of the Winds, and Xihe Li, the legendary Fire Elemental.

Her mother and aunt had spoken about those illustrious ancestors as if they were close relatives who lived down the block. The stories were passed down her maternal family line the same way her mother's jade combs had been. As a result, she'd grown up with knowledge of the Elementals as part of her reality. Nevertheless, it had come as a shock when she had inherited in her teens.

Recalling those first heady days playing with her new abilities brought a smile to her face. Gia had called her a prodigy. And she *had* been a natural, able to take to the winds within the first few weeks. It was a skill that took months or years to master, even among those who had been born with their abilities.

She still had a lot to learn, but things were going well. Her sisters were pleased with her progress. Logan, however, couldn't wait to be completely healed so she could get back out there. Downtime was great, but work was better. She loved her job.

Very hungry now, she threw her quiche in the oven, and then turned the music up loud.

CONNELL STOOD outside the two-story house, just beyond the lit windows. He was shrouded in darkness.

The devil take it.

She was dancing again. He stifled a groan. This was getting ridiculous. He'd been tracking the Air Elemental for more than two months. He'd started in England after hearing about what happened at the Burgess estate. Word had come almost immediately about the stripping of the Burgess heir.

Normally, the seven families would hush up that kind of disgrace, but a retainer had spread the story. For some reason, the sitting patriarch hadn't done anything to squelch it.

That was how Connell had known whom to search for. He didn't care that her actions might have been justified in the Burgess case. If the rumors were true, those damn witches had done something terrible to deserve being stripped of their power. But he didn't know what it was, and he didn't care. All he knew was that *he* hadn't done a damn thing wrong, and he'd still been targeted. It didn't make any sense. But that didn't matter anymore. He wouldn't leave until the Elemental restored him.

After he had found her twice in London clubs, *found and lost her*, he had tracked the Elemental through Italy, Rome, and then a small town outside of Milan. After that, it had been Canada, where he'd arrived too late. He'd missed her by only a few minutes, but she'd left a path of destruction in her wake. Not to mention some roided-out male witches, groaning and moaning like little bitches on a muddy field outside of Quebec.

His admiration had kicked up several notches after that, but he didn't let it stop him from pursuing his goal. The only time he'd come remotely close to catching her was when she stopped to dance the night away at some club. She'd given him the slip the second time when a bunch of groupies had rushed the pretty boy actor she'd been with. They had disappeared, ushered out by the bodyguards the guy employed.

It had pissed him off more than words could say, seeing her waltz off with that douchebag. It had pissed him off even more that he'd spent all that time afterward tracking the stupid actor, expecting the Elemental to appear again, only to be disappointed.

Perhaps it had been a blessing he hadn't found her right away. Connell wasn't reacting the way he should when dealing with an enemy. To his complete disgust, he was as hard now as he had been in that club.

Inside, the Elemental changed rooms. He shifted to another window to follow her. When he caught sight of her again, he wanted to groan aloud. She was dancing on a table now, those graceful, fluid movements enough to drive any man mad.

Connell closed his eyes and willed his arousal away. He was successful, but it took him longer than he cared to admit. When he looked again, the Elemental wasn't in sight anymore. Sniffing the air, he decided she was still in the house. There wasn't a scent outside except his own.

He went to the door on silent feet. Christ Almighty, she hadn't even bothered to lock it. Anybody could walk right inside.

Suppressing a sigh, Connell started to open the door. It rebounded on him with enough force to knock him backward. He hit the ground hard, his head snapping back and bouncing on the ground twice before he could blink.

The Elemental was on him, her small form crouching on his chest, an arm raised above him, ready to pound him with a tiny fist.

"Who are you?" she hissed before her little nose wrinkled and her expression became confused. "And what's wrong with you?

4

"You're what's wrong with me, you crazy bitch!" Connell growled, hyper aware of how damn cute his mortal enemy was.

She was in a word—*adorable*. Finally up close to her, he could see all the details he had missed before. She was definitely Asian, but mixed, a little over five feet tall.

Despite her diminutive size, she was perfectly proportioned. She had creamy skin that looked smoother than silk. Her eyes were the color of honey. As he'd thought in the club, her hair was black, but it had a streak of blue. It was longer too. The gossamer strands were an asymmetrical curtain that fell below her shoulders.

He'd never been attracted to petite women before, preferring ones he could stand next to without feeling monstrous.

Ironic, that.

However, this woman could probably drive a fist clear through his head, no matter how much she resembled a fragile doll.

Logan stared down at the Were a moment longer. She'd sensed him only moments before. She wasn't sure how he'd almost gotten the drop on her, and it was pissing her off. But she'd worry about that later, once she'd dealt with him. And whatever it was that had brought him to her.

He was just all wrong, despite the fact he was *all right*. He had wavy, dark brown hair and light green eyes that almost seemed to glow in the dim light. A Were's eyes were supposed to glow yellow like a wolf, but only when they were agitated—certainly not green. His face had well-defined cheekbones and a straight Roman nose.

And he was to-die-for gorgeous.

Underneath her, his body rippled as he attempted to get up, high-lighting his heavily muscled frame. Her uninvited guest had to be at least six-foot-four. This guy could go *through* the door of the safe house if he wanted to.

But there was something terribly wrong with him. She could see it in his aura. The natural red and gold was jagged with a sickly green edge, as if something had taken a bite out of it. She hopped off him and retreated a few steps, cocking her head to one side to give him a thorough once-over. Something majorly bad had gone down.

"What happened to you?" she asked with a frown.

"As if you don't know, you crazy..." he started, pointing at her as he got up.

"Don't call me a bitch again if you want to keep that finger," she warned. "What happened to you? Your aura looks like it went through a blender."

The stranger blinked, surprised. For some reason, her concern confused him. That only lasted a second before his mouth hardened into a flat line. "If you didn't do this to me, one of the others like you did."

Logan studied him in silence. In addition to being ridiculously hot, the Were was damaged. It was clear to her now. He'd lost his second form. But none of them had hit a Were this year. As far as she knew, none of their kind had been stripped since she'd become an Elemental.

She and her sisters made damn sure they kept each other informed about that sort of thing. Not to mention the fact that action against Weres was largely unnecessary. Other shifters were a different story. But werewolves were pretty good at policing their own. The pack system was an archaic patriarchy that thrived on an overdose of testosterone, but at least it did a decent job of taking care of its own problems. After a fashion...

Logan had been raised by two very strong women. Whenever she had had to deal with any Weres, she practically choked on the alpha-male vibes. *Give me a black witch any day.*

"What are you staring at?" the stranger spat at her.

Scowling, she crossed her arms. "None of us stripped a Were."

"Yes, you did. You did it in Somerset. Don't try to deny it," he yelled at her, his temper still hot.

Logan narrowed her eyes. "Those were witches. And *they* had it coming. They broke the covenant, and a child died because of it. A second kid came this close," she said flatly, holding her thumb and index finger a hairsbreadth apart.

The Were froze. He actually appeared to be digesting the new information. Maybe the stripping had removed some of the stupid that came with the urge to get on all fours and howl at the moon.

"No Elemental came after you," she continued. "If we had, you would be normal. Just plain old vanilla human. But this..." she said, her gesture encompassing him. "This is wrong. You're in pieces." She was unable to resist squinting at his aura again, although it felt like she was peeking under his skirts, so to speak.

The edges of his mostly red aura were screaming. The sickly green was edged in a hint of yellow. It must be driving him mad. She didn't know how he was still on his feet, let alone upright with the wherewithal to get in her face.

Her observation seemed to offend him. "I can't shift anymore," he growled. "Not for months. One of your kind took my wolf. I'm here to make you give it back," he finished, stepping up to tower threateningly over her.

When she didn't blink, he reached out, putting his massive hands on her shoulders in a tight grip. Logan looked at his hands and suppressed a smile.

It was time to teach this dog a new trick.

CONNELL TRIED to drag the Elemental toward him, but she didn't budge. Instead, she glanced at his hands. For a second, he could have sworn amusement flashed across her face. Then she was gone—wind whipping him in the face so hard it stung.

Fuck!

He turned around in a circle, scanning the air and the land around him. God, he couldn't lose her now. He needed to get his wolf back. Not having the extra other in his head was tearing him apart. The empty space inside him was like a crawling emptiness. Sometimes, it was in his head. Other times, it was in his heart.

I can't believe I lost her.

He'd had her in his hands, and then *poof*. At this point, she could be anywhere. A strangled sigh escaped from deep in his chest. It sounded pathetic and broken, even to him. He checked the house to make sure she wasn't there, and then he walked back out to his rented jeep. Damn it, he was going to have to start tracking her all over again.

"Hey, what's your name?"

Stunned, Connell tripped. Pivoting on his heel, he turned to see the sprite standing on a huge boulder in the distance. He was so damn surprised to see her that he lost his tongue. He just stared at her like an idiot.

Apparently, she agreed. "I can't keep calling you tall, dark, and stupid, now can I? *What...is...your...name*?" she repeated, over-enunciating each word.

He was too relieved to get upset over the fact she was talking to him as if he were slow. "Connell Maitland."

The imp turned away and started addressing the air around her, "He says he's one of the Maitlands. American accent, so one of the

Colorado ones. Yeah. It's severe. I haven't seen anything like it. It's like his wolf was torn out of him somehow. He thinks *we* did it. Hold on a sec—" Her words broke off as Connell started to run toward her.

A gust of strong air slammed him down to the ground before he cleared the rise.

"Stay there," the sprite ordered in a glacial tone.

Frigid as the wind, he thought as he regained his footing. Hell, everything about her should be ice-cold. Instead, he felt like he was burning up around her. It was disconcerting. So was the hard edge in her voice. That kind of steel shouldn't be coming out of such a tiny, doll-like girl.

"Yeah, yeah. It's fine. He's on a leash," the imp said a touch smugly.

Connell growled low in his throat. At least that hadn't changed. Prey the world over would still react instinctively in fear at that sound.

But the imp didn't even blink. And she *had* heard him. She just hadn't cared. She kept on talking like some gossipy housewife on the phone. Except she was addressing no one.

"Who the bloody hell are you talking to? Invisible fairies? Can anyone even hear you?" he asked incredulously.

The Elemental ignored him and kept talking. "Yeah," she said with a tiny sigh. "I'll look into it. No, don't worry. One hundred percent. I promise."

The imp hopped off the rock and started toward him. "Come inside. I need to examine you."

"You know what's wrong with me. You did this," he said, but the accusatory note in his voice was weakening.

The imp rolled her eyes before giving him a clinical once-over. "If we had stripped you, you wouldn't be hurting. You can come inside and let me examine you, or you can get back into your jeep and drive away with your tail tucked between your legs. Your call."

Connell narrowed his eyes. Her voice was so bloody calm. It made him want to hit something. He snarled instead.

"Too soon for tail jokes?"

When he didn't say anything, she shrugged. "Suit yourself. I've got stuff in the oven."

She walked ahead of him and headed toward the house. He stood there, trying to get his temper under control, but the imp didn't wait. She was walking inside before he'd made up his mind.

What the hell was going on? One of their kind had done this to him. At least, that was what he'd believed since he'd heard about the Burgess clan. Even his father had believed only an Elemental could be responsible. No one else could have done this. If a witch had stripped him of his power, he'd be dead, not hunting down an imp in Provence.

Stealing magic was a violent act. Even he, the future chief of the Colorado Basin Pack, wouldn't have survived an attack from a witch powerful enough to strip him.

He stepped back onto the porch. There was a big crack in the solid oak door where it had hit him. It was a good thing he still had some of his supernatural strength—not as much as before, but some. Otherwise, he'd have broken some bones with that hit. Quite a few bones if he was entirely human.

What if it was true? Would he be vanilla right now if the imp had done this?

Don't trust her.

He wanted to...a lot. It was a strong instinctive impulse that he had to fight as he stepped inside the house.

The room he entered was a small living room. It was cozy with comfortable furniture in warm earth tones. The walls were white with an ancient hardwood floor that had been polished by both care and age. Off to the side, a door was open to a makeshift gymnasium with exercise mats and a set of free weights. But more interestingly, the walls were covered with an assortment of knives and wicked-looking swords.

What the hell? Did the imp not register him as a threat? She had just left an arsenal in easy reach for him.

Fuck, this is so insulting.

He stomped through the door. The next room was an informal

dining room with a long wooden table and six chairs. But no tiny Asian sprite.

Growling under his breath, Connell walked through a door on the other side of the table. He found himself in a modern and airy kitchen. It was another incongruously warm and welcoming place. The whole damn house was like something out of a freaking sitcom from the fifties, one set in rural France.

The imp didn't even bother to turn to face him as she put something in the oven.

"Oh, for crying out loud," he muttered.

He could be holding one of her own swords at this moment. Did she not have any sense of self-preservation? No caution at all?

He sighed and leaned against the counter. The kitchen smelled great, like melted cheese. The smell was coming from a quiche cooling on the rack. He glanced at the bowl next to her. Dinner was ready, but dessert was still in preparation.

The imp bustled here and there. He watched her without a word, trying not to be annoyed at how non-threatening she found him. No one else he'd ever come up against had turned their back to him. Of course, none of them could disappear into thin air either.

Minutes passed, and a new smell began to fill the air. "Are you making *cookies*?"

Connell had spent months tracking the imp, and now she was playing Suzy Homemaker, baking *cookies*. Was this really happening? Everything felt surreal. He watched her bend down to open the oven, half-expecting her to start glowing or sparkling like a cartoon fairy.

"Chocolate chip and walnut," she replied, setting down a baking sheet.

A dozen large, gooey cookies were on the rectangular sheet. Connell's stomach rumbled audibly, but he ignored it.

The imp lifted a brow. "Do you want one?"

"No," he said curtly.

His stomach growled again, and he closed his eyes in irritation. He'd had a huge lunch at a nearby inn, but he was used to four large meals a day, at least half of which he ate communally with the pack.

Connell took a deep breath. "I don't believe you didn't do this. Or one of the others like you. If it had been a witch, I'd be dead right now."

The imp cocked her head and stared at him with that same unnerving calm from before. He shifted, suddenly more warm than angry.

Why did she have to be so damn cute? He didn't even like Asian girls. He went for tall, busty blondes like Riley.

Don't waste time thinking about that mess, he reminded himself.

"I don't think that's necessarily true," she said, still studying him. "And I can't tell what's wrong with you yet, so I'm not ruling anything out. Witches included. How long have you been this way? Start at the beginning."

Her tone made it a command. He wanted to shake his head in disbelief. The imp looked like jailbait, and yet she issued orders like a general. She had the innate authority to back it up too. Connell was an alpha, but he wanted to bow down to her. It was unnerving.

"How old are you?" he asked suspiciously.

"How old do I look?"

The answer was so cheeky that he wanted to grab her. But putting his hands on her was a bad idea.

When he didn't answer, she dropped her shoulders. "Start at the beginning," she repeated, a trace more gently this time.

Frustrated, he ran his fingers through his hair until it stood on end. Could he trust her? Did he even have a choice?

"If you want me to help, you have to explain what happened to you."

He stepped to her aggressively, eyes flashing green fire. "I didn't come all this way to chat, little girl. I came here so you could fix me. Even if you didn't do it—if an Elemental didn't strip my wolf away—you can put it back. You have that power. It's what you're supposed to do."

Connell expected her to warily back away. But the imp stood her ground and met his stare. Her eyes were kinder than he expected, filled with sympathy.

He *hated* it.

"That *isn't* what we do. Elementals aren't healers. We're soldiers. I can't fix you, not yet. I don't even know how this happened. You have to tell me. And it's Logan, not little girl."

Connell blinked. "Like the airport?"

Logan scowled at him. And like everything else about her, it was adorable. *Shit.* He was not attracted to cute.

"Like the Wolverine," Logan snapped with a ferocious frown on her face.

Still adorable.

Connell flared his nostrils. What the hell was he supposed to do now? There was no trace of a lie in her scent. And despite losing his wolf, he could still tell when others lied to him. Like Riley. And he knew from first-hand experience what a skilled liar she was.

Logan had to be telling the truth. And if she wasn't, he didn't have another alternative. The witches his pack contacted after his attack hadn't known how to help him. The healer his father had found had taken one look and said it was beyond his skill. He had nothing to lose by telling Logan what little he knew.

"I don't know how it happened. Whatever it was, I was out for most of it," he said, reaching for the quiche at the end of the counter. It was ham and tomato, conveniently cut into quarters. He inhaled one piece and reached for another.

"Help yourself, why don't you?" she said in a neutral tone as he bit into the second piece.

"I've tracked you through four different countries. *I'm hungry*," he growled.

The thick wedge was good. So was the dirty look Logan was giving him. It made him feel alive again.

"You know you're replacing that, right?" she asked, her hand on her hip.

He didn't answer in favor of plowing through the third piece of quiche. Generously, he left the last quarter for her. He was reaching for the cookies when the imp took a mixing spoon and smacked his hand. *Hard.* Smiling, he grabbed the cookie anyway.

Logan's face was flushed red now. His smile grew wider. Connell was suddenly enjoying himself. She tapped her foot, waiting for him to finish the cookie with crossed arms. When she uncrossed them and started drumming her fingers on the counter, he started talking.

"Three months ago, I was taking a night run in the woods outside the family compound. You know where it is?"

The Elementals supposedly kept tabs on his kind. They knew where all the major concentrations of Supes lived. She nodded once, and he continued.

"I was alone," he said, not bothering to mention why. Most of the pack ran in pairs or groups, but Connell often ran alone when pack politics and family obligations got to be too much. He'd been running alone a lot in the last few years.

"Go on," she said, reaching for the last piece of quiche before hopping on the counter.

Following her lead, he sat on the marble counter he'd been leaning on. "I was about twenty miles from the pack house in the densest part of the woods. There was nothing unusual. No strange sounds other than those of the forest. No one was near. I would have smelled them. All I remember was a bright light. It was a little greenish in color. And then I was out. I woke up the next day in human form. And it was gone. I couldn't change back. My wolf was gone," he finished, dropping his head into his hands.

He couldn't meet her eyes. If he saw pity in them, he'd go ballistic.

"Are you sure you would have noticed anyone nearby if you were running?" she asked. "Your kind moves faster than normal wolves. What do you clock out at? Forty-five or fifty mph?"

"Seventy," he said, looking up to see her skeptical smile.

"Like cheetah speed?" she asked.

Most werewolves only ran ten or twenty miles faster than normal wolves. Seventy mph was unheard of, but he'd always been advanced.

"I said seventy." It was close to a growl. How dare she doubt him?

"*Okay*, right, so you're sure? No unfamiliar smells?" she asked

He reviewed the night in his head and shook his head. "No."

"And no familiar ones that shouldn't have been there at that time of night?"

Connell frowned as he replayed that night in his head. He hadn't given her question much thought before.

He shook his head. "No, but I'm not sure anymore. It happened fast, whatever it was. I just saw a green light. Next thing I knew, I was waking up buck naked on the ground, my face in the dirt. I must have inhaled a sandbox worth of soil before I woke up."

Both Logan's brows rose at the *buck naked*, but other than that, she said nothing. Her eyes were on him, but she appeared lost in thought as she mulled over what he'd said.

Connell took advantage of the sprite's inattention to study her. She was wearing a wine-red tank made out of some silky material that was fitted at her breasts, but floated around her with the breeze. Her dark blue jeans were tight, but they didn't seem to constrain her movement. She'd still been able to knock him on his ass outside, despite the fact they looked painted on. And she was wearing black riding boots that were going to feature in some secret sexual fantasies for a long time to come.

He quashed the sudden impulse to run his fingers over the delicate features of her face. Logan looked too damn young for the thoughts he was having.

She only looks young. They all do. The imp was probably older than he was.

"And there was nothing on you?" she asked abruptly, snapping him to attention. "No residue of any kind? No marks?"

"No," he said.

The most grievous injury of his life hadn't left a scar.

"You're sure?"

"Yes," he hissed, hopping off the counter.

She did the same and said, "Come with me." She led him back into the living room and gestured to a clear space between the couch and the stairs. "I need to examine you."

Connell nodded and reached up with both hands to take off his coat. He whipped off his T-shirt in time to take in her wide, startled eyes.

5

Logan stared at Connell's bare chest in amazement. She hoped her mouth was closed. His chest was sculpted like a fashion model in a magazine, but there was no pretty-boy softness to this man.

Even now, damaged as he was, he was dangerous. A predator. And weren't injured predators always the most deadly? This man was lethal. Yet, he was standing there half-naked and gorgeous with his shirt in his hand.

"Why did you take your shirt off?" Her voice was weaker than she'd hoped it would be.

"You said you wanted to examine me," he said, gesturing to his chest.

"I meant a closer examination of your aura...but I may as well look for marks you and your people might have missed," Logan said with a shrug, trying her hardest to sound nonchalant.

She stepped up to him and peered closer at his abdominals. "It's like it's photoshopped. Is that a ten pack?" she said, poking one of the raised ridges before she could stop herself.

CONNELL DIDN'T ANSWER the imp. Instead, he coughed as a sudden rush of blood left his head and headed south at breakneck speed. It was almost as if she'd shocked him with electricity at her touch, but she didn't seem to notice.

And it was only a pinky, for Christ's sake.

Logan finished staring at his chest like he was some sort of bug under a microscope and stepped around him to inspect his back. She poked at some old scars and asked him how he got each one. He told her about his time in the Special Forces, as well as the scars earned as an enforcer for the pack.

Most of the wounds he'd sustained weren't severe enough for him to scar. A werewolf healed through the change to wolf and back. That meant most marks disappeared on his kind, but he'd had a more adventurous life than most. He was his father's right hand, an alpha in his own right.

His father was Canus Primus, or chieftan, of the largest groups of Weres in North America and Europe. Douglas Maitland was responsible for the safety of his people and those of the neighboring families that had settled under the shelter of the Colorado Basin Pack. He depended on Connell and his men to put down any threats posed by rogue wolves and the few Otherkind stupid enough to tangle with them.

"What about this here?" Logan asked with a feather-light graze at the base of his spine.

He suppressed the shiver her touch incited. "What? There's nothing there."

Logan touched him again, tracing a small line. "It's very thin. Only a nick really. It looks older than three months, but your kind heals fast. It's hard to say how old it is. But the fact that it's small is unexpected. Something like this ought to have disappeared on one of you by now."

"I don't know. I haven't seen it. Do you have a mirror?" he asked, trying to twist around enough to see it.

"There's one on the bathroom door," she said, coming around to face him.

Her eyes lingered on his bare chest for a moment before she flicked them back up to his face. He wasn't sure, but he thought she might have been smelling him too. It filled him with a rush of pride, and he couldn't help teasing her. She'd led him a merry chase across half the globe. It was only fair.

"Should I take off my pants now?" he asked, voice neutral.

The color that stained her cheeks was a victory, the first he'd had in a long time.

But Logan only frowned and straightened up. "I think you should go to the bathroom and drop trou. Give yourself a good once-over. There's a lot of damage to your aura, but no sign of what caused it. Check and see if you have any other unexplained marks. Doesn't matter how small."

Her tone was professional, but the blush on those cheeks wasn't. Connell gave her a slow grin, feeling more alive than he had since this whole mess started. Actually, since before then.

"You don't want to help?" he invited, leaning toward her. "You could take a closer look. Make sure I don't miss anything. While you're at it, you can convince yourself that nothing's been airbrushed or cosmetically enhanced..."

***

LOGAN TOOK in the flirtatious grin on Connell's face and felt her face get even redder than it already was. None of Michel's most practiced moves had ever turned her on as much as one smile from this man. He was carnal sin on two legs.

Except he prefers four.

Narrowing her eyes, she reminded herself how much she disliked Weres. She schooled her expression. "Something tells me you're used to handling yourself just fine," she said with a meaningful glance at his groin region.

Her voice was sweeter than sugar, but her insinuation didn't put him off. Instead, his smile deepened, and she was suddenly in danger of not being able to catch her breath.

"Are you *sure?*" he teased.

"Bathroom's up the stairs, first door on the right." She pointed, all business.

Connell backed away with a long, lingering look. He was wearing that panty-melting smile when he turned and headed up the stairs.

"Don't forget to check the soles of your feet too," she called after him, her voice perfectly even. Once he was gone, Logan let out a long, hard breath. Damn, that man was *hot*.

She wished she had taken Michel up on one his many offers to take her to bed. Recent sex might have acted as a shield against Connell's supercharged pheromones.

Well, you didn't sleep with him, and there's no point regretting that now.

Sighing, she dematerialized, heading outside for a quick trip to the air currents. It was better than a cold shower any day.

———

CONNELL STARED at himself in the mirror for a long moment.

Logan. Her name was Logan. And she was a revelation. She smelled good. *Really* good. Like a summer storm or a crisp breeze blowing over fresh snow. It was heady stuff. A little weird too. Her scent seemed to change constantly. Yet, it stayed identifiably hers.

He still missed his wolf, but for a few moments with her, he'd felt whole, complete.

Connell shook his head and stripped down. What was wrong with him? He was kidding himself—he wasn't whole. Now that he wasn't with Logan, he could feel the empty space in his head again. The longer he focused on it, the more broken he felt.

And Logan could see the damage—what he was missing. That was all wrong. Someone like her should only see him at his best. He sighed. He had better forget about taking the sprite to bed, at least for the moment. Once he got his wolf back, well, that was a different story.

The overhead lights were bright, which was a good thing. He

stood under their glare and checked out his own backside with care. Other than his tattoo and an old mark from a nasty bullet wound, there was nothing. His ankles, feet, and soles were clear too. The only thing he couldn't account for was the tiny scar Logan had found.

Craning his neck, he used the mirror and took a long look at the little line on his back. It was at the base of his spine where the sacral chakra was supposed to be. The mark was thin, almost surgical in its precision. And Logan was right. Something that small should have faded by now. But maybe the reason it hadn't was due to the unpredictable nature of his healing ability since his attack. It might not have anything to do with his lost wolf.

He pulled on his clothes and went downstairs to search for the sprite, but Logan wasn't there. Her scent was all over the house, but she was gone.

For a second, his heart seized. Forcing himself to relax, he stalked around the living room.

She just stepped out, he told himself. He didn't think she would leave without telling him. She hadn't technically agreed to help him, but her actions had implied as much. And she was a direct link to the most powerful forces on Earth. If she couldn't help him, then he wasn't going to get better.

Scanning outside through the living room windows, he resisted the urge to growl. The predator in him, the side that had nothing to do with his wolf, didn't like that Logan wasn't there. Connell wanted her with him at all times. He didn't bother to analyze why the impulse was so strong. It was only natural after he'd chased her across two continents

Calm down. Logan was coming back. She wouldn't ditch him now. But first, he would teach her a tiny lesson about ducking out on him without a word. He snorted to himself and went to finish the rest of her cookies in retaliation.

IN THE AIR, Logan whispered to her sisters. Like Serin, she could communicate over long distances when in her non-corporeal form. So could Gia and Diana for that matter, but their communication was limited—Gia's by geography and Diana's by the amount of time she spent in her medium. If Di was using fire to travel, she moved too fast to communicate with the rest of them.

Her sisters weren't available to talk in real time, so she left an update—one the winds would carry to them. Summarizing what he'd told her, she conveyed her confusion about Connell's state. But she didn't mention the detail that had been nagging her since his explanation.

I've tracked you through four different countries. Logan sniffed. He'd just gotten lucky.

Four times.

Pushing away that thought, she descended with a thump outside the kitchen door. Connell was impatiently shifting around inside. She walked in and noted with irritation that every last one of her cookies was gone. Giving him a dirty look, she took her usual seat on top of the kitchen counter.

"Any other scars or marks I should know about?"

Connell gave her a crooked grin that threatened to melt her into a puddle on the floor. "Aside from my tattoo?"

"You have a tattoo?" she asked in surprise, flushing hot.

She had seen every inch of his chest and extremely muscular back. There had been no trace of ink there. *Where was it?*

It took special effort for a Were to keep a permanent mark on their skin for more than a few years. Their self-healing ability made any tattooing or branding temporary.

He leaned closer and put his hands on either side of her, trapping her against the counter. "You'll see it eventually," he murmured into her ear before he pushed away.

Feeling foolishly weak in the knees, she frowned. "Excuse me? Wasn't I the enemy a few minutes ago?"

Connell shrugged. "More like twenty. Things change. Try to keep up," he said in a gruff, sexy tone somewhere between a growl and purr.

Since when was a growl sexy?

Logan was irritated with him. She'd never gotten so hot and bothered around a man before. The new feeling of being off-balance was ticking her off.

She made her tone clipped and frosty. "I think it's best for all concerned if you keep your pants on around me. I am the Air Elemental, after all. It gets quite chilly around me sometimes. Sensitive bits tend to suffer in the cold."

Connell's grin only grew broader, and he made a show of scenting the air as if he was smelling her. And enjoying it. *Ugh.* Her threats didn't seem to faze him at all. She decided it was time to get back to business.

"I need to examine the area where your wolf was taken. You should give me the exact coordinates. In the meantime, you should return to your people. When I have something, I'll find you."

His flirtatious swagger disappeared in a blink. "No. No way. There's no chance in the seven hells I'm letting you out of my sight until I get my wolf back. Besides, I should be there to show you what happened. I'm not going to cool my heels with the pack and wait while you investigate," he growled.

Logan paused for a moment "I see," she said softly.

"What do you see?" he bit back.

She shifted to the bowl, intending to replace the cookies he'd eaten by baking more, but it was empty. He had eaten all the raw cookie dough. With pursed lips, she slammed the empty bowl down on the counter.

Connell's eyes glinted, and she had the sense he was laughing at her. Feeling a little vindictive, she said, "I'm guessing things aren't too comfortable at home just now. Pack hierarchy is determined by strength. Your position must have been compromised when your wolf went walkabout, and some of your underlings are probably getting ideas."

Connell visibly bristled with irritation, but he ignored her comment. "It took me a long time to find you, girl. I'm not letting you go anywhere without me."

Logan sighed. He was going to make things as difficult as possible. *Of course he is, he's a* Were. His tight, sculpted abs had made her forget that fact for a moment.

"Look, I work alone. Frankly, I can make it there and back a lot faster without you tagging along."

He took a step closer, invading her personal space to tower over her. "Not gonna happen," he snapped, reaching out to grab her arm.

LOGAN LAUGHED AT HIM, an unexpected sound of unadulterated delight. "How are you going to stop me?"

She was gone with a sudden fresh breeze, disappearing from under his grip before he realized his mistake. The wind whipped around in the little kitchen. He tried to track her by scent, but she seemed to be everywhere.

Shit. He had to stop giving in to the impulse to manhandle her. He couldn't do this alone. Losing his wolf wasn't like taking down some rogue Weres, or searching for terrorists in the desert with his old Special Forces team. There wasn't an enemy to fight, at least not yet.

Connell needed someone with access to magic. High-level magic. And there was no way he could trust a top-tier witch to help him. One of their kind would either waste his time or stab him in the back if it benefited them somehow. This was his best and possibly only chance.

"Okay, okay. I'm sorry. I'm used to working alone too," he shouted to the empty air. "I respect that. But I still think it's best if we travel together, so I can show you everything. It's pack territory. You'd have to stop and make a formal request from the chief to visit in any case."

"And since he's your father, you think you should be there to smooth things over?"

Connell spun around. The imp had rematerialized behind him on the other side of the kitchen island. His sense of smell hadn't been able to differentiate her scent from the traces she'd left in the room. She spent a lot of time here, enough to mark the place.

Or maybe his keen sense of smell was failing now—unless Elementals were too subtle to be pinned down.

He told himself that was what it was. It had to be some super defense mechanism against his kind. They were the Supernaturals' police force right? It was why she knew he was the chief's son and next in line to lead the pack.

Connell swallowed down the defensiveness he felt and decided the truth would serve him best. "Something like that. Not to mention the fact the pack thinks you're the enemy. We got word that those witches had been stripped just after my wolf was taken. They all think it was you or one of your kind."

Logan sighed. "Of course they think that. I would too if I were them. But even if that's the case, I'd soon set them straight. If you insist on being there, you could join me once you catch up after I check your location in the woods. In my personal experience, it's generally easier to ask for forgiveness than permission anyway. I can get there in a fraction of the time. All you have to do is tell me where to look."

Connell wanted to howl in frustration. He ran his hands through his hair, tugging it back, an old sign that he was nearing the end of his tether. But getting angry and exerting his dominance was not going to get him anywhere this time.

"I would appreciate it if you stayed with me until we get my wolf back. You were almost impossible to track the first time. If you disappear on me—if something gets in your way—I'll have to start all over. So..." He trailed off, choking on the words.

"So what?" Logan asked, that damn eyebrow reaching for the sky.

"So please stay with me," he said quietly, his voice cracking on the please.

It wasn't a word he used very often, and it showed.

LOGAN BIT BACK ANOTHER SIGH. Connell was clearly frustrated. The telltale gesture of rubbing his temple with the heel of his palm was telegraphing his feelings more effectively than the scowl on his face.

Asking for help might actually be killing him. It was certainly making the flaring red in his aura darker. He was in pain, and her refusal was making it worse.

Crap. She was going to have to give in. But letting him tag along meant spending a lot of hours at his side.

Logan had done a job or two that required her to keep company with another Supernatural for a while—one or two vamps and even a ditzy gremlin. But no Weres. And no one like Connell. He was just so...male.

Suck it up. This is your job.

"*Fine.*" She huffed. "But we need to move quickly. I was taking some downtime, and I have other cases waiting. We always do," she added.

"Is that how you refer to them? Cases?" he asked, following her as she left the room.

"Yeah. Why?"

"It's nothing. You sound a bit like a policeman. Policewoman. Whatever. Hard picturing you with a badge," he said. "I thought you'd be taller too," he muttered.

Logan did sigh this time. Her size was a major problem in her profession. She'd give anything to be tall and statuesque like Serin or Diana. Gia was small, but she was still taller than Logan was.

"Five-foot-two is a perfectly respectable height." She sniffed, and Connell smiled.

Irritated, she turned her back and marched up the stairs, calling behind her. "How did you get here? Do you need to book a flight back to Colorado?"

His heavy footsteps followed her up the stairs. She could feel those intense green eyes on her as she threw open the door to her room and began to pack a few things in a bag. The doorframe creaked as he leaned against it.

"We'll be taking the pack jet."

"*We?*" Logan asked, turning to him with a frown.

He scowled at her. "You agreed to stay with me. So we take the plane together. I know you'd rather do your Harry Potter thing and just show up at the Colorado airport, but I'd feel more comfortable if you were with me. Maybe we can brainstorm what to do next."

Logan wrinkled her nose. "I've never flown *in* a plane before."

Surprise flitted across Connell's features before he shrugged. "It'll be a piece of cake for you. Probably easier than playing Superman."

6

A scant few hours later, Logan wanted to strangle Connell. Maybe punch, kick, or bite him. Although, she wouldn't do the latter because she had a sneaking suspicion he'd like it. And he was having too good a time as it was.

He was watching her now, his eyes dancing with smug amusement as she twisted and shifted uncomfortably in the small, but luxuriously appointed jet.

She had been fine until the moment the cabin had been pressurized. Then all hell had broken loose in her head. As the plane climbed to its cruising altitude, a weight settled on her chest as an unfamiliar feeling grew in the pit of her stomach.

With some surprise, she realized the new feeling was panic. Completely discomfited, she focused on taking deep breaths, but the more she tried to calm herself, the more her tension grew. Her skin grew clammy. The edges of her vision started to blacken. She wanted to claw the walls of the cabin until they gave, and she could reach the calm, cold air outside.

The fact Connell was genuinely enjoying her discomfort was another nail in the coffin. Logan squeezed her eyes shut and sank deeper into the plush leather chair, hands gripping the armrest.

She spent another few minutes with her eyes closed, trying to will herself to sleep, but it wasn't working. Her chest felt tight, and she was breathing a little too fast, almost panting. She felt a hand on her own. She opened her eyes to see Connell watching her, unsmiling. All traces of smugness had been wiped away. Instead, his amazing green eyes were filled with genuine sympathy and concern.

"Are you okay, Logan? Can I get you something?"

She shook her head and squeezed her eyes shut again.

"Are you sure? I think maybe you need a drink. Do you like scotch? Or whiskey?" he asked, his voice low and soothing.

She ignored him, sitting stiffly in the chair in spite of her reclined position.

"Logan?" Connell sounded worried now.

His arms went around her, and her eyes flew open. "I have to get out of here," she gasped before dematerializing and whipping around the cabin in rapid movements.

But there was nowhere to go as long as the cabin stayed pressurized. She was trapped.

Connell watched the wind whip around the cabin as it knocked napkins off the table to the floor with considerable force. He felt like shit for teasing Logan now, but he hadn't expected her discomfort to escalate into a full-blown panic attack.

Feeling helpless, he stood, his arms out in front of him, as the wind continued to circle in the small cabin. His concern for the sprite turned into worry for himself and the pilot. If Logan didn't calm down, she was going to depressurize the cabin and possibly take down the jet.

The wind whipped past his head. Closing his eyes, he instinctively reached out. Not bothering to analyze the stupidity of his move, he grabbed at the gust of wind. Suddenly, Logan was there, in his arms.

He didn't know which one of them was more surprised as he

looked down at her. For a moment, they simply stared at each other —his eyes wide and her rosy lips an O of surprise.

"How did you—"

He cut her off by doing what he'd wanted to do from the first moment he'd seen her dancing at that club.

He kissed her. *Hard.*

His lips crashed down on hers, taking her mouth aggressively, possessing it with a growl that came from deep inside him. Logan was too disoriented to shove him away. Instead, she lay limp in his arms, her mouth soft and pliant under his.

Connell took advantage of his imp's confusion to plunge his tongue into her mouth. The world narrowed down to that touch—his tongue stroking hers. She was like nothing he'd ever tasted, and he was two seconds from tearing their clothes off when she pushed him away. He didn't make it easy; he didn't want to let her go. But it soon became clear that he didn't have a choice.

He landed on the leather couch with an *oomph* as most of the air in his lungs was expelled by the force. That much strength in such a little body was unnatural. It was like being moved by a forklift.

Logan was standing over him with a confused expression on her face. "Huh," she said.

Connell sat up straight. "What does that mean?" he asked.

He wanted to grab her again, but the dent he just made in the couch was a good reminder not to do it again without permission. But later...she would beg for his touch. He'd make sure of it. In the meantime, he waited with uncharacteristic patience for her to answer.

"It means huh," she replied, sitting on the sofa opposite the one he was in and cocking her head at him.

She was watching him as if he were a curious specimen of insect. Other than mild interest, there was no reaction to what had happened. And annoyingly, it also didn't appear as if she wanted to do it again.

"*Okay,*" he rumbled as she reached up for the nearest bottle on the bar next to her. He frowned. "What are you doing?"

"I think I need that drink after all," she said, pouring a large measure of his favorite twenty-year-old scotch into a glass.

"Fine. Just don't get drunk," he muttered. "You don't even look old enough to be drinking. I feel like I'm contributing to the delinquency of a minor."

Logan snorted at that, but she didn't respond. He took that as a silent confirmation that she was older than she looked.

Meanwhile, Logan downed scotch that was older than she was.

THE IMP SLEPT through the landing. She had drunk about a third of a bottle of scotch before stretching out and falling asleep. Connell couldn't believe it. He'd gone from being worried about her to total irritation.

He wanted to grab her tiny, sleeping body and shake it. Among other...far more illicit things. But she was passed out and sleeping like a total innocent. Judging from her body weight and the amount of alcohol she'd consumed, she was going to be out a while.

With frustration he couldn't bury, he shook her awake. "Mmr-rph," Logan hummed as she turned away to face the back of the couch.

"Wake up already," Connell growled.

She finally opened her eyes to meet his glare. "What is it?"

"We're here," he said shortly, crossing his arms and towering over her.

"Oh, okay," Logan murmured in a languorous voice that vibrated along his body in an unnerving fashion.

As if it couldn't get any worse, the imp proceeded to stretch in moves a seasoned yoga instructor would eat their own foot to achieve. Christ above, there was only so much a man could take. He breathed a sigh of relief when she stopped. Standing, she grabbed her pack and gracefully stepped to the open cabin door.

Logan was too damn chipper as they walked through the crowded airport. She was wearing yet another tank top, a navy-blue one overlaid with a fine black mesh decorated in a baroque pattern. Black leather pants and short, steel-toed biker boots were paired with gradient shades that darkened the golden glow of her eyes.

Given how much she'd drunk, the imp had no right to that spring in her step. She looked completely fresh and dewy, like she was about to do a photo shoot.

"Why aren't you hung-over?" he asked.

"Why would I be?" she asked, her tone teasing and light.

"Because you drank enough of my best scotch to fell a horse. And you can't weigh more than a pony—one of those Shetland ones."

Logan stopped dead in her tracks, turning around to glare at him "What did you say?"

Connell frowned. "What's wrong?" He scowled.

"A Shetland pony weighs four hundred pounds or more," Logan bit back.

"Is that right? They look so little and cute," Connell mused aloud.

When an apology was not forthcoming, Logan rolled her eyes and stomped away, muttering. "A Shetland pony. Way to make a woman feel sexy after you shove your tongue down her throat..."

A normal man wouldn't have been able to hear her. Grinning like a fool, he decided not to enlighten her of the fact that he'd retained his superior hearing.

"So you can drink anything and not get a hangover?" Connell asked after a while as they entered the terminal, refusing to apologize.

Ponies were cute.

"Yes," Logan replied, only a faint trace of smugness in her tone.

"Seriously? Not ever?"

"Do you get hangovers?" she countered.

He did, but not often. He and the pack had to really tie one on before he felt the effects. Nevertheless, they were Scots by heritage, and he had woken up enough times in his teens, praying to the porcelain gods. However, he wasn't about to admit that to her.

"I'm a Were," was all he said.

"And I'm an Elemental." She shrugged.

Connell grunted, but he let the matter drop. Instead, his eyes wandered over Logan's tight body as she negotiated through the crowd.

Her grace was abnormal. Despite the number of people milling around, Logan always managed to find a path through. She stepped lightly through gaps in the crowd without ever touching anyone. It was almost like a dance, the way the wind found its way through space around objects.

People didn't bump into him either, but not for the same reason. Strangers took one look at his massive frame and the expression on his face, and they quickly got out of the way.

At first, he let Logan get ahead of him—until he noticed the looks other men were giving the sprite. Suppressing a growl, he moved behind her as they headed to the exit. He walked close, shooting black looks at every man who glanced Logan's way until their wandering eyes skittered away from her.

They were almost out of the airport when Logan stopped short in front of him, causing Connell to crash into her back.

It should have been enough to send her flying, but it was like hitting a concrete wall—or a reinforced concrete beam. The average unreinforced wall would have given way when hit with a two-hundred-and-seventy-pound werewolf. But Logan didn't even budge. Instead, she arched her back to give him an annoyed frown before turning away again.

Amused despite himself, Connell didn't acknowledge his clumsiness, nor did he back away from her to give her some space. He stayed pressed against her, tempted to sling an arm around her and usher her into the nearest bed. However, it was clear her attention was elsewhere. When he followed her gaze, his body instantly tightened in anger and challenge. Logan was looking at another man.

The enemy was young and blond with thick, wavy hair and glasses that gave him the appealing air of a scholar. When Logan continued to study the stranger, the impulse to walk over and pound the smaller man into the ground grew stronger. Was it an ex-boyfriend? It had better not be a current one.

If his mate didn't stop checking out another man, he was going to have to put her over his knee.

Connell froze. *Fuck.* Was it possible? He'd been wrong about Riley. Disastrously so. But this...this felt right. He humphed. *An Elemental for a mate?*

But how could he be sure when he didn't have his wolf? A Were could choose a woman, only to find out later that the wolf did not accept her. Both the man and the wolf had to agree. If the wolf chose first, the man's heart inevitably followed. But it didn't always work when the order was reversed.

If the wolf did not approve of the woman, there was little the man could do except give her up. And that could get very ugly. He'd seen that with his own eyes. And how could he know if the wolf would agree that Logan was his mate when it was gone?

No. He must be wrong. His lust was doing the talking. Everything in his body was going haywire, including his judgment. For Christ's sake, he wanted to get into an Elemental's pants. If that wasn't proof of his insanity, then nothing was.

Watching Logan's eyes follow the other man, he decided he didn't care if she was his mate or not. While he was with her, he wanted her attention on him. Complete and undivided.

But Logan had other ideas. She continued to stare at the other man as if he was the most fascinating thing on God's green earth. Connell's growl was a low rumble in his chest. Any second now, his control was going to snap, and he was going to find himself beating the other man into a bloody heap.

"Who is that? Do you know that guy?" He didn't bother to hide the jealousy in his voice.

"No," Logan said, still too distracted to look at him.

Connell growled audibly. "*So why are you looking at him?*"

"Because I have to follow him," she said, meeting his eyes. "Can you pick a place for me to meet you later?"

"You are not going anywhere with that guy," Connell said, the cords of his neck standing out in stark relief.

The imp shot him an exasperated look. "I'm not going *with* him.

I'm going to *follow* him," she explained as if she were talking to a small child.

"You can't be serious. No. We have work to do," he insisted, grabbing her arm and trying to haul her closer.

It didn't work. He couldn't move her an inch.

Logan smiled. "Connell, you don't get to say no." She laughed at him. He glared at her, and she subsided. "Look, I know you feel you should be a priority, but it's part of the job. Even when I'm on a case, there are often little interruptions."

"Which is why I insisted we travel together. As for that shmuck, I don't care if it's him or that pretty-boy actor you hook up with. Your job is me right now."

And I'm going to be your after-hours occupation too from now on, he added silently.

"This is not a hook up," she shot back. "It's work. The scene of your attack is three months old. It can wait till tomorrow."

She shrugged off his hand and stepped past a pillar to get closer to the other man.

"But—" Connell began, but she was no longer there to hear him.

A telltale draft of wind, one that had no apparent source, whipped around him for a second before disappearing.

"I am going to spank you so hard," he called after her, hoping like hell she could still hear him.

To his surprise, a middle-aged woman on his right stopped short. Her wide eyes took in his bulging biceps and the flat pecs outlined by his T-shirt.

"Okay," she agreed with a confused smile.

7

Connell ran through a steady stream of swear words in his head as he followed the blond man from the airport to a suburban neighborhood.

He'd had to boost a car from the long-term parking to make sure he didn't lose the guy, but his quick action saved him the trouble of running the imp to ground.

The trip had taken him several hours away from the pack compound, but he wasn't about to let the sprite go off anywhere without him. Still seething, he watched as the man parked on a quiet residential street and pulled a large suitcase from the trunk of his car.

He didn't know what Logan was up to, but he believed what she had said. Her interest in the younger man wasn't personal. It was related to her work, although he couldn't figure out how. The guy was human. There was a remote possibility he was some kind of witch whose talent was hidden by a clever charm, but he didn't think so. He had enough faith in what remained of his sense of smell to be sure.

Well, ninety percent sure.

After the man had entered a nondescript beige house, Connell prowled the perimeter. There was no stink of the Otherkind anywhere near. But he had a sneaking suspicion Logan was close. He could catch a faint whiff of her scent here and there on the breeze. It would have been comforting if it wasn't so damn frustrating.

He wanted to shout at the wind, to yell at Logan to show herself, but he knew better than to ruin whatever it was she had planned. The human might be some kind of criminal.

There were rumors that the Elementals sometimes concerned themselves with human crimes. He didn't know why. Humans policed themselves far more effectively than the damn vamps or Fea did. As far as he was concerned, Weres were the most effective and honorable of the Supernaturals, at least when it came to taking care of their own.

Connell had turned the corner out of the guy's yard, rounding a tall, wooden fence to an empty alley, when the wind picked up. He was carried to the ground with a hard crash. He grunted and blinked up at Logan, who had a fist in his T-shirt.

"How do you keep finding me?" she hissed in a quiet whisper.

He grinned at her. She sounded pissed. "This time, it was easy. I followed him."

The hard set of Logan's features eased a little, and she rolled her eyes at the sky as if she were pleading to the gods for patience. She was starting to do that a lot.

"I have business to take care of. Why don't you go hole up somewhere? Like a hotel, or better yet, a bar," she said. "Maybe drunk, you will be easier to deal with."

"I said I wasn't going to let you out of my sight. What part of that was confusing?" he asked, resisting the urge to grunt as she hopped off his chest.

For such a little thing, Logan weighed a ton. *Maybe four hundred pounds wasn't far off*, he thought. He wasn't about to mention that, though. Not that it mattered. Logan was spacing out again, staring at the sky. It was obvious she wasn't even listening. He got up, trying not to take it personally.

"Hey," he said, putting his hands on her shoulders, some of his fingers grazing the soft skin at her neck.

For a second, he could hear a buzz of whispers in the air. *Weird.*

He let go. "Are you even listening to me?" Man, this girl was putting a serious dent in his ego. He wasn't used to being ignored. "I asked you a question," he prompted.

"*No, I'm not listening,*" she ground out through set teeth. "I told you. I'm busy. And keep your voice down."

She cocked her head, and the next thing he knew, she was climbing on top of him.

"Um, Logan?" he asked in confusion. The sprite had just gotten right up on his shoulders and perched there to peer over the top of the wooden fence.

"Shh," she whispered, waving a hand in his face in a shut-up-or-else gesture.

Connell was tempted to bite one of her cute little fingers, but he was distracted by the warm pressure of her legs on his shoulders as she shifted around. It didn't last long. Before he could start to enjoy it, Logan hopped off and landed soundlessly a few feet in front of him. She rounded on him with her hands on her hips. He stopped himself from picking her up to resume the physical contact. Touching was good. The glare she was giving him was not.

"Is there anything I can say to make you go away?" Logan asked, her eyes sweeping over him.

"Nope. Not a thing," he said with a cheerful smile.

"That's what I thought," she replied as she grabbed him, pulling him up into the clouds.

8

Connell was screaming, only no sound was coming out. And it was fucking cold. He felt weightless and freakishly formless. Trying to curl into a ball with a body that wasn't there anymore, he rolled and shifted as the air buffeted him with surprising force. The wind felt solid as it smacked him around like the ocean's surf during a storm.

To make matters worse, he couldn't hear above the roaring sound of the wind. The noise filled the world, and then he was plunging down to the ground.

The trip down was faster than a free-fall. It was more like being caught on the tailpipe of a rocket as it hurtled through space. Images of Major Kong riding the nuclear bomb flitted through his consciousness for a second before he came together with a loud pop. The sensation was something like waking up, except it hurt like hell.

"Ow! Fucking *shit*," he shouted, rubbing his head.

"Oh, come on. That didn't hurt," Logan said from the other side of a chain-link fence.

"Of course it fucking hurt. What the hell did you do to me?" he growled.

The evil imp had the gall to smile at him. "We took a little trip.

And it only hurt because you *think* it hurt," Logan said nonsensically as he rubbed his aching head.

"What the hell does that mean?" he asked. Looking around, he still felt dazed.

The imp didn't answer him. Awareness of his surroundings came. He was on his ass, sitting inside a pen in a row of pens. There was a wall of cages opposite. Blinking to clear his vision, he checked out his neighbor in the next pen.

It was a very surprised-looking Chihuahua. "A *kennel*? *Seriously*?" he snarled, getting to his feet.

"Well, it seemed appropriate," Logan replied with a shit-eating grin.

Incensed, he grabbed the mesh door between them, intending to tear it away, but the door didn't give. The cage must have been used to house bears that wandered into suburbia.

"Look," Logan said. "I'm sorry, but I need to take care of our friend from the airport. I don't need a massive wall of beefcake getting in my way. I'll meet up with you later."

She gave him an almost apologetic smile before vanishing with a rush of wind, her scent washing over him as she left.

"Damn it," he swore, kicking the steel door.

He was getting tired of her disappearing on him. Images of him physically restraining her flitted through his head, and he lost some of his anger.

The fact she was tied to his bed in his fantasy certainly helped...

IT WAS GOING to be full dark by the time he got back to Logan and the beige house, Connell realized with gritted teeth.

In the end, getting out of the pen had been no problem. Once Logan left, he'd stopped being gentle. A few hard kicks had done the trick. The door had broken apart at the joint, wide enough for him to step through. But afterward, he'd felt bad about the destruction.

He didn't know where the staff of the shelter was, but the fact that he had busted out of one of their pens and no one had come running meant the place was understaffed. The only witnesses were four-legged.

All the cats and dogs were strangely quiet as he did his best to put the door back into some semblance of working order. It wasn't a great fix, but it would do temporarily. He dropped several hundred-dollar bills on a crowded desk on his way out to pay for a permanent repair.

The animals remained eerily quiet as he left, their silence grating on his nerves. If he'd still had his wolf, they would have howled and screeched the walls down. As it was, they seemed confused, like they couldn't decide if he was friend or predator.

Connell was surprised as hell when he exited the kennel and discovered how far they'd traveled. In what had seemed like only minutes, he'd been dropped more than a hundred miles away, in the tiny town of Cañon City. Stunned and a little dizzy, he realized how far he'd been flung through the sky without the protection of an airplane.

The imp had chosen well. She'd dropped him in the middle of nowhere, in a town without a cell phone tower. He couldn't get a signal to call a cab, no matter how high he held his phone above his head. Disgusted, he dropped his phone back into his pocket and walked to a gas station. There, he was able to call for a car.

After a further delay, the rental agency dropped off a truck. The four-wheel drive came in handy. There was some pretty tough terrain between him and his goal. He spent the drive back plotting and planning exactly how he was going to punish his imp.

DUSK HAD FALLEN when Connell finally pulled into the right street. He was greeted by blue and red flashing lights. For a moment, panic seized him before he realized the lights were cop cars. There were no ambulances out in front of the beige house.

Relaxing, he got out of his truck to join the shifting crowd that had gathered to watch the spectacle. It was unlikely that Logan had gotten hurt. The guy she was after was fully human, after all. But the instinct to protect her was very strong, the way it would be if she were his mate.

He told his instinct to shut the hell up, but his eyes still darted over the crowd looking for her crown of black-and-blue silk hair.

He spotted her with a group of nosy neighbors behind a string of yellow police tape. Logan masked her expression well, but he could feel the satisfaction that was rolling off her as he approached. She didn't turn around when he came up behind her.

"What did you do?" he asked quietly, resisting the urge to grab her and put her over his knee. Instead, he settled for putting his hands on her shoulders to pull her close. To the rest of the crowd, they would look like a concerned couple conversing.

Logan tensed under his hands. "He's not dead," she said. "I took some of the nasty things he was hiding and made them a little more visible. Then I called the cops. Anonymously, of course..."

Connell huffed. "No wrath of the gods this time? You're just going to let the human cops have him?"

She shrugged "Sometimes, it works better that way."

"And an anonymous call was all it took? The humans believed some random tip?"

"Well, they may have been under the impression that Mr. Whelan had a woman chained up in his basement at the time of the call. I gave them enough details to make it necessary for them to check it out," she said, tilting her head back far enough for her hair to brush his chest.

"Whelan is our blond friend?" he asked. Logan nodded. "*Was* there a woman in his basement?"

"No damsels in distress were harmed in the making of this little scene. In fact, when they got here, the cops realized Mr. Whelan liked pretty young men instead. Parts of them anyway. They found some of those parts in his freezer."

Connell made a face. Humans were a lot more twisted than he'd realized. Some of them were getting as bad as rogue wolves. But that still wasn't sufficient reason for Logan to shut him out of her plans.

"You could have told me what you had planned," he said from between his teeth. "I could have helped."

Logan twisted to meet his eyes, her expression thoughtful. He should have been angry with her, but he couldn't work up the energy. *Not to fight with her anyway.*

She turned away, and he gave up on getting a response. *Not even an apology.* "So are you done here?" he asked.

"Not quite yet," she murmured, keeping her eyes on the police officers going in and out of the house.

After a moment, there was an increase in movement at the door. Whelan was brought out with his hands cuffed behind his back. A grizzled-looking detective led him to a squad car with a rough hand. When he was putting the smaller man into the backseat, he shoved Whelan's head against the hood. Connell could hear the thud from across the street.

Logan grinned a little wickedly. "I may have added some naked pictures of the head detective to the pile of evidence."

Connell resisted the urge to laugh aloud. "And just where did you get naked pictures of the detective?" he asked, deciding to go with amused instead of jealous since the detective in question was an overweight bald man pushing fifty.

"Oh, I have my ways," Logan said, turning on her heel and walking away from the crowd.

"Over here," Connell said taking her arm and leading her to his rental truck.

The car he'd boosted was near enough the front of the beige house to be discovered and returned to its rightful owner. They would take the rental from now on.

The imp frowned at the truck. "You know my ride is quicker."

A breeze ruffled his hair. "Yeah, right," Connell huffed, opening the door for her. "I'm not doing that again in this lifetime so don't get ideas. It's too bloody painful."

Not to mention how utterly terrifying it was being formless. No mouth to scream or even breathe. The utter lack of control he felt as the wind carried them. Wolves weren't meant to travel like that.

"*Fine*," Logan said, rolling her eyes as she climbed into the passenger seat. "You can drive this time. But you should reconsider. Air travel is much faster and safer. It only hurt because you thought it should. It's a mind-over-matter kind of thing," she said, buckling her seatbelt and putting her feet up on the dash.

"Sure it is," Connell muttered as he got in the driver's seat.

He pulled away from the curb, leaving the police to finish what Logan had started.

* * *

THE IMP HAD FALLEN ASLEEP AGAIN. She'd dropped off ten minutes into the car ride, like a little kid. He'd woken her when he'd pulled into a burger place for some fast food around half an hour ago. She had eaten an impressive amount of food—three double cheese-burgers and a large order of waffle-cut fries. He didn't know where she put it all.

After eating, Logan fell asleep again, curled into the bucket seat of the truck like a cat. He kept one eye on her as he drove, marveling at her ability to get comfortable anywhere. Even though he wanted her awake and talking to him, he took comfort in the fact that she at least trusted him enough to go to sleep around him. Connell found that strangely satisfying.

The detour to stop a murderer had taken a lot longer than he'd realized. Not that he begrudged Logan for the time spent. If he'd known what she was up to, he would have helped. Next time, he would make that clear.

And there would be a next time.

Scanning the road ahead, he came to a decision. They weren't going to reach the pack's compound tonight. On impulse, he pulled onto the highway. With luck, his buddy, Jack, was off on assignment, and his cabin would be empty. They could spend the night there and be on their way to the compound early in the morning without going too far out of their way.

The fact that there was only one bed in the cabin might be a problem...but not for him. And really, if Logan had wanted to have some input on their accommodations, she should have stayed awake.

9

L ogan woke up when he slammed the truck door shut behind him. She sat up and peered out the cab window.

Connell had stopped the truck in front of a small, rustic cabin halfway up a mountain. The passenger door opened, and he gestured for her to get out.

"The pack's house is much smaller than I imagined," she said with a little yawn, staying put.

"This isn't pack property," he said, the corner of his mouth quirked up. "I need to get some sleep, and the compound is still three hours away. I don't want to get there in the middle of the night. I want the pack alert when we arrive, or someone might do something stupid. And something tells me you don't drive much."

Frowning, Logan hopped out of the truck. He didn't blame her for her obvious skepticism. The cabin did look pretty rundown from the outside.

"Your summer home is...charming, but we have a pretty big place a little ways from here. One that's habitable." She gestured to the cabin walls. "Those gaps in the wood mean this pile is drafty, to say the least. That doesn't bother me that much, but those openings are large enough for some of the local wildlife to join us. And I don't want to bunk down with a raccoon tonight."

Connell pulled his bag out of the truck with a smirk. She was exaggerating the size of the holes. He continued up the stairs. "This is my friend, Jack's, place. We served together. And it's tight inside. The outside is just camouflage to discourage thieves," he called back as he stepped onto the porch.

"Still looks a little small. Sure you don't want to come to our place? It would be a quick trip."

Despite his reluctance to make another voyage in the clouds, her offer was tempting. Connell was intensely curious about Logan. Seeing her in her space would give him a lot more information about her. And he wouldn't mind getting a closer look at the types of weapons Elementals kept around.

But a bigger place meant more than one bed. And if all went well, Logan would be bunking down with an animal tonight. *Him.*

The interior of the cabin was much nicer than the exterior. Snug and well made, it had all the amenities—along with reinforced bulletproof windows and walls. Logan studied the security enhancements before letting out an impressed whistle.

"Jack built this place himself," Connell informed her as he punched in a security code in the high-tech panel next to the door.

"Jack takes his security very seriously," she observed, completing the small circuit around the cabin.

It was pretty small, but it had been designed for maximum efficiency. Shelves lined the walls on two sides. On the third side, a nook had been carved out for a small kitchen.

"And apparently, he never sleeps," Logan added.

There was no bed.

"Over here," Connell said, going to the wall.

He pulled on a cleverly concealed handle disguised as a log in the wall. A sturdy-looking Murphy bed appeared.

"There's only one?" Logan asked, eyeing the bed as if it had sprouted tentacles.

"Yeah, you don't mind right?" Connell asked lightly.

He didn't give her any time to answer before stripping off his shirt. Dropping it on the floor, he took a sneak peek at Logan's wide eyes before walking into the bathroom.

"Well..." she started, but he ignored her and closed the door behind him.

Breaking out into a huge grin, he stripped off his pants and got into the shower. It was going to be a very good night—if she was still there when he got out of the shower.

Just in case she wasn't, he turned the water to cold.

LOGAN WAS IN THE CLOUDS, trying to get a grip. Connell hadn't propositioned her, she reminded herself. The fact that he oozed pheromones and charm was simply a side effect of whom and what he was.

Weres had the reputation of being the most carnal of all the Supes for a good reason, and Connell was a prime example of their kind. He probably couldn't stop from flirting with every woman he met.

She kept telling herself that rather sternly, but her anxiety didn't lessen. And her worry was transmitting out into the aether.

"Logan? What's wrong?" Serin asked.

Logan wished fleetingly that it had been Diana communing with her element. Until recently, she and Diana had the same amount of experience with men. *Zilch.* But then, Alec had come into Di's life—and had refused to leave it. Now Logan was the only inexperienced one in their small sisterhood. Talking to Serin or even Gia about something like this was a little like talking to her mother.

"Nothing," she said. "Just a little keyed up."

"Are you at the Maitland compound?"

"Not yet. We'll get there tomorrow."

Serin wasn't stupid. "I see. And you're with the Were. Is he giving you any problems?"

"Not a problem per se," she hedged. "He's...a big flirt."

Across the aether, Serin laughed. "Men flirt with you all the time. You're pretty good at shutting them down. Unless you don't want to shut this one down?"

Damn, the woman was perceptive. Logan hummed noncommittally.

"I see."

"Stop saying that. I'm not going to do anything stupid. He's a case, nothing more," Logan said.

Serin sighed. "I don't know. You sound...different. This Were has succeeded in getting your attention. And he's done it in record time. He must be something special. Even that actor you were stringing along couldn't seal the deal. And you're the one who always says you only live once..." She trailed off, her voice distant.

I knew it! Something was definitely up with the Water Elemental. And Logan would bet anything that something was Jordan. Under normal circumstances, Serin would have been lecturing her to be cautious. If she was actively encouraging Logan to get involved with Connell, then something was off.

Maybe her sister was seeing the light about her own relationship? It was essentially an arranged marriage, after all. How many of those worked?

"Serin, you know you can tell me anything, right?" she said.

"Don't change the subject." Serin laughed. "You've been itching for a fling for a while. Don't think I don't know what you and Diana talk about behind my back. I know you think I'll disapprove—and there was a time I would have. But fuck it, doll face. Do what you want. Fling away."

Okay, this was not the Serin she knew. This was Serin 2.0, and Logan *loved* her. Not that she hadn't loved her before. But she had two mothers—her mom and Aunt Mai. A third had been a little much.

"Well, that's...new. I hope you're not trying to live vicariously through me. One little change, and you can get your groove back too."

"I'm not dumping Jordan," her sister said in a tired voice. But there was a tiny hint—a *not yet* in her words.

"Course not. I don't know what I'm going to do about my little two-hundred-and-seventy-pound problem, but if I figure it out, I'll let you know."

"You do that. And try not to worry so much. You're a big girl. You can take care of yourself."

Wow, it must have been a *huge* fight.

"Uh, okay. Thanks," Logan said, grateful for the vote of confidence, even if it had been brought about by Jordan.

"All right, sweetie. I have to go. Stay safe. If he gives you any trouble, I'm sure there's always a handy tree to throw at him," she finished.

"Aww, that's the Serin I know and love. Don't worry. I'm good now."

"All my love," Serin said before withdrawing.

Feeling better, Logan decided there was no reason to worry. She was in charge. Connell was a puzzle, but not one she was afraid to solve. He was able to track her, and she was damn near impossible to track. Not as bad as Serin, but *difficult*.

No normal Were should have been able to do that. And there was the fact he was able to travel with her. Another nearly impossible thing—but there were exceptions to the rule. There was still room for doubt, but she wasn't going to figure out anything hiding in the clouds. She rematerialized on the porch and walked inside, confident in her ability to handle one flirty werewolf.

The sight that greeted her almost made her swallow her tongue.

"Hey," Connell said casually.

He was stretched out on the bed, flipping through a hardcover book. There was a small towel wrapped around his hips...and nothing else. Washboard abs gleamed under the overhead light.

Logan moved into the room, trying hard for nonchalance. "If you're done with the shower, I'm going to use it. I'll be quick," she said, grabbing her pack.

She went into the bathroom and shut the door, taking a long, hard breath once she was on the other side.

SHE SHOWERED IN RECORD TIME. Heat coursed through her body that had nothing to do with the warmth of the water. She washed carefully, her skin more sensitive than usual. So were her breasts and other more secret places.

Logan was sorely tempted to take the edge off her arousal, but she was pretty sure Connell would smell it if she did. Of course, he could smell her unfulfilled desire just as easily. She didn't know which was worse.

Refusing to dwell on it, she jumped out the shower and briskly toweled off. She pulled on a tank top and boxer shorts from her pack. Pausing a moment, she inhaled deeply before opening the door.

Connell sat up in bed. He'd put on a pair of shorts himself, but he hadn't bothered with a shirt. *Man, he loves to display that ten pack.* Logan's hands itched to touch it, but before she could give into temptation, Connell shot up from the bed.

"Whose are those?" he snarled, putting his hands on her arms with a hard grip.

Confused, Logan shrugged him off with a frown. "Whose are what?"

"*The boxer shorts.* Where did you get them?" He towered above her almost aggressively.

"At Target, you douchebag."

Connell's head drew back in surprise. "What?"

"I said I bought them at *Target*," Logan said, shaking her head in exasperation.

The possessive note in his voice stroked something deep inside her, but she wasn't about to let him get away with being an ass.

"Oh." Connell backed away.

He sat on the bed, avoiding her eyes. His face was flushed, but Logan wasn't willing to let him off the hook. She walked to the side of the bed to stand in front of him.

"Even if these belonged to another man, it's not your business," she baited him.

His eyes flashed dangerously. Quicker than she could blink, she was flat on her back on the bed with Connell's hard body over her.

"Everything about you is my business," he growled before taking her lips with his in a hard kiss.

10

Hours later, Logan shifted next to him in the bed. "You know those boxers are way too small to belong to man. I got them in the boy's department," she said.

Connell lifted his head to look for the pieces of her shorts. He'd flung them across the room. Tearing them off might have been overkill, but he'd wanted to make damn sure she wouldn't be able to wear them again.

He didn't like seeing her in men's clothing that wasn't his—even things she had bought herself. And she wouldn't need anything to sleep in when she was with him from now on. He ran possessive eyes over Logan's naked body, which he quickly followed with equally possessive hands. She was pressed to his front like a blanket, but even with so much skin-to-skin contact, he couldn't stop his arms from wrapping tighter around her.

At least his grip had gentled. Sex had blunted the hard edge of his hunger enough for him to relax his hold on her. But it didn't stop him from splaying his hands on her naked skin to try and touch as much of her as possible. It was an instinct stronger than anything he'd ever felt. And the contentment he was feeling at this moment was strange —considering his condition.

He felt great. Amazing. Better than he had since he'd woken up alone in the woods all those months ago.

Did sex with an Elemental heal you? Connell did a mental self-evaluation. No. He was still wolf-less. And the hole in his head was still there, a glaring flaw that was probably glowing like a neon sign to Logan. But it was as if the volume on it had been turned down somehow. Like what he had first felt after spending time with her at the French safe house, only stronger.

He grunted. "I don't like other men's clothes on you," he said. "Even if you bought them. If you need something to sleep in, you can wear one of my shirts."

The better to mark her with his scent. That Harry Potter dematerialization thing she did made it fade. He was going to have figure out a solution for that.

Logan yawned and stretched languorously across him. "And what will you wear?"

"When I'm with you—nothing," he replied.

She laughed. "*Hmm.* You may have a deal."

11

Logan woke up boiling hot. She could barely breathe. Groggily, she moved to shove her blanket away, but it didn't give at all. Startled, she realized her blanket was flesh and blood. Very naked flesh. Cracking her eyelids open wider, she saw Connell pressed against her, fast asleep.

He was wrapped around her like a vine, somehow managing not to smother her with his massive bulk as he slept. And not quietly either. His breath was a low-frequency whistle that wasn't quite a snore. In fact, he sounded like her dog Nico used to when he slept at the foot of her bed as a child.

Sighing, she watched Connell sleep with a mixture of anxiety and satisfaction. He was an amazing lover. She was glad that he had been her first. There was a sense of rightness being there with him, touching him. *He must feel it too*, she thought, her hand going to the bite mark at the base of her neck. It hadn't hurt—well, not a lot—but she was very conscious of it.

Logan was still young, and she had planned to sow some serious oats before committing to one man. However, it appeared the Mother had other ideas *if* Connell was her mate. And despite how good the past few hours had been, she still thought it was a big *if*.

It was simply too much of a coincidence that she found her mate right after Diana met Alec. Things just didn't work that way. It wasn't like the Mother manipulated the events in their lives, but an Elemental meeting a mate meant change. And the Mother didn't like a lot of change—not all at once. Still...the fantasy of being able to keep Connell was too tempting not to indulge in.

She traced a line up his abdomen, running her finger over the ridges of hard-packed muscle there. Her mind drifted until she daydreamed about introducing him to Diana and her mate. The fantasy fell apart a little there. Connell and Alec meeting couldn't end well, even if Alec was atypical enough to keep company with Weres. Dmitri was proof of that. But Connell was probably not a fan of vampires. Not if he ran true to hairy form.

Things were about to get very complicated. Connell was second in command to one of the largest Were packs in the world. Only the Russian pack was bigger. Logan needed to figure out what the hell this thing with him was going to be—if it was going to be anything at all. In a way, Serin was lucky. She had known who her mate was for years before they got together.

Okay, you need to think clearly. Sex hormones were messing with her head. Connell wasn't her mate despite the little love bite she was currently sporting. The timing was off. And his bite hadn't broken the skin.

Didn't she read somewhere in the archives that there had to be a blood-and-saliva exchange for a wolf-mate bond to take? That hadn't happened. He couldn't even shift. Maybe he had decided a little bite wouldn't hurt since he didn't even have his wolf.

That had to be it. He didn't think he was her mate. He had simply been playing since it had been safe to do so. She was working herself up for nothing.

Stomach tight, Logan decided she needed a little air. However, extricating herself from the huge arms wrapped around her without waking him proved complicated. Giving up, she dematerialized straight into the clouds over the cabin.

So much for the casual in casual sex, Logan thought with a disquieting pang. She should have just slept with Michel. Choosing to take a Were as her first lover was monumentally stupid. She didn't know anything about Connell. It only felt like she did. As usual, she had jumped in with both feet without looking.

"*Hey!*"

Connell's voice sounded as if he were standing next to her instead of on the ground in the one-room cabin. And he must have been yelling at the top of his lungs. Or that deep bass voice carried with preternatural resonance. *Unless it's a mate thing.*

Shut up, she told herself.

He hadn't slept long. Dawn was starting to lighten the sky in a faint glow, the black night giving way to a deep navy blue. Unable to stall any longer, Logan descended through the cabin's chimney and rematerialized on the kitchenette counter, lounging with a casualness she wasn't feeling.

CONNELL WAS PACING in the nude when the sprite rematerialized in the kitchen area.

He'd snapped awake the second Logan had disappeared from the bed, annoyed he hadn't been able to hold her during those first few moments of wakefulness. At least she'd puffed away without getting dressed, a sight he'd been looking forward to.

Except, she was somehow wearing clothes now. Connell frowned, checking out the dark jeans and sleeveless turtleneck she'd paired with the smallest combat boots he'd ever seen. Seeing clothes instead of all that glowing, naked skin he'd been expecting, he felt a little cheated. Especially since her top covered his mark at the base of her neck.

"Where did you get those clothes?" he asked.

"From my bag," Logan answered with a one-shoulder shrug as she swung one tiny, booted foot up and down.

"*How* did you get them?" he asked, eyes narrowing.

He hadn't dressed in the hope of more mind-shattering sex before they left for the compound.

Logan shrugged. "I called for them. It's a simple spell when I go non-corporeal. They show up when I pop back if I haven't taken them with me. Doesn't work for weapons or people. Those have to be with me when I go. But I can call for the uniform," she said, leaning back to grab a jar from behind her.

She opened it and sniffed, the scent of peanut butter filling the air.

"Oh," he said. "How...disappointing."

What was even more disappointing was her scent. Or the lack of his. He should be all over her, but there wasn't even a trace of it on her now. Every time she took to the air, it was like she took a shower. Or ten.

Hell. It was going to take a lot of work to keep her continuously marked.

No time like the present to start, he thought as he got up and stalked over to her. Logan's appreciative eyes took in his naked body, and he glowed with pride. Resisting the urge to preen, he lifted her to him.

"If you can magic them on, you can just magic them right off," he said, tossing her back on the bed.

Logan laughed. "What happened to getting an early start?" she asked with a giggle as he climbed over her.

"Fuck it."

"I'd prefer it if you didn't refer to me as an *it*," she said cheekily before she disappeared.

Before he could blink, she was back underneath him, all silky skin without a stitch of clothing.

"*Okay.* I take it back. That could come in handy," he murmured as he pulled her body flush against his.

Logan's laugh filled his ears...but he made sure she wasn't laughing long.

12

"I can't believe we broke the bed. What will your friend say?" Logan asked, peering at the broken support underneath the mattress.

He grinned. "Something along the lines of congratulations. This frame was double reinforced steel. Jack's a pretty big guy. It took a lot of down and dirty acrobatics to break this. He'll be impressed."

"Charming. Is Jack in your pack?" Logan asked as she lifted the frame to inspect the damage more closely.

Connell raised a brow at her, and she put the bed down.

Oops. She should have waited for him to get off the bed. Never a good idea to remind a guy that his new lover could bench press two of him.

He exhaled slowly before answering. "No. He's a human I served with. Mostly human anyway. My team was all Weres, but we often worked with another one that was humans of mixed heritage."

Logan nodded in understanding. When a Were said mixed heritage, he meant descended from a shifter line in some way—humans who hadn't inherited enough to sustain a change. They were often large and strong with bodies like rugby players, slightly bulkier than normal Weres. Full-blooded werewolves were sleeker, but their muscle mass was denser. Their mixed relatives were often too distantly related to be aware of their lineage. Most became soldiers or professional athletes.

"Hmm," Logan said as she finished examining the broken frame. "Hope he's an understanding guy, because I don't think we can fix this without welding tools. And if he's anywhere as big as you, then a fix like that wouldn't last long."

"I'll leave him some cash to pay for a replacement," Connell said as he stripped the sheets and threw them in a hamper she hadn't noticed.

He was shining with a post-coital glow that made her want to jump him all over again. Or at least lick him up and down.

Good thing he doesn't smell like wet dog, Logan mused, and then wondered if that would change once he got his wolf back. A lot of things might change...

She watched Connell pensively as he pulled the mattress off the broken frame. He shoved the metal pieces together enough for the whole assembly to fit inside the concealed wall space again, leaving the mattress on the floor in front of it. Logan pulled on her clothes while Connell rummaged through his bag for shorts.

After he was dressed, he ransacked the cupboards and made a breakfast of powdered eggs with some beef jerky in lieu of bacon. Logan took one look at it and went for the peanut butter. She ate it with some crackers she found in the cabinet, along with a fistful of dried Captain Crunch, while sitting cross-legged on the kitchenette counter.

Connell sat next to her on the only bar stool, staring at her with a little too much smug satisfaction. Reaching over, he snagged the peanut butter jar from her with a lightning quick flick of his wrist. Even his fingers looked muscular.

Was she looking at her mate right now? If she was, the Mother had one twisted sense of humor...

CONNELL WASHED his dish and dressed slower than usual. He'd been so determined to get Logan to the compound, but now, he could barely summon the enthusiasm to leave. After last night, he wasn't sure he wanted to share her with his pack.

It would normally have been a point of pride to take his mate to the compound and have her meet his family. But he'd left a mess at home, and he wasn't looking forward to cleaning it up. Not with Logan around to watch.

At least Riley won't be around to fuck shit up. He relaxed a bit. If his ex were gone, then things would be a bit easier. He could handle everyone else if she wasn't around to spread her poison.

"We should get going," he said, stacking dishes in the small rack next to the sink to dry. Even he could hear the reluctance in his voice.

Logan frowned at him. "Are you all right?"

"Are you still coming with me?"

"Yes."

"Then I'm all right," he said, grabbing their gear and taking it out to the car.

He opened the passenger side door for her. She disappointed him by flashing over the distance in a blink, appearing in the car and buckling her seatbelt in a soft, fluid motion.

Damn. There went his scent. He locked up the cabin and got into the driver's seat, slamming the door a little harder than necessary.

"Is something wrong?" Logan asked innocently, a little Mona Lisa smile playing on her lips.

She knew. The little minx knew he'd done his damnedest to ensure she smelled like him all over, and that it was erased when she dematerialized.

"Everything's fine," he ground out, throwing the truck into drive.

"Uh-huh," she murmured, getting comfortable in the seat the way only a small person could.

He shook his head at her, the motion abrupt. Snaking out his hand, he pulled down the neckline of her turtleneck and scowled. The half-bite on her neck was gone too. *Double damn.* Elementals healed faster than Weres. How would everyone know she was his if he couldn't mark her?

Inhaling deeply, he relaxed. He couldn't mark her permanently, not *yet*. When he got his wolf back, he would be able to take care of that. The bite of a wolf claiming his mate was bulletproof. It never failed, no matter who or *what* you were.

He drove in silence, but he wasn't annoyed this time when Logan fell asleep after a few minutes. Her trust in him was gratifying. Leaning down, he picked up her pack and reached inside the front pocket where he'd seen an earbud cable peeking out earlier. Fishing out a small MP3 player, he scanned the playlists. He didn't recognize very many of the artists.

Choosing something called *L'exode* by blob at random, he put the volume on low and connected the player to the sound system. He was surprised when a soft, haunting composition filled the air. He almost skipped to the next track, but the song resonated in his brain, a mixture of anxious purpose and classic beauty that made him keep it on.

Logan stirred during one of the crescendos, but she didn't wake.

It had started to rain, but the cabin of the truck was warm and comfortable. In spite of the circumstances, it felt good to drive his mate home.

***

LOGAN WOKE up as soon as Connell put his hand on her arm. She smiled at him.

"I was going to hassle you for sleeping most of the trip, but when you smile like that, I forget to be annoyed," he said, his eyes zeroing on her lips before lifting to meet her gaze.

She wrinkled her nose at him. "You have only yourself to blame. You didn't let me get much sleep last night. Besides, I learned the hard way that I need to catch my Zs whenever I can. You never know when something's going to start that keeps you up for days."

Yawning, she sat up straight before looking around with a frown.

They were at the top of a rise overlooking an isolated valley. Nestled in the middle of a bare field was a long, two-story building. It was the only structure in sight. Mountains rose up on all sides a few miles away.

"Is this the compound?" she asked, mouth pursing. "I thought there would be more buildings. You know, more Camp David and less...barn."

"We're not at the compound. While you were asleep, I got a call. We've detoured fifty miles. This is the howf, although we call it the longhouse for obvious reasons," he explained with a gesture to the long, rectangular building.

"A *howf* is a meeting place, right? Shouldn't it be in your compound?"

"We have one there too, but we need more than one. The Basin Pack is a coalition of several smaller packs. My father isn't just the alpha for the local pack; he also functions as the chieftain for all the ones in this part of the country. All told, there's close to nine hundred of us. If you count those who defer to my father as counselor, then there are triple that across the Americas. Depending on the parties concerned, we shift around for the *howf*. This place is used for particularly big meetings. It used to be neutral territory before the packs were united under my father."

"I thought your grandfather united the packs," Logan said, toying with the felt of the seat cover.

"My grandfather started it, but he couldn't finish it. My father did that. And since then, his position hasn't been challenged. Not seriously anyway, not in decades."

He paused. "It's a little weird hearing an outsider speak so knowledgeably about us. Werewolves are a little xenophobic. We don't share our internal affairs with others as a rule."

"It's my job to know these things," she said, looking at him from underneath her lashes. "So why did we detour?"

Connell's face tightened. "My father called a meeting for all the packs in his purview. There's been another."

"Another what?" Logan asked, perplexed, before her face cleared.

"Another member of the pack lost their wolf?" She put her feet down on the floor, her adrenaline surging.

He nodded grimly. "My father's third, Malcolm Ingram, called me. He was surprised to hear I was on my way back. The attack happened the day before yesterday. It's a cub this time—the youngest son of my father's best friend Bishop Kane." Connell shook his head as he drove closer to the *howf*. "His name is Sammy. He's only seven."

So young? "I'm so sorry. How is he?"

"Alive, but from the sound of things, he's even more messed up than I was. He was taken to our house, and a healer was summoned. But they weren't able to do anything for me, so the chances they can help him are pretty low. Not unless we can figure out who or what is doing this."

"I should see Sammy now," Logan said, looking askance at the longhouse.

"I know, but he's stable for now. The healer is with him, and you and I need to make an appearance here. The packs are feeling pretty threatened. Tensions are running high. Before things blow up, my father is hoping to diffuse the situation."

He slowed the truck down to face her as he spoke. "It was different when it was me. I was a soldier and an enforcer. The others —even the ones who like me—are used to the idea of me getting hurt. This is something else."

Logan nodded darkly, her stomach muscles tensing. "A second case involving a child is disturbing. If it's a Supernatural at fault, this is a clear violation of the Covenant. Not that it wasn't before when you were first attacked, but the fact that it's a little kid makes it doubly so."

He agreed with a murmur. They were almost at the longhouse. To one side, she could see a large group of cars parked on the flattest stretch of open land. Most were trucks and SUVs. Connell pulled up next to a flatbed and turned off the engine.

"The meeting will have started by now. We're the last to arrive. I should warn you. I told Malcolm you were with me and that your kind wasn't responsible, but tempers are running hot inside. Most won't believe you're innocent, not right away. Not until they've heard you speak, so they can smell the truth of your words. They want someone to blame. You should tread carefully. And..." He broke off with a headshake.

"And what?"

He looked uncertain for a moment. His hesitation was so uncharacteristic that she sat up straighter.

"What is it?"

"Well, it's just that there's a lot of very pissed-off werewolves in that building. Male wolves. Women aren't allowed at these meetings. And there are at least two or three men from each pack, which means there are something like a hundred wolves in there. And most aren't used to deferring to a woman. My father in particular..."

"So what are you saying?" Logan asked, even though she had a pretty good idea of what was coming.

Connell gave her a concerned glance. "I would recommend that you be...respectful. I know you can handle yourself in a fair fight, but there are too many wolves in there if things get out of control. If things go south, do your Harry Potter thing and meet me at my house. I wrote down the address," he said, handing her a slip of paper.

She wanted to roll her eyes, but she knew Connell was trying to protect her in his own way. Trying to look appropriately grateful, she took the slip of paper and put it in her pocket as she got out of the truck. Connell took a defensive position in front of her as he led the way to the longhouse.

Logan smiled through her annoyance, but it faded when she remembered what he'd said. *No women allowed.* She sniffed to herself. *This should be fun.*

The shouting of many male voices could be heard from outside. Connell opened one side of the double doors. Gesturing for her to stay behind him, he slipped inside the shadowy room.

Logan followed him, her eyes adjusting instantly from the bright sunshine outside. The room was one large rectangle. Even though it was tall enough to be two stories tall, it was only one. Instead of a second level, there was a catwalk around the entire room. Massive wood rafters occasionally crossed the sturdy-looking walkway. Hanging from every corner were werewolves of every shape, size, and description.

Except female.

Most of the men were massive and muscular like Connell, although none matched his height or muscle definition. She could have been biased on that last, however. There were even some kids there, teenage boys and a scattered handful of preteens here and there. Only the youngest male cubs were absent.

Too many people were talking at once, or shouting, in order to be heard over one another. It was like a wall of sound, one with a lot of bass.

No one had noticed them yet. Connell was scanning the crowd for his father. Logan knew him as soon as she spotted him. He was the older version of his son, tall and handsome, except his eyes were blue and his dark hair was threaded with silver at the temples.

Douglas was in the center of the maelstrom, leaning on a wooden support beam that bisected the room in half just opposite the door. He seemed content to let the assembled crowd get all the shouting out of their system until he saw Connell. His eyes locked onto his son's face in relief, but it was short lived.

When he saw Logan standing next to Connell, his expression changed. It was wary for a fraction of a second, and then all emotion melted away. He did inscrutable much better than his son did. It could have earned him a fortune at the poker tables.

Douglas stepped into the middle of the room and held up his hand. The assembled group of Weres stopped shouting, although a low grumbling continued in the background like the sound of a rough ocean.

She and Connell were finally noticed by the others. Logan could feel the censure of so many eyes on her body like so many pinpricks.

If looks could kill.

Although not everyone was looking at her as if they wanted her dead. Some glances were dismissive; others were confused.

"Welcome back, son," Douglas said, moving to embrace Connell.

"Is this her?" called out another voice. "Is this that *thing*?"

Logan turned in time to see the hulking shape of another Were rushing toward her. Connell reacted, moving to stand in front of her, but Logan dematerialized to stand in front of him instead. The Were crashed into her, his speed checked hard when she put out her hand. Instead of using her wind power, she grabbed the man by the neck, lifted him up, and tossed him aside like a rag doll. He hit the wall opposite with a crash.

It all happened in the blink of an eye.

Logan leaned back, bending at the waist to look up at Connell. "Was that respectful enough, do you think?" she asked, unable to stop herself from sounding cheeky.

A pin drop could be heard in the formerly noisy room. Connell put a hand over his face and sighed as Logan struggled not to smile. She turned back to Douglas.

"I hear you have a problem," she said.

Douglas gave Logan a thorough once-over. Although Connell was a good three inches taller, his father also towered above her. She gave him her warmest, friendliest smile, and his eyes dilated slightly, but he didn't move to welcome her in any way.

If she were a different kind of Supernatural, he would have been doing a damn fine job of intimidating her. In fact, for a split second, the instinct to drop her gaze in submission almost overwhelmed her. But only for a second. Maybe two.

Douglas' authority was innate and powerful. It radiated from him like an aura, which was mostly red and gold like his son's. It wasn't hard to see why he was the man who had been able to unite so many different warring packs into a workable coalition. Given the volatile temperament of the average Were, it was a serious achievement.

"Connell said you and your kind weren't involved." Douglas said in a voice full of gravel.

Logan immediately wanted to offer him a hot tea or a lozenge, but that would have to wait.

"We weren't," she said in a clear voice that carried to every corner of the room. "I told Connell this already. No Were has been stripped for decades. Killed, yes," she said, spinning to check out the others in the room over as they did the same to her.

Her announcement started the grumbling again, but she continued undaunted.

"The last was a rogue in the Andes who was attacking village children," she continued. "And as you know, we don't interfere in your internal issues—we restrict our punishments to those outside pack law. But no shifter has been stripped of their second form since before I was born."

"Why should we believe that?" the man she'd knocked down shouted.

His voice was strong, even though he was still struggling to get up. Logan scanned him. It didn't appear as if she'd broken anything of his.

"That's it, big guy, shake it off," she said in an undertone as the Were got to his feet.

He walked a little unsteadily to stand next to the chief, aggression and distrust coming from him like a bad smell. He was as tall as Douglas, with inky-black hair a little shorter than Connell's. Dark green fatigue pants were paired with a black T-shirt that showed off an impressive set of biceps.

"She's lying," he barked.

Logan's voice dropped several degrees in temperature. "I thought your kind could smell a lie?"

The murmur of voices around them grew louder as the assembled group of Weres argued, mostly about her scent. A few brave souls got closer, making a show of sniffing the air around her.

She waited, giving everyone a chance to decide if she was friend or foe before smirking back up at Connell. "Glad I showered," she said under her breath.

He smiled in spite of himself when a few of the cubs snickered. A Were's hearing was almost as good as their sense of smell, and even the youngest one in the room had caught that.

"You don't smell like anything," a wrinkled Were with grey hair said.

Several others around the room nodded their agreement.

"Not true. She smells like the wind," Connell corrected. Douglas glanced at him sharply, but he didn't say anything. "And she was with me when Sammy was attacked," he finished with a meaningful glance at the angry Were.

The stranger scowled. "You saw how fast she moves. The way she disappears. She could have attacked Sammy and been back before you knew it."

"She can only move as fast as the wind. There wasn't enough time. And if what Malcolm says is accurate, Sammy's attack happened when we were still in Provence, France," Connell stated inflexibly.

The other man bristled. "That doesn't mean anything. There are four of them. It could have been one of the others!"

"She said it wasn't, and I believe her," Connell shot back, putting a protective hand on her shoulder.

For a second, Douglas's eyes flared in surprise, but his son didn't notice. The chief watched them, his eyes trained on that small point of contact, but his face cleared when Connell stopped touching her.

"Look, I'm sorry about your brother," Logan told the angry Were, trying for diplomacy now that she'd established her position of strength. "I'm here to help in any way that I can."

Murmurs of surprised speculation followed. Logan cocked her head, listening to the whispers on the wind until she caught the right name.

"Yogi, can you tell me what happened to Sammy?" she asked politely.

Yogi's head drew back in surprise. He glared at Connell. "Did you tell her my name?"

Connell shook his head. "They did," he said, pointing at the sky.

"Who are they?" Yogi asked, staring at Logan like she was something that crawled out of a gutter.

Connell shrugged. "I don't know. I don't want to know."

Logan pressed her lips together hard, masking her surprise. Did Connell just insinuate what she thought he had? Did he know how she got her intel?

No, that's impossible. She'd misunderstood, or he had. It didn't matter. She had a mystery to solve, and they were wasting time.

Clearing her throat, she repeated herself. "What happened to Sammy?" she asked again, raising her voice, although she was careful to keep her tone civil.

Yogi looked over at Douglas. The chief shifted his weight and gave a tiny nod. Yogi crossed his big arms and let out a frustrated breath. He put a hand on the back of his head.

"I don't know. He stumbled home yesterday. We had been searching for hours. He'd been missing since early morning. We tried tracking him, but all the traces were old, and we ended up running in circles," he said, vibrating with tension and anger. "But then he came home on his own, collapsing in the yard. He had a raging fever, and he couldn't speak. A bunch of us went back out when we found him. I thought we could track his attacker. But we never found where he'd been assaulted. His scent appeared less than a mile from our house like he'd dropped there out of the sky."

He glowered at Logan when he said that.

She ignored his glare. "Did he have any marks on his body? Any fresh cuts or scars?"

Yogi shook his head. "None that I saw."

"I should see him as soon as possible," Logan said, turning to Douglas and Connell.

Connell nodded. "I'll take you there now," he said, putting a hand on her shoulder to lead her out.

"*No.*"

Connell turned to his father in surprise. Douglas shook his head at his son. "No," he repeated. "I need you to go out with a team to Kane house. Start there. See if you can find any trace of where the attack took place."

"He doesn't even have his wolf," Yogi protested indignantly.

"Even without it, he's a better tracker than you, son," Douglas said with an apologetic pat on Yogi's back. "But you go with him. I'll take her to Sammy."

Yogi nodded, accepting the chief's orders without question. Logan's mouth quirked.

Handy that. Being chief had its perks. No one argued with you. She stepped away from them, giving the trio a little space. Connell began to question Yogi about their search, throwing out the names of men he wanted in the new hunting party.

"Max, Derrick, and Leeland. You too, Malcolm. I want you with me," he said, calling out to a blond-haired Were standing against the wall.

Some emotion she couldn't identify crossed Malcolm's face, but he stood at attention and nodded. He moved to join the other men Connell had appointed to the search party.

She waited a little apart, letting the others see her. Normally, given her small size and unfortunately non-threatening appearance, she would be trying to appear more intimidating. But she'd just knocked one of their largest warriors on his ass. Anything more would be overkill. Instead, she crossed her arms and studied the crowd. There were a number of people continuing to give her dirty looks. But not all. Some were relieved. And all the cubs were curious, whispering like mad as they eyed her up and down.

Logan could feel Douglas' eyes boring a hole into her. A few minutes later, he gave a small signal, and the Weres scattered. A few hung back to talk to Douglas and some of the other elders. Logan went to the truck to retrieve her pack, Connell close at her heels.

"Father will have to stay behind to talk to the others for a little," he explained. "I know you could whip over there in a few minutes, but it would be best if you didn't step into the chief's home without his invitation. And sorry about Yogi. He's a bit of a hothead, and this situation is taxing his control."

Logan shrugged, "It's understandable under the circumstances. Can I ask how he got saddled with Yogi when Sammy got a nice, normal name?"

Connell smiled wryly, "He didn't. Sammy is short for Sammael."

Logan clucked sympathetically. "Still, Yogi is somewhat ironic, isn't it? He doesn't strike me as a terribly Zen person."

"I always figure Bishop was trying to invoke the power of a name the first time around. He himself went through what my father called *a difficult period*, which is his way of saying a tear of epic proportions. But my father saw him through it. They've been best friends since they were cubs. I think Bishop was hoping his son would avoid something similar to what he went through. And Yogi's not that bad. He has a short fuse, but he cools down quick. Sammy is a sweet boy. Yogi is twenty years older than he is. There's a sister too, but she's off at school."

"Their dad's name is Bishop. I'm beginning to see a trend," she said, slinging her pack on and turning to the longhouse.

Men were starting to trickle out of it in little groups. They stared at her and Connell as they walked to their cars. She edged away from him, trying to act casual.

He frowned. "What are you doing?"

Damn. Logan's mouth tightened. "Um. It might not be a good idea to...you know...be close in front of everyone."

His expression darkened. "Why?"

Logan made herself keep his hot gaze. "It might complicate things."

"We've already burned that bridge," he growled, stepping close and wrapping his hand around the back of her head.

In the next heartbeat, she was gone, flashing to sit on the hood of the car while he stared at his now-empty hand. He turned to her with a scowl, but she held up her hand.

"Don't get mad," she admonished in a whisper. "I just think it's a better idea to stay on the down-low in front of the other members of your pack. Especially the chief."

The scowl deepened, "I don't see why."

Logan was exasperated. "We should be careful until we decide what it is that we're doing here. I'm not used to this sort of thing, you know."

Connell paused, his face clearing and growing thoughtful. "How not used to it?"

Logan made a face at him. "Never mind."

He rocked back on his heels and studied her. "I know exactly what I'm doing with you," he said.

"And what might that be?" she asked, trying to sound unconcerned.

But he only smiled cryptically as his father and a group of men stepped out the door of the longhouse and called to him. He walked away, still smiling.

Jerk.

Her hands fisted, and she resisted the temptation to smash them into the hood of the car. Forcing her hands to relax, she crossed her arms and stretched out, her back on the windshield while she waited for Douglas.

A group of seven or eight intimidating Weres had gathered around Connell and the chief. They didn't resemble each other at all. Some were stocky, others were tall and lean, but all of them were muscular. Each had a hard edge, an air of menace that would have made a normal person cross to the opposite side of the street.

All hunters down to their furry toes. Or was it only hobbits that had furry toes? She hadn't noticed any extra hair there on Connell, but then, she hadn't been looking at his feet.

Stop thinking about it. Him. She was about to get a ride from his dad, the chief, for fuck's sake. Time to get her mind out of the gutter.

The group of hunters left, departing in black SUVs with coordinated movements like a trained military team. No doubt, these men had been part of Connell's Special Forces unit. But even after they left, there were still stragglers around Douglas Maitland, waiting for a word with their leader.

Logan sighed. How long was this going to take? She hadn't expected Weres to stand around so long, gossiping like old women. If she hadn't had to wait for Douglas, she could have been there by now. The fact that she didn't want to spend any quality time alone with the chief had nothing to do with it.

Eventually, Douglas dismissed the last hanger-on, tossing a pair of keys to him before walking to a blue SUV. He stared at her, and she shifted with the breeze. Now she was sitting on top of his car while the other Were drove off in Connell's rental.

Douglas and Logan stared at each other. There was no trace of fear or curiosity in his eyes. Just a resigned wariness.

"Are you ready?" he asked, ignoring her position and climbing into the front seat of the car.

Whipping inside, she sat in the passenger seat and buckled up without bothering to open the door. "Yes," she said.

He didn't say anything else. Compared to him, Connell was downright chatty. He started the car and drove them away without another word.

LOGAN WASN'T USED to feeling awkward. Being driven by someone else was weird enough. So far, Connell had been her only chauffeur since she'd left home to take up her position. Now his father was driving her to his home in a taciturn silence so thick you could cut it with a knife.

She wasn't even slightly tempted to fall asleep.

"So you're the Air Elemental," Douglas observed in his deep, gravel-chewing baritone.

They were only a few minutes from their destination by that point. Logan nodded once. She could do the strong and silent thing too.

"I knew one of you once," he said unexpectedly. "Her name was Gia. She was—"

"She still is," she replied, cutting him off.

Curious. Gia had never mentioned knowing the chief.

"Oh," he said.

Logan waited for more, but Douglas was done speaking.

"When did you meet her?" she prompted.

Douglas turned into a gated drive, a series of buildings appearing in the distance. The silence stretched so long Logan thought he wasn't going to answer.

"A long time ago. Before Connell and his sister were born."

Logan nodded again, a little disappointed to hear that Connell didn't have another brother waiting in the wings. *Relax,* she told herself as they pulled up to the main house. She didn't care that Connell was the next in line to lead the pack. Or that there didn't seem to be a spare male heir lying around.

The pack house was a sprawling three-story structure at the center of a compound full of buildings. It looked like a cross between an army base and a ski lodge. Douglas turned off the engine and sat there for a moment before opening his mouth.

"Look, my son appears to trust you, and I believe it when you say you're not involved, but I've met your kind before."

Logan's lip quirked. "Meaning what exactly?"

"I know you have...limitations. I don't want my son getting his hopes up."

She hoped he was talking about the missing wolves. "If someone is targeting your pack, there is something I can do," she said, matching his serious tone. "I can stop them from doing it again. Why don't you show me where Sammy is?"

Douglas didn't bother replying. He just turned around and went inside.

Oh yeah, Logan thought dourly, following him up the porch stairs. *This is going great.*

13

The front door of Connell's childhood home opened directly onto a large mudroom.

"This must come in handy," she said to the chief. "Given the number of muddy werewolves who cross this threshold..."

Douglas paused and grunted.

An actual sound! It was progress, she thought, following him farther into the house.

The impression she'd had of a rustic lodge was solidified when the tiled mudroom gave way to an open space full of leather and wood paneling. Huge redwood beams supported a twenty-foot ceiling. Three staircases led to a second floor from the living-room area, and a massive fireplace dominated the living room.

In front of it was a big, three-sided leather couch, on which sat two women. One was a teenager. The other was roughly Connell's age. The latter looked so much like him that she had to be his sister. She was tall with the same dark hair and light green eyes. On him, it was striking. On his sister, it was devastating. She looked like a supermodel. Logan felt like a short troll next to her.

"Mara, this is Logan. Your brother brought her here. He'll be back soon. He's out with the other trackers trying to find where Sammy was hurt," Douglas said.

Mara rose up from the couch in a fast, fluid motion, moving toward them aggressively. "I don't fucking believe this. We don't hear from him for months, but now he's back, bringing home some skank he picked up God knows where. What is wrong with him?"

Despite Mara's petulant tone, her voice rang with the authority of an alpha. *What a fun household.* On second thought, Connell probably deserved a sister like this.

"Language, Mara." The chief sighed. "And this isn't a woman."

"Hey," Logan protested, turning to him with a glare.

"I mean, she isn't Connell's woman," he corrected.

Logan bit her tongue, and Douglas took a deep breath. He was starting to look tired, his broad shoulders fractionally less straight than before. "She's the Elemental he was tracking. He found her."

That shut Mara up...for about two seconds. "You're fucking kidding me, right? She's like fourteen years old," she said, gesturing to Logan in disbelief. "And she looks like a fucking anime character."

Logan sighed. "Story of my life."

She dematerialized. A split second later, she reappeared in front of the tall brunette, giving her a narrow-eyed inspection. Mara reared back, but not in fear. Logan smiled. In spite of the other woman's bitchy attitude, she rather liked her. Mara reminded her a teensy bit of Diana. Except the female Were said *fuck* a lot more.

"I could prove it by taking you up to the currents now, but your brother was kind of a pussy about it." She squinted at Mara again. "Hey, are you and Connell twins? Because I'm definitely getting a yin to his yang thing in your auras."

No answer. Logan flashed to Mara's other side, checking her aura from another angle. While Connell's was red with some gold, his sister's was mostly gold with some red, like an inverse mirror image. "Yup. Definitely twins."

Douglas coughed in what could have been confirmation or reluctant amusement. "Logan, why don't you go upstairs and check on our patient? Mara, why don't you take her to the guest room?"

But the brunette didn't move. She was staring at Logan with something like deep fascination.

Okay. "Should I wait for wolf girl to find her tongue or should I show myself up?" she asked in an aside to the chief.

"I'll take you."

Logan turned. It was the teen from the couch who had spoken.

"I'm Salome, Sammy's sister," the girl said. "He's upstairs with Riley. The healer left a little while ago."

"And?" Douglas asked.

Salome looked down and shook her head.

"Sorry," Logan said, her mouth turned down in sympathy. "I don't know if I can do anything either, but I need to examine him as soon as possible."

Salome nodded, the dark circles under her eyes deepening with the movement of her head. She started up the stairs. "This way," she called behind her.

Logan saluted with exaggerated formality. Mara was still standing there frozen, her mouth open when she moved to follow Salome.

"Did she just call Connell a *pussy*?" she whispered as soon as Logan reached the top of the stairs.

"Yes, she did," Douglas answered flatly as she followed her guide around the corner.

If they said anything else, Logan didn't hear it. She was too busy checking out Connell's childhood home. The upstairs was a maze of hallways. She didn't know how many pack members made this place their home, but the house had a lot of bedrooms.

"He's in here," Salome said, opening a closed door at one end of the second floor.

The little boy was on the left side of a large bed, asleep with his hair plastered to his head. A tall, leggy blonde was sitting next to him, but she stood when they entered.

"Thanks for sitting with him, Riley," Salome told the blonde. "This is the Elemental Connell was tracking. She's come to help. Logan, this is Riley, Connell's mate."

14

W here the hell had all the oxygen gone? Had she accidentally sucked all the air out of the room? Were the wolves still breathing? *Was she?*

The block of ice that had once been her stomach was radiating cold, freezing her from the inside out. Could they tell? Did she look as shocked as she felt?

"*Oh.*"

She couldn't think of anything else to say. Why weren't the winds commenting right now? Was it true? Or was it a lie?

The fickle currents were silent. *Bloody figures.* They were useful only when they wanted to be and sometimes even got in the way. Maybe silence was the better outcome in this case...

Gathering herself, Logan straightened and looked at the pneumatic blonde with what she hoped was a neutral expression. "It's nice to meet you. Please get out."

Suspicion and distaste flashed across the blonde's face and took up residence there. "Why?"

"I would like to examine the patient alone."

"All right," Salome agreed with a polite nod before moving to step into the hallway.

Riley frowned, her model-perfect features distorting. "I don't think so. One of our kind should be here at all times when *it's* here."

Well, at least Logan had a good reason to hate her now. She smiled sweetly at Riley before picking her up and unceremoniously dropping her on the other side of the door.

Salome and the blonde gave her a stunned glance, one Logan didn't stop to enjoy before slamming the door shut in her face. After, she shuddered, drawing in a deep breath.

What the hell? How could Connell do this to her? Why hadn't the winds told her about his mate? Why hadn't he?

Fuck. Bracing herself against the door with one hand, she counted to ten.

"Are you okay?"

Logan turned around. The little boy was awake. His voice was weak and hoarse, scratchy.

Get ahold of yourself. This is why you're here. Forget about the man and concentrate on the crime.

Shoving her feelings deep down, she focused on the child in front of her. It took a major effort of will to turn off her emotions, but she wasn't an Elemental for nothing.

However, it was harder than she would have imagined to ignore the pain blindsiding her.

"I'm fine," she said, her voice steadier than she'd hoped.

She walked to the bedside table and poured him a glass of water from the carafe sitting there. "Here," she said, giving him a sip of water, which he took gratefully.

He signaled that he was done, and she put the glass down. "Who are you?"

She smiled at him and introduced herself. "My name is Logan. I'm an Elemental. I'm here to investigate what happened to you and Connell."

Saying his name aloud made an icy shard shoot through her chest, but she pushed it away, embracing the numb coldness that followed. *It's temporary, like your mistake with him. A brief lapse in judgment. It's going to be okay,* she reassured herself.

That felt like a lie.

She refocused on Sammy. He was the reason she was here and she owed it to him to give him her best.

"I'm going to examine your aura now," she said, walking over and taking his hand.

He was hot to the touch. The little boy exhaled sharply when she made contact, and for a second, she was worried she'd hurt him. Technically, touching him wasn't necessary, but it did make the connection more immediate. His naturally blue aura was streaked with purple, except for where it was torn with the same sickly green she'd seen in Connell's.

"Is this worse? I don't need to hold you to do this," she said in concern, starting to let go of his hand.

"No!" he protested weakly. "It feels better. Don't let go."

Logan frowned. She didn't have any healing ability, so maybe his response was psychosomatic. "Okay, we'll just hold hands for now," she said with a smile, covering his hand with hers.

He was an adorable little boy, with dark eyes and hair and a slight cocoa cast to his skin. He was still a little sweaty from his fever. She put her other hand on his forehead, but he didn't feel that hot.

Sammy sighed again, moving his head as if he was rubbing his head against her hand, like a little cat. Logan was surprised, but she didn't say anything to call attention to his action. It might embarrass him.

"Can I take a look at your back?" she asked him.

He nodded and tried to roll over, but he was too weak. She helped him and lifted the top of his pajamas to reveal his waist.

Well, fuck me. There it was—a tiny cut at the base of his spine. It wasn't a scar, but a fresh cut. Was it a mark from a knife? Something ceremonial that was used in some sort of ritual?

Whatever had done it, it didn't seem to matter if the subject in question was full grown or a child. Sammy's aura had the same damage as Connell's did. It had the sickly green signature at the ragged edges, but it was tinted with a white-hot edge instead of a yellow one.

Shit. The damage was similar to Connell's at first glance, but it was worse. More had been taken, and what was left of his aura was eroding.

Logan's stomach gave a sharp lurch. Sammy's aura was bleeding away into the aether. The leak was barely visible, less than a trickle under her trained eye, but it was there. And if she didn't do something, he was going to die.

She probed the wound meticulously, looking for traces of a spell. She remembered what Diana had told her about the spell that had affected the vampire's human servant during her first investigation with Alec. That curse had manifested like an octopus, digging into the man's aura and wiping away much of his memory and personality.

Unfortunately, this was nothing like that. There was no hidden spell woven into the fabric of Sammy's aura. There was only the damage from where the wolf had been torn away, just like Connell. It was as if a blind man had performed surgery.

Was it her imagination or was the white edge turning yellow?

"Sammy?"

His eyes had closed and his breathing had evened out, his body relaxing. He felt cooler. Logan told herself that she'd bored him to sleep, but she was starting to wonder. Could she affect his aura? Was it possible that she could heal him?

Logan heard herself telling Connell she wasn't a healer, but she ignored her own voice. She had to stop the aura bleed. But she didn't know how. At a loss, she checked Sammy's temperature with an actual thermometer. He was only a few degrees above average for a wolf, so she covered him with a sheet and threw open the window.

Gia, she called.

There was no answer. She sent out a call to her other sisters, but they were silent, no doubt busy with their own cases.

"Okay," she said, biting her lip.

She was on her own for the moment. And she had to make a decision. Sammy was too young to survive this kind of damage, despite the drop in his fever. That was only temporary. It would spike again, and he'd burn up without the protection of his aura.

If this was how Connell had looked right after his attack, it was a miracle he was still alive—his status as card-carrying asshole notwithstanding.

There it is. Her hurt was safely tucked away. All she'd needed was a little perspective. Connell's cheating ass was now in a little box marked '*do not open*'. She'd deal with her feelings about him later. Right now, she had work to do.

Except she didn't know what that should be. She closed the window and stared at Sammy's sleeping form.

Crap, he was so little. Normally, her blood would be boiling, and she'd be in the air hunting down whoever had done this to him. But she couldn't leave him.

Impulsively, she picked up the little boy off the bed. She had an idea. She was going to envelop Sammy with her power. Connell had said dematerialization was painful, so that was out, but there was another way she could try.

Making sure the blanket was still wrapped around him, she sat on the bed with the child on her lap. Settling him more comfortably, she called the winds.

MARA GRITTED her teeth and suppressed the urge to unsheathe her claws.

Riley had been trying to convince her to go upstairs for the last ten minutes. Apparently, she didn't trust the Elemental any more than Mara did, but the fact that Riley wanted her gone was enough to give Logan the benefit of the doubt.

Turning a deaf ear to Riley's continuing complaints, Mara focused on comforting Salome. But it wasn't easy to ignore her brother's ex. Riley had always embodied what she'd hated the most about pack females.

The voluptuous Were was power hungry and vindictive...but only around other women she saw as rivals. And Mara was one of those women.

Around men, Riley was whatever they wanted her to be, a chameleon who would pretend to love whatever they did. She excelled at making herself the center of attention. The behavior would last until the men were gone, and then Riley's true nature revealed itself.

It made Mara sick on behalf of her sex.

Their father had no idea how badly Riley had hurt her brother. Mara wanted nothing more than to throw the blonde bitch out on her ass. But her hands were tied. She had to put up with the other wolf given the situation with Sammy, Riley's cousin.

Mara wanted to believe that the other Were was genuinely concerned for the cub, but she knew better. Riley was playing the family card to stay in the thick of things...and around Connell now that he was back. After all, Riley hadn't shown her face until they heard he was on his way home. She obviously regretted cheating on him and wanted to patch things up.

Please God, don't let Connell take her back.

Unfortunately, it was a real possibility. There weren't too many options out there for her brother. Most of the pack in the vicinity was related to each other in one way or another. As a group, they were discouraged from mixing bloodlines too closely, but any safe union between principal families was strongly encouraged.

Despite her wish to the contrary, Mara knew Riley was the likeliest choice as a mate for Connell, the future alpha. Or at least, she had been before the selfish cow had blown up her relationship with him.

There was also one other thing Mara was worried about. If Connell regained his wolf, and Riley managed to sucker him into forgiving her, Mara would be stuck as her subordinate for the rest of their lives. That was the way pack hierarchy worked. A female's position was determined by her mate's rank. It was almost enough to make her wish Connell's wolf would stay lost...

Feeling guilty for that selfish impulse, Mara was startled by a loud crash. She leaped to her feet. The noise had come from the upper floor.

"I told you," Riley hissed at her in triumph.

Shit. She didn't answer, hesitating as Riley and Salome ran up the stairs. Mara looked around for her father, but he was probably still outside pacing, his cell phone in hand, waiting on an update from Connell. Swearing, she decided not to delay by going to get him.

The noise grew louder as she made her way upstairs to the guest suite they'd converted into a sickroom for Sammy. Salome glanced her way from the open door, her eyes huge.

Fuck. Mara's heart picked up, and she sprinted the final few steps to the door.

She hadn't believed Connell would bring home someone dangerous, but when she took in the scene inside the guest room, her stomach dropped like a stone.

Logan was sitting on the bed in the center of the room with Sammy in her lap. It was almost like a scene from a painting—idyllic and calm. But they were in the middle of a cyclone.

All the loose objects in the room were spinning crazily in a circle around them. The winds were contained to the room, and the noise was crazy loud, like a roaring beast.

"She's killing him!" Riley yelled over the noise.

The blonde Were rushed into the room, but she was promptly struck in the chest by a table lamp whipping out of nowhere. Riley hit the ground, hard.

Mara could swear Logan's lip twitched as Riley struggled to get up. But the force of the wind was keeping her on the ground. Mara started forward to help when a large hand restrained her.

"Riley, get out of there," her father said calmly. She hadn't even heard him come up behind them.

Riley's face screwed up. "But she's—"

"It's all right," he said. "She's not hurting him. Get out of here."

Mara raised startled eyes to her father. *Are you sure?* she mouthed. Douglas nodded curtly.

Crawling on her hands and knees, Riley scuttled to their side.

Once she was at the doorframe, she was able to stand. Dusting herself off with a frown, she rounded on Douglas. "What is she doing?" Riley asked in a shrill voice.

"She's helping," her father rumbled, reaching out for the doorknob.

He closed the door with a thud, and the sound of the rushing wind ceased.

Was that normal? She hadn't heard the wind from downstairs. What she'd heard was one of the flying objects hitting the wall. But not the strange magic wind.

"Everybody, downstairs," Douglas ordered.

Behind him, Riley's face twisted in an incredulous expression, but she followed him down when he led the way. Salome hurried to join them, but Mara lingered, throwing a last glance at the closed door of the bedroom.

When she went downstairs, her father was alone in the kitchen, sipping a coffee. She didn't say anything about the strong smell of whiskey that came from the mug. Instead, Mara poured her own cup and sat down to drink it.

She always took her coffee black, unlike Connell, who put so much crap in it that it was more like he was having dessert in a mug. But whenever she called him out for it, he would smile smugly and say he needed the calories. She hated that it was true.

The silence stretched so long she cracked. "Do you know what the Elemental is doing?" she asked her father.

Douglas exhaled audibly. "I think she's trying to wrap him up in her energy somehow—a bit like I tried to do."

Mara nodded. As the chief, her father had the ability to focus the energy of the pack. He used it sparingly, most often in battle to infuse his wolves with strength. But sometimes, he was able to tap into it when a wolf was injured beyond his or her own ability to heal. The energy of pack had amazing healing ability when it was directed properly. Her father had that skill; however, it hadn't helped with whatever had been done to her brother.

It had been a shock when Douglas had been unable to help him.

Then Sammy had been struck down, and she'd hoped, this time, he might have better luck. That hope had dwindled quickly.

The fact that both Sammy and Connell were still alive and breathing was a miracle. But it was one that might not last. Among the old guard, there was a lot of doubt that Sammy would survive. Connell had been a soldier, and he was the strongest wolf in the pack. Or at least he had been. But Sammy was only a cub. Some of her father's friends had been blunt about his chances when he'd been brought in.

Even Bishop, Sammy's father, was acting as if he were already gone. He was focused on hunting down the person responsible. He and a few others kept scouring the woods, going out repeatedly instead of spending any time with his boy. Mara suspected he was avoiding the sickroom because he couldn't handle his son's inevitable death.

Except it may not be inevitable.

"What do you think of Logan?" she asked.

Her father scowled, his eyes distant. "What I think doesn't matter. It's what your brother thinks that's the problem."

Mara's brows drew together. "What do you mean?"

Her father focused on her for a second before turning away abruptly, as if he'd just heard a noise.

"Nothing," he muttered, but he hurried to the back door.

Wondering if the search team was back, Mara sprang up to follow him. However, there were no cars coming up the drive.

Her dad started down the stairs, scanning the horizon. Or she thought so at first. His gaze was low as if he were looking for something on the ground.

"What's wrong?" she asked, confused.

Douglas didn't reply. He was scanning the ground intently.

"Dad?"

He held up a hand for silence, stooping to put his ear to the dirt.

Oh God, he's lost it.

Maybe the stress had finally done him in. She was about to take his hand to try to lead him into the house when he straightened up and dusted himself off. He joined her on the porch steps and crossed his arms resolutely—almost as if he were posing.

Mara nearly bit her tongue in surprise when the ground began to give way a few feet from the steps. It wasn't like a sinkhole. Instead, it was like the ground had liquefied. It rippled like the surface of a pond disturbed by a dropped stone. But there was no sign of what had caused the disturbance—not until a head emerged from the center of the quickening sand.

That head was followed by the rest of the body, complete with arms and legs. It was a woman. Her hair and eyes were dark black, set against light, cocoa-colored skin. Her cheekbones could cut glass. The stranger was more striking than beautiful, with an ascetic reserve found in those with Native American blood—although her face looked like a mix of indigenous and European features.

Mara blurted out the first thing that came into her head. "Why aren't you dirty?"

The stranger glanced down at her clothes and smiled. "Practice." Then she turned to her father and bowed slightly. "Greetings, Douglas Maitland, Chief of the Colorado Basin Pack."

Her father stood up a little straighter. He inclined his head with equal formality. "Hello, Gia."

What the hell was this? Did her father know this person? And what was with the whole rising-from-the-ground trick? *Shit.* This was another Elemental. Earth, if she had to state the obvious.

Gia's smile warmed her face, and Mara had the inexplicable desire to drop her head. The power emanating from the other woman was odd. It was soothing, like a warm summer's day. But that didn't mean her energy wasn't potent. It was fucking powerful, the strongest she'd ever felt from anyone, her father included.

"I would ask how you have been, but Logan's been keeping me updated," Gia said politely. "I am sorry for your trouble."

"Thank you," Douglas replied gruffly.

"May I see Logan?" Gia asked, her hands respectfully clasped behind her back.

Her father nodded, and he stepped aside. The Earth Elemental snaked past them, pausing to nod at her. Mara watched her pass, wide-eyed.

Snake is the wrong word to describe it, she thought. Gia and Logan moved the same way. Quick and fluid. It was different from the way wolves moved. Mara had always believed her kind was the fastest and most graceful of all the Supes. She knew better now.

Her skin tingled in the aftermath. "Should we show her up to the sickroom?"

Her father shook his head. "She doesn't need help. They always know how to find each other."

15

"I *fucked up.*"

Gia had just closed the door behind her before Logan greeted her with that pithy confession.

Her counterpart was sitting next to a sleeping boy. He was quite young, a wolf cub a little over seven years old. There was stuff all over the floor as if a small cyclone had gone through it. Or a small child—but something told her the little one on the bed wasn't the culprit.

She smiled at the junior Elemental. "I'm sure you haven't done anything wrong. Is this our patient?"

"Yes, this is Sammy, short for Sammael. He's the second victim. He wasn't doing too good, so I tried something, but now he won't wake up," Logan said, her voice tinged with panic.

"Calm down, sweetie," Gia said. She leaned over the boy, stroking his forehead with her hand.

"What if I made him worse?" Logan asked, her dark honey eyes wide.

"If you didn't intend to harm him, then you didn't," she assured her.

Logan scowled. "You don't know that!"

Gia smiled. Intent was everything when it came to their gifts. "Call it an educated guess. Move over so I can confirm it."

Still frowning, Logan stood to make room for her at the side of the bed. Gia sat next to the cub, taking both his little hands in hers.

Gia closed her eyes and felt around. It was a deep sleep, one not entirely natural. "Hmm," she murmured.

"Hmm, what?"

This was interesting. "What exactly did you do?"

Logan shuffled her feet, a nervous move Gia hadn't seen her do since her training. "I could feel his aura bleeding away, so I wrapped him up with my energy. I was hoping it would stop up the leak somehow."

That explains it. Gia huffed. "Well, I think you've succeeded. Only you've done a bit more."

Logan bit her lip and started pacing. "What did I do?"

"I'm seeing traces of *your* aura weaved into his, right over the tear. It's this silver bit here. I didn't think this was possible. But it's stopped the bleed, so it must be."

She'd learned a little of healing techniques under the Mother's tutelage, but this sort of fix was like nothing she'd read or seen. *That doesn't mean it hasn't happened somewhere. It just means it wasn't written down.*

She sent a silent prayer of thanks to the Mother for letting the boy live. Over the centuries, she'd seen a few victims drained of magic. But they had been dead when she found them; their aura's gone, returned to the earth. Gia sighed, not unhappily. There was still so much more to learn about the world.

Logan stopped short in front of her. "Crap! Have I sprung a leak in mine now?"

Gia squinted at her. "I don't think so," she said and laughed. "I think you've done the magical equivalent of a skin graft—but with auras. Unlike other Supes, ours are capable of regenerating—but only to a point, so I wouldn't try this again. You haven't damaged yours. It also hasn't healed the boy, but he's stable, at least for the moment."

"Can you wake him up?"

Gia frowned down at their small patient. "I don't think that would be a good idea. His sleep is a reaction to the treatment. It's his body's way of trying to protect him through the healing process."

"Like a medically induced coma, but supernatural?"

"Yes," Gia said before her forehead creased. "Was this how the other one was too? I know he was walking around and everything, but does he have an aura bleed?"

Logan flushed and shook her head. Gia searched her expression. Why was her sister blushing?

"Connell's injury must have been shallower somehow," Logan said quickly, avoiding looking her in the eyes. "Or being an older alpha allowed him to heal faster. He's already on the mend. My theory is that the perp didn't cut away as much that first time. I don't know why he took a child this time instead of another alpha. Maybe he's trying to refine his technique and was looking for an easier mark. But I don't know why he would keep trying so soon, unless—"

"Unless the first attempt didn't go as planned. Like he or she successfully cut away the magic, but couldn't absorb it," Gia finished for her, still analyzing that flush on her sister's cheeks. "It's as good a theory as any other. So...where is Connell?"

"Looking for the site of the second attack with some others."

"And he's doing well enough for that?"

"It would seem so. He hasn't lost all of his wolfy abilities either. Still stronger than a human. And his sense of smell seems to be intact." She shrugged, still studiously avoiding looking at her. "What happens in those cases where the perp couldn't absorb the magic? Does it roam around loose in the aether?"

Gia considered that. "In theory, but I don't know of a way to funnel it back into a body once it has been severed. Not in cases where a witch took the magic. There simply hasn't been a case where the victim survived before," she said before studying her counterpart.

Something was definitely off with her sister. "Is everything okay?"

Logan's eyes snapped up to hers. "Not exactly. But I don't want to talk about it."

Gia leaned back, bracing herself on one hand as she examined Logan. "Are you sure?"

Logan blinked and let out a harsh breath. "Let's just say I let this case get personal. It was a mistake. I've made a bit of a mess, but I'll deal with it. It won't stop me from completing this mission. I promise."

Oh. This is about Connell. Yes, that sounded right. If he were anything like his father, he would have been enough to turn any Elemental's head. Gia sighed.

Ah, Douglas. He had gotten grey, with some new lines around his eyes, but he was still the same man—attractive and virile. But some things weren't meant to be...

Of course, she wasn't Logan. And Connell wasn't Douglas. But she'd been around long enough to know that history sometimes did repeat itself. "All right," she said quietly, deciding to let it go for now.

She might be jumping to conclusions in any case. Best to let Logan play this one out as she wished. It was her case after all.

"What do you want to do now?"

"Can we leave him?" Logan asked, gesturing to Sammy's still form.

Gia took another long look before nodding. "He is stable. I don't believe there's more we can do for him right now."

"Then let's go do what we do best," Logan said, straightening up. "Let's go hunting."

16

Logan was glad that Gia was with her when she informed Douglas of Sammy's new condition. The Earth Elemental stood silent at her back while the assembled wolves towered over her, trying to intimidate her.

There were more of them now. A lot of pissed-off males who hadn't been part of the search party were milling behind Douglas, no doubt egged on by Riley. The blonde Were was shooting daggers at her from behind the chief's back.

The announcement that Sammy was now in a coma didn't win them any fans in the increasingly hostile group. That included Douglas, who was frowning at her.

Damn, she hated when he did that.

Despite her show of concern for Sammy, Riley didn't run upstairs to check on him when they came down. It was Mara and Salome that hurried off to verify that Sammy was unconscious. Mara came down alone while Salome stayed upstairs to sit with her brother.

"It's true," Mara confirmed. "We can't wake him up."

Riley's pretty face contorted, and she stepped up to Logan and got into her face. "You've done something to make him worse! I told you we couldn't trust her or any of them," she said with a sneer, turning back to the room at large.

The Weres behind her paced and whispered. One male even growled. He tried to move to the side, presumably to flank her and Gia, but a glare from the Earth Elemental froze him in his tracks.

Logan wiped the excess spittle, courtesy of Barbarella's snide twin, from her cheek with a moue of distaste. "I haven't done anything to harm Sammy. He was dying. I didn't heal him, but he is better now. Stabilized at least."

"I don't believe you," Riley snarled.

"I don't care what you think," Logan spat back, baring her teeth.

She stared her rival down, but Riley didn't budge. They glared at one another while the shifting group of men paced restlessly.

The tension in the air jumped up a few notches. Logan smiled and cracked her knuckles behind her back. She wasn't about to start a fight with the bitchy Were, but she'd sure as hell finish one.

"Riley," Douglas snapped, and the big blonde retreated behind him.

Disappointed, Logan sighed and rocked back on her heels.

"What my sister said is true," Gia said, breaking her silence. "The child's aura was bleeding away into the aether. Logan somehow managed to weave some of her own into the wound, enough to stop the bleed. Sammy's coma is protective, not unlike a medically induced one."

Douglas' face cleared slightly. "How did you do that?" he asked, turning to Logan with narrowed eyes.

He still sounded suspicious, but he seemed to believe Gia.

Logan shrugged. "Hail Mary," she said honestly.

Douglas' lips thinned. "But he's not healed?"

She shook her head. "We don't know how. What I did is a stopgap. If he makes it, he'll be like Connell. Wolf-less."

He crossed his arms and stared down at her. "And you can't put his wolf back?"

It was Gia who answered. "There is no way to do that as far as we know, but there's also no way to graft your aura on someone else's either."

Douglas huffed before nodding. "We haven't heard from the search party yet, but I expect them to check in within the hour."

Logan sucked in a breath, her chest tight at the reminder of who was heading that search party. An hour was too soon. "We'll start without them, at the site of the older attack. Can you give us directions?"

"Shouldn't you be able to divine where it is?" Riley sneered.

Logan ignored her. Douglas did too. "It's near the stream, thirty-four clicks southwest, then bank hard left for one and a third."

"Got it," she said, pivoting to extend a hand to Gia behind her.

Her sister took it, and they were off in the air.

Logan took more pleasure than she should have giving Riley a good, harsh blast in the face as they went out.

It was a quick trip in the currents. They landed in a small clearing surrounded by a thick copse of trees. Logan could hear the faint sound of running water nearby to the south, but she couldn't see the stream Douglas had mentioned.

There wasn't anything special about the place. No stain of violence. No telltale ripples of magic in the aether. If she'd been scanning from the sky, she would have missed it.

Logan took a long look around and sighed deeply.

"Relieved to be out of there?"

She looked up at Gia. The Earth Elemental was watching her instead of looking around for clues.

"I could have taken them had things gone south," Logan assured her.

Gia laughed lightly. "I'm sure that's true. But it's not what I meant. You seemed uncomfortable, especially with that difficult female. And you don't usually let anyone get to you like that."

Logan wished Gia wasn't so perceptive. Diana would have let her tiny show of aggression go, but the Fire Elemental was kind of a smash first, ask questions later kind of girl. Gia was a talker, always had been.

"She's Connell's mate."

"*Oh.*"

There was a wealth of information in that one syllable.

"And I slept with him."

"Oooh."

Logan rolled her eyes. "I told you I made a mistake—a huge fucking monster one. And it keeps getting bigger and bigger, and now I think my head is going to explode. Also, I'm pissed off. I want to kick Connell's ass into the middle of next week. If I thought he'd survive, I'd do it too."

"I take it he didn't mention having a mate?"

"No, he didn't," Logan said, her eyes wide. She exhaled and crouched down, eyes on the ground. "What am I going to do?"

Gia knelt in front of her and waited until Logan looked up before speaking. "Finish the job and forget about him. What's between him and that female is not your problem."

"How do I do that? I thought—well, never mind what I thought..."

"You thought he might be your mate. Mainly because he was acting like he was."

Logan frowned. "How did you know?"

Gia's face clouded. "It may have been a mistake to let you take this case after all. I know Connell came to you, but Serin or I should have taken it over."

Her heart dropped. "Why do you say that?"

Gia patted her arm. "It's not a reflection of your abilities. But there are some unforeseen complications when dealing with Weres. I should have warned you. In a way, this is my fault."

Logan's head was starting to ring. "What are you talking about?"

Her sister smiled, but it was a sad and distant expression. "I've never told you this. Actually, I've never told anyone, but that may have been an error in judgement. I didn't want to embarrass him."

She was starting to feel dizzy now. "Who?"

Gia grimaced and sat down Indian style in front of her. "Douglas. The same thing happened to me with Douglas."

Logan's mouth dropped open. "*Really?*"

"Well, not exactly the same thing. I didn't sleep with him. I had a mate."

"Oh," Logan said in understanding. "This was when Marco was still alive."

"Yes," Gia said, a sad smile on her face. "It was a case, forty years ago, right after Douglas succeeded in uniting the packs. The union was fragile. A rogue Were was trying to break it before people could get used to the new order. She had allied with some witches, and they were attacking Were families that didn't join them as well as any stray humans who got in their way. I helped clean it up out of self-interest. Uniting the packs meant less fighting and fewer rogues being created when their packs were wiped out. I stayed here for weeks trying to ferret out the witches. It was a longer case than most, but Marco understood how important it was."

Logan nodded. Marco had been Gia's mate for hundreds of years. Unlike others in their sisterhood, Gia didn't put down the mantle when she met him. She and Marco had grown up together, friends long before things had turned romantic. But he had been gone a long time, since before Logan had been born.

"During that case, I worked closely with Douglas," Gia continued. "I got to know him pretty well. But I hadn't anticipated his interest in me. Or mine in him for that matter. However, when all was said and done, I went home to Marco as I always did. My mate was a good man, and he deserved nothing less than my complete devotion. But don't think I wasn't tempted. Back then, Douglas was very much as he is now, strong and handsome. Age has tempered him, made him more contained and careful. But picture him a little brasher, a little more aggressive. It was a potent combination."

"Sounds familiar," Logan grumbled before running her hands over her face. "So this is normal?"

Gia laughed. "I didn't say that. We like what we like. And our sisters liked what they liked. Otherwise, there would be a long history of wolves and Elementals mating, and there isn't one. Both Di and Serin have worked Were cases and have been...unaffected. But when it comes to the wolves, the converse may be true. They might not be able to help it. It seems our kind holds a rather strong appeal to a certain class of alpha."

Logan threw up her hands. "What the hell does that mean?"

"I think—and this is just a guess based on my own experience— that males of Douglas and Connell's ilk, those at the top of the food chain, are compelled to take a female mate like them. An alpha female for an alpha male. It's built into their biology. We're not in their hierarchy, but a little above it. We don't register as alphas to them, but something more."

"So the reason Connell can't keep it in his pants is not his fault? It's mine?" Logan asked sarcastically.

"I didn't say that," Gia said, fiddling with her braid.

Logan grimaced. "And is this supernatural appeal strong enough to make a Were break his mate-vow?" she asked in a low voice.

Gia's eyes were sad. "I don't know, sweetheart."

17

Connell jumped out of Yogi's truck and hustled up the back porch steps. His sister was outside, pacing back and forth. When she saw him, her eyes lit up, but they dimmed when she saw Malcolm coming up beside him.

For a second, the blond Were paused, his eyes gravitating to Mara before skittering away. He put his head down and went through the kitchen door with the rest of the search party to get something to eat.

Connell lingered, reaching for her as the door closed. "I missed you, rugrat," he said, hugging her tight.

Mara smacked his back with a free hand before tightening her hold on him. "Me too, asshat."

Connell smirked and ruffled her hair. She wrinkled her nose and swatted his hand away.

"How are you?" he asked.

"I should be asking you that," Mara said with a frown. "You look... better. Sort of."

Connell humphed. He was better than he'd been when he'd left home to track Logan, but nowhere near as good as he was with the imp. In fact, his skin had been itching more and more the longer he went without seeing her.

"In a way, I am I guess, but it's not permanent." At least, he didn't think it was. "Is Logan inside?"

Mara shook her head. "After helping Sammy, she took off with that other one to the site where you were attacked."

He frowned. He had expected Logan to be here. The idea of her running around without him made him uncomfortable. "What other one?"

His sister shrugged, but her eyes widened. "Another Elemental showed up. Earth. Dad knows her."

"*What?*" he asked, confusion swamping him. His father had never mentioned knowing an Elemental.

"He's being pretty tight-lipped about it."

"What else is new?" Though Connell was his right hand, the chief only shared what he deemed fit.

Still, he could have mentioned knowing a freaking Elemental. They must not be on good terms, or he would have sent Connell after the one he knew.

He set aside thoughts of future complications and asked about the cub. "How did Logan help Sammy?"

Confusion flitted across his sister's face. "We're not sure how she did it. I don't think she knows either. But Sammy was a lot worse off than you were. Logan said his aura was bleeding off into the aether. Somehow, she managed to weave bits of her own into his, enough to stop that. Dad's confirmed it—although he's confused as hell as to how it happened."

Damn. Connell chuckled. Of course they were confused. "That sounds about right. Nothing that woman does surprises me anymore. I've learned to expect the unexpected in a short amount of time. So... what did you think of her?"

Mara's head drew back, and she scented the air. "Why?" she asked suspiciously.

Crap. His sister would be able to smell his arousal when he talked about Logan. Well, his mate's request that they keep things on the down low was unrealistic. They were werewolves, for Christ's sake.

He smiled at his sister, relaxing for the first time today. "I want you to like her."

His sister's eyes narrowed. "Well, she thinks you're a pussy, so I already do."

Connell's mouth turned down, and Mara laughed. "Did you really fly with her?"

Oh, that. "It's not flying. It's disintegrating and getting pushed along by the winds at supersonic speeds. And you wouldn't like it either. It hurts like a son of a bitch."

Her eyes widened. "Actually, that sounds fucking cool. I didn't think Elementals could take on passengers."

He wanted to tell her that he was special, but he didn't know for sure. Maybe Logan could pick up anyone at will and whip them through the clouds. Which got him considering something else. He wanted to tell the entire pack that Logan was his mate, but there was still a chance it wouldn't happen. Not if he didn't get his wolf back... but he could tell Mara. He told her things he didn't share with anyone else.

Connell's position as pack enforcer didn't encourage close friendships. He had plenty of friends and several brothers in arms he trusted with his life in battle, but no one he could talk with about his hopes and fears. No one but Mara. She was his sister and closest confidant despite the supercharged form of sibling rivalry that was common in Were families.

"There's something else," he said, looking around before leaning in and lowering his voice to just above a whisper. "Logan is mine."

Mara squinted at him. "What the hell does that mean?"

He took a deep breath. "I think she's my mate. We're together. Well, sort of. She's dragging her feet a bit, and I wasn't able to claim her—but I will once I get my wolf back."

Mara huffed a laugh and rolled her eyes to the heavens. "Only you would lose your wolf and still manage to score with an Elemental."

Irritated, he grunted at her. "It's not like that. She's *mine*. And she doesn't do casual. In fact, I don't think she's very experienced at all," he added, wondering again how many lovers had preceded him.

Not many, he decided. *And if I ever find out their names I'll make them regret they ever touched what is mine.*

He was so busy plotting deep dark revenge that he didn't notice Mara was frowning until she kicked him.

"Ow."

"Connell, how old is Logan?"

"You know her kind doesn't age," he said dismissively. "She's probably older than me."

His sister frowned. "That doesn't feel right." Her expression cleared, and then darkened once more. "Also, there's something you should know—"

A step on the other side of the door alerted them to the presence of another wolf, but the intruder's scent preceded them.

Connell resisted the urge to snarl when Riley pushed open the screen door and joined them on the porch. Had his ex-girlfriend been listening to his private conversation?

Good. The bitch should know she no longer had a place in his life. "What the hell are you doing here?" he growled.

Riley straightened up, a wounded expression flitting across her face. "I'm here for my family, or did you forget that Sammy is my cousin?"

He suppressed a snort. *Like you ever gave a shit about him before.* Unfortunately, the family tie was there. So long as the Kane family was okay with her presence, Riley could come and go as she pleased. Pack rules. But he didn't have to pretend to be happy to see her.

"Sammy is in my father's care and is now in Logan's as well. You're not needed." He leaned closer and lowered his voice to a flat and more menacing register. "Don't overstay your welcome."

He inclined his head meaningfully at Mara, gesturing that she should follow him inside, but Riley stepped up to him and put her hand on his arm.

"Connell, we need to talk," she said, her large blue eyes filled with tears that didn't fall.

It was an artful display, one he might have fallen for once upon a time. *Not going to work now.*

"We have nothing to say to each other," he said, shaking off her hand.

A lightning-fast smile flashed across Mara's face, but it was gone in a blink. He pushed past his ex and made his way into the mudroom, his sister at his heels. Bypassing the main entrance, he pulled her to the side door, the one that led to his father's office.

"Did Logan meet Riley?" he asked worriedly.

Mara nodded. "Salome introduced them...and no one but Malcolm and me knows you're not together anymore."

His sister's eyes tightened slightly at the mention of his father's third, but it was the only thing that gave her away.

"Have you two talked lately?" he asked softly.

Mara straightened. "No, why would we?" she said nonchalantly.

Her attempt at casual didn't fool him. Connell wasn't the only one hurt by Riley's infidelity with the other alpha.

His instinct was to comfort his sister, but there was little he could say that would be welcome. Mara would see the sympathy as an admission that he thought her weak, and she would despise it. Besides, Mara and Malcolm hadn't happened yet—and now they probably never would.

And you have a much bigger problem now.

Logan thought he had a mate. He needed to tell her the truth—even if it meant admitting how he felt about her. There was no way he could risk losing her over something like this. Riley was a cheat. She had shown her true colors when he'd lost his wolf, but the flaws in her character had always been there. He knew that now.

"I need to get to Logan. She's going to be pissed I didn't warn her about this. But Riley was supposed to be back East."

His ex had run after he'd tore into her about Malcolm. Riley always took off when things got sticky for her. Connell had expected her to waltz back a few months after he returned. If he had managed to get his wolf back, she'd have had her tail between her legs. And if he didn't, she would have resumed pursuing Malcolm. Either way, she'd continue to chase the top alpha in the pack—whoever it might be.

Mara hesitated. "As much as I dislike Riley, do you really think you should pursue Logan? I mean she's an Air Elemental. You spent months chasing her all over the world. Should you go for someone who won't be able to settle down?"

He hadn't wanted to think about that yet, but of course, Mara forced him to. "I will make it work."

He had to. There wasn't a choice. Not since he'd laid eyes on his sprite. *Once you get your wolf back*, he promised himself.

Mara looked skeptical. He put a hand on her shoulder and squeezed it, willing her to have some faith in him, before making a move to leave.

"Father will want your report," she reminded him.

"It will have to wait," he decided, his mind on finding Logan. "Besides, Malcolm will have already given his. He'll have told him what we found."

His sister's brittle nod when he mentioned Malcolm again made him ache with sympathy, but he didn't say anything. *The devil take it.* He was crap at all this emotional stuff.

"So did you find something?" she asked.

"Yes. Ask the others about it. I have to run." The need was urgent now. Every second that he was away from Logan felt wrong.

And there was always the chance she'd be pissed enough to leave now that there was a second Elemental who could take over for her here.

Not wasting another second, he turned on his heel and ran out the door. He headed for the garage and climbed on his little-used motorcycle. Next to his wolf, it was his fastest means of transportation in the woods.

———

MARA WATCHED her brother leave with mixed feelings. Despite his overbearing nature, she loved Connell with all her heart. She had thought the mess with Riley had hurt him, but it seemed like he was setting himself up for a much bigger fall.

Maybe it will be all right.

The Air Elemental might have real feelings for him. Women fell like bowling pins around Connell. What if one of them happened to be able to fly? Was that so outside the realm of possibility?

Lost in her thoughts, she didn't hear the heavy footsteps coming up behind her.

Mara spun around when she realized she wasn't alone. Annoyed at being caught off guard, she was ready to bite the head off the person intruding on her solitude.

Seeing Malcolm, she closed her mouth, lips forming a tight seam. She gave him a curt nod and fixed her eyes on the distant tree line. When he just stood there like an ass, she cleared her throat. "I need to speak to my father. Excuse me," she said, moving away.

It was the longest sentence they'd exchanged in months. She didn't intend to make it any longer, but his hand shot out, grabbing her arm.

"Mara...I..."

"*What?*" she bit out when he didn't say anything more.

"I made a mistake."

"Yeah, no shit." She snorted, shrugging his hand off. "But that's between you and Connell. It has nothing to do with me."

"Mara, I was drunk—"

She rolled her eyes. That was a piss-poor excuse for a Were, and he knew it. They metabolized alcohol too quickly for it to be a viable reason for that level of screw-up.

"Well, I had been drinking," he amended, a little more honestly. "But it's no excuse for what I did. I...I don't even like Riley."

Then why did you fuck her? she thought, her vision darkening

Her temper had always been close to the surface. It had taken her years to gain control over her emotions, but at the moment, Mara felt like she was going to explode. Taking a deep breath, she counted to ten. She wasn't about to humiliate herself by making a scene.

She and Malcolm had never even been on a date. That didn't

seem to matter, though. She was raw, stuffed to the brim with feelings she could barely justify.

Neck corded, Mara spoke as calmly as she could. "Again, I don't know why you're telling me this," she muttered from behind gritted teeth. "It's my brother you need to make amends to. Riley was *his* girlfriend."

Malcolm shuffled on his feet. It was a disconcerting gesture for someone so large. "Maybe we could have dinner sometime?"

Is he fucking kidding? After almost two years of half-hidden glances and built-up expectations that went absolutely nowhere, he was finally asking her out? Now, after he'd slept with her brother's girlfriend?

If it had been anyone but Riley.

"No, thank you." She spun on her heel, ready to get the hell out of there.

Malcolm stepped in front of her, his hands up. "I don't mean now," he said. "I mean later...maybe next month?"

Mara closed her eyes. Her head was spinning, and her stomach hurt.

"Or the month after?" he asked, a pleading note in his voice.

She cracked an eyelid and squinted at him. Would she ever be able to look at him and not feel betrayed?

You're not the one he betrayed. He owed you nothing, she reminded herself. But the knot in her throat wouldn't let her get the words out.

"I have to go," she whispered hoarsely, breaking past him without looking back.

She hurried inside, eager to find a place to be alone. But that was easier said than done. No sooner had she reached the landing than she was intercepted by her father.

Mara surreptitiously wiped at the moisture in her eyes. *The wind outside made them run.*

It didn't matter. Her father was too preoccupied to notice. "Where is your brother?" he asked.

"He left again," she said, unsure of what to tell him. Connell wouldn't want the chief to know about this idea that Logan was his mate, would he?

"To go to the Air Elemental."

She nodded, wondering vaguely why he didn't mention the second Elemental.

Gia had made an immediate and lasting impression on her. Earth had the gravitas that came with true power, and though Mara had little to justify her opinion, Gia struck her as wise. She was a soothing and calming presence.

I wish she were here, she thought, surprising herself. *Or Logan.* Right then, she would have welcomed either Elemental. *I guess I like them. Go figure.*

When her father didn't say anything, she started to become concerned. The chief looked tense, more brooding than usual.

"What's wrong?"

"I think your brother is in trouble."

More than he was already in? *Oh, shit.* He knew... "Because he likes Logan?" she asked quietly.

"No, because he thinks he's in love with her."

18

Gia turned her attention to the southwest a split second before Logan did. Someone was coming. A motorcycle was approaching at top speed. Instinct told her it was the wolfless Were long before the shape of the man came into view, and Logan's shoulders tensed.

Concern for her sister was paramount, but Gia bit her tongue as a muscular young man—one uncomfortably close to Douglas in appearance—pulled off his helmet and climbed off the bike.

As much as she wanted to guide her sisters and protect them from harm, life's lessons had to be learned firsthand. Whatever happened next, however Logan chose to deal with this situation, Gia couldn't interfere. It wasn't her place.

It was difficult to remain silent as she read the pain in her sister's eyes as she watched the damaged Were approach. However, Connell didn't seem to have that problem.

"Logan, I can explain," he called out, hurrying up to them.

Logan had been kneeling, looking for trace evidence on the ground, but she stood straight and narrowed her eyes at Connell. And then Gia saw something that made her proud and reminded her why the Mother had chosen Logan as her sister.

The Air Elemental fisted one hand, her expression wiping clean. There was no hint of the pain she had been feeling moments before —Logan had always been exceptionally good at compartmentalizing.

"Explain what?" her sister asked in a perfectly neutral voice.

The Were's reaction was telling. He looked hurt. And very worried...

Maybe this isn't what I thought it was, Gia considered before the Were opened his mouth again.

"About Riley—"

He didn't get another word out. Logan didn't flinch, but her fist tightened. With a flick of her fingers, the Were was gone—his molecules dancing in the air like dust in the wind.

It was Gia who flinched as the aether filled with Connell's shouts and the occasional howl.

Well, that answered that question. When push came to shove, Logan wasn't the type to wallow in hurt. She was the type to get even.

The aether reverberated with another howl, and she winced. "Um, Logan, sweet, I don't think he likes that."

A slow, wicked smile appeared like the dawn on her sister's face. "*I know.*"

Gia bit her lip to keep from laughing, although she wanted to point out that Connell's ability to travel in the winds was significant. *Perhaps he is something to her after all...*

If this ability only extended to Connell and his family, then perhaps Gia had misread the situation. Or it was part of Logan's natural ability to take a non-mate into the currents. It wasn't a common gift, but the youngest Elemental had always been advanced.

Only time would tell. Deciding to leave the two to talk, she wandered close to the stream. Hopefully, it wouldn't be too long before Logan tired of tormenting the Were—even if he did deserve it.

She'd hate to have to explain to Douglas that his son had acquired a raging case of post-traumatic stress at her sister's hands.

THE ANGER LOGAN was feeling cooled with the breeze. She was in control—now that she'd proved Connell's fate was literally in her hands.

It was a reminder they both needed. Getting involved with him had been a mistake, but she had committed to helping him. And she was going to do it if it killed him.

Her mental balance restored, Logan let Connell come together. He collapsed in a heap next to a large fir tree. Whatever hurt she had felt at learning that Connell had a mate was locked away. She would do her job and leave him to the blonde if that was what he wanted. And if it wasn't, it didn't matter. His personal life was no longer her concern.

"I don't need an explanation," she said coldly. "What's between you and your mate is your business. I'm here to do a job, one that you temporarily distracted me from. That's over with now. It's time to find out what the hell is going on with these attacks."

It felt good to lay down the law, but Connell didn't appear to appreciate the return of her professionalism.

"Riley isn't my mate," he gasped, rushing the words as if he was worried she would blast him again. He paused, wheezing slightly. "She's my ex, but not everyone knows we broke up yet."

Logan held up a hand. "I don't care," she said, and it really sounded as if she meant it.

Connell scowled. "You should. *You're my mate.* That woman is not! She's a cheating whore."

Her head drew back. He *did* think she was his mate? Somehow, that superseded the fact Riley had cheated on him.

The wind filled with sound, the spirits of air and earth weighing in on Connell's truthfulness. Ignoring the contradictory hisses and whispers, she blinked, clearing her head.

"I'm not your mate. It's not real, what you're feeling," she said, somehow managing to keep the wistfulness out of her voice.

Connell's expression turned thunderous as he got to his feet. "I know what I feel, and it is real. *You are mine.*"

A tiny, weak part of her thrilled at the words, but Logan couldn't accept them. "Once this is over and I'm gone, you'll go back to feeling normal again. Whether that includes feelings for your former mate—"

"I will never want her back," Connell broke in. "She's faithless. The second my wolf was gone, she was playing up to the next alpha in line. Malcolm felt terrible about it, but he confessed to me that she'd seduced him. And I could still smell a lie. She didn't know that. But what Riley did doesn't matter. Not anymore. Besides, the problems were there before. I never loved her, and I never claimed her."

What the hell was she supposed to say to that?

"Not really my business," Logan said slowly.

Connell looked like he wanted to put her over his knee, but he didn't make the mistake of touching her. "Stop talking like that," he said, his voice a low rumble.

"Actually, that's a good idea," Logan said, circling him with something of her old swagger. "We should stop talking about anything that isn't about your case or Sammy's."

"Logan—" he said, starting toward her.

"*Connell.*"

It was her tone that stopped him in his tracks. He stood silently, his broad shoulders relaxing after a moment before he let his hands down. "*Fine.* We won't discuss our relationship. Not yet. But once this is settled, we'll be having a very *long* talk."

Logan blushed in spite of herself. It was clear that Connell didn't intend for there to be much actual conversation if he had his way.

Well, he's not getting his way. She was getting hers.

Connell paced in front of her, throwing her the occasional smoldering glance while muttering under his breath. After a minute, he put his hands on his hips and faced her, a wall of aggressive testosterone and muscle. It almost looked as if he were going to leap on her anyway when a delicate throat was cleared.

Logan swung her gaze to Gia, who had stepped away to give her time to deal with the new arrival. She shot her older sister a grateful glance, and Gia nodded before turning to Connell.

"Hello, Connell Maitland, son of Douglas. My name is Gia."

Connell looked confused for a second as he assessed the small Hispanic woman in front of him.

Logan could see the play of emotions across his face. It was hard to believe so much raw power could be contained in one small body. But Gia was the real deal, and Connell could see it. It was in his eyes. He lowered his head and nodded, but his respectfulness didn't last. He turned back to Logan, and all the annoying male aggressiveness was back in an instant.

"I found the site of Sammy's attack. It's only a few miles from the Kane house," he announced.

Finally, a lead she could follow. She turned to her sister. "Will you come?"

Gia turned to her, her gaze flitting between her and Connell with a small smile on her face. "Yes, for now."

Logan held out one hand to her sister and reluctantly extended the other to Connell. He reached out to clasp her hand in his much larger one. They were gone in the breeze, Connell's motorbike temporarily abandoned.

19

The winds read Connell's direction and deposited them at a small glen surrounded by young trees twenty kilometers to the east. Unlike the location of Connell's attack, the stain of violence was still fresh, although it was much smaller than Logan had expected.

"Almost nothing," Gia said, her nose wrinkling.

Logan turned to her and nodded in agreement.

Every hair of the Earth Elemental's braid was still in place. She was completely unaffected by the trip. Logan resisted the urge to smirk at Connell, who was holding his head as if his ears were ringing.

"Are you okay?" she asked him, a superior little smile on her face.

Connell shook his head like a dog and glowered at her. "I'm fine," he said defensively. "It gets easier and easier."

Logan pursed her lips and focused on their surroundings. Turning around in a circle, she examined the space around them, absorbing what information she could from the winds, but they were silent except for the odd bit of swearing here and there.

Dry pine needles littered the ground on a mostly dirt floor. This late in autumn, there was little green besides the sparse pines mixed in with the bare hardwoods.

"Why isn't it bigger?" she asked.

"What do you mean?" Connell asked.

"The act of tearing an aura apart should have left an echo of violence that we could see even from space," Logan exaggerated. "Instead, this is small and already fading."

"Yes," Gia said, her eyes closed as she focused on the terrain.

Though Logan had seen it multiple times, it was always awe inspiring to watch Gia work. The voices Gia referred to as her "wind talkers" were spirits of the dead—most of them anyway. She suspected the loudest voices were members of her family line, but that was just a guess. Gia's gift was different. She was listening to the earth, absorbing what information she could glean from soil and stone.

It was one thing to have a pet rock; it was another to have it talk back to you.

"There's something here," Gia said eventually. "But it's not on the scale it should be. It's no wonder there's nothing left where you were attacked. In fact, I'm somewhat surprised that we can detect anything at all after seeing this."

She gestured to the trees around them. With a nod of agreement, Logan ran a frustrated hand through her hair while Connell paced the small diameter of the clearing.

"I don't feel anything like that," he said.

Logan frowned. "Then how did you find this place?"

"Fear. I can smell it. This place reeks of Sammy's fear and something else..."

He trailed off and looked around, his pain for the little cub apparent in the tightness of his features and the stiff set of his posture. Subdued now, Logan felt sorry for him despite her lingering hurt feelings.

"What's the something else?" Gia asked after a beat of silence.

Connell rolled his shoulders and glared at the trees like they were responsible for his current predicament. "It's faint, but there's a trace of something like...surprise. Shock."

He scowled and passed a hand over his face. "You need to find the person responsible. I need someone I can beat into a bloody heap."

Gia smiled at him sympathetically, but Logan's lip curled. "No, that's my job," she said.

Connell crossed his ridiculously defined muscular arms. "I'm the enforcer in these parts."

"One without a wolf," she pointed out bluntly, making his expression darken. But she wasn't in the mood to pull her punches.

"All right, so what does this tell us?" she murmured, more to herself than the others as she studied the lingering traces of magic in the air. She turned to Gia. "There are no ley lines around here, are there?"

"None close enough to make a difference," her sister confirmed.

Gia started walking around the circle, bending occasionally to touch the earth or turn over a stone. Meanwhile, Connell paced in the opposite direction like a caged animal.

Look high.

Logan snapped her eyes up, following the breeze that whipped her long hair around. The winds had been silent since entering the clearing, but now a voice she recognized rose up from the aether. *Look high*, it repeated.

Pivoting on her heel, she scanned the tree trunks around them, a glint of something metallic catching her eye. Adrenaline carried her across the clearing to the tall trunk of a pine tree. A fragment of something silver was embedded in the rough bark about two and a half meters up.

Connell had been watching her. He moved behind her and put his hands on her waist to lift her above his head, high enough to reach the object.

Twisting to give him a venomous look, she flashed out of his arms. She reappeared clinging to the trunk right over the object, holding herself with one hand while her heels dug into the bark.

Prying the thing out with her free hand, she took hold of it before dropping to the ground. Turning it over, she held it up for Gia to see. Both she and Connell crowded closer.

The object was a flat piece of metal only a few centimeters long. It was shaped like a spike, with a jagged bottom from where it had broken off something larger.

"There's something familiar about this," she said, handing it to Gia.

Gia hummed. "Perhaps. The metal is terrestrial at least. Most of it. It's a composite. It does contain iron from a meteorite. However, it's only a trace."

"But doesn't it feel good?" Logan asked.

Connell harrumphed. "How in the seven hells can it feel good?"

Even Gia was looking at her funny. Logan shrugged.

"It just does," she said, taking the piece when Gia handed it back. She held it between her fingers. The sensation was difficult to explain —it felt like home.

"Yes, that's it..." she said, holding up the spike. "This thing feels familiar. Like it's mine."

Connell face darkened at her words. "Are you telling me it belongs to you?"

"No. That's not what I mean." She shook her head. "I've never seen it before." She turned to Gia. "But don't you feel something similar? A connection?"

Her sister shook her head. "Not quite. There's a sense of familiarity, of course, but not one of belonging or possession."

A large hand reached out. Logan inhaled and handed the piece to Connell. No sooner had he taken hold of it with the tips of his fingers than he swore loudly and dropped it.

"Son of a bitch," he said, sucking on his fingers.

Logan and Gia watched him, eyes wide. "What happened?" Logan asked.

"Did it burn you?" Gia asked.

Connell did one of those headshakes that reminded her of a dog again as she bent to pick up the fragment.

"Fucking shit, yes," he growled. "But it wasn't hot. It was cold, like sub-zero." He narrowed his eyes at Logan. "And I think you're right. It's yours somehow."

It wasn't what he said, so much as the way he said it, that made her stomach drop. She stared into Connell's handsome face and could see the heat in his eyes dying as he looked at her. In its place, suspicion grew.

Despite her acceptance that Connell wasn't her true mate, the distrust in his eyes hurt like hell.

Gia looked from one to the other. "What precisely do you mean?" she asked.

He scowled. "I can hear the buzz in the air when I touch it—the same one I hear when I touch Logan when she's listening to the winds. Spirits or whatever the fuck. The ones that give her intel."

"You can hear them?" Logan asked, unable to hide her dismay, but he didn't answer her.

What did that mean? Not even her sisters could hear the voices on the wind—not unless she was sending them a message. Then they heard her voice—but not the spirits that had filled her ears since childhood. How could Connell hear them?

He'd hinted that he could at the *howf*. But she'd immediately dismissed the notion. Nothing in their long history suggested that another type of Supernatural—mate or otherwise—could hear the wind spirits.

Only witches of elemental lines were susceptible. Those that did were marked. Often, they inherited the Elemental mantle, but not always. It was a rare gift, one often disguised as a curse. And not all Air Elementals could hear them for the Mother's sake!

She turned to Gia, her confusion and pain clear to her sister. The Earth Elemental didn't appear alarmed, only intrigued.

"Interesting," Gia murmured before cocking her head at Logan and gesturing at her to step away from the contentious Were.

They walked to the other side of the clearing, and Logan leaned in to hiss at supersonic speed.

"What the hell is going on, Gia? Not even a mate should be able to hear the winds. And he's definitely not my mate. You said so yourself!"

Gia's mouth turned down at the corner, and she rocked back on her heels. "Well, that isn't exactly what I said. But you're right. In any case, this is unprecedented. And it's a hell of an important clue."

She reached out for the fragment, and Logan handed it over. "Do you think it belongs to us?" Logan asked.

Gia nodded. "Somehow, I think it might. I'm going to take this to T'Kaieri to search the archives. There is something about this thing—a suggestion of a memory if you will."

"And you think there's a record in the archives that will explain what it is?"

The Earth Elemental took a deep breath. "I hope so. The fact that you're drawn to it is significant in of itself. But combine that with the fact the Were over there associates it with your wind talkers, and I'd say a trip to the island is imperative."

Logan wrinkled her nose and glanced over at Connell. "I suppose that means that I have to stay here?"

Gia grimaced. "If it wasn't for the child, I'd say we both could go, but you're the one who has made a connection with the cub. Also, if this piece is part of a larger whole and it's still in the area, then you stand a better chance of finding the thing than I do."

Shoulders slumping, Logan nodded. "Trust you to be logical and reasonable about this."

"I'm sorry, darling. But he's not stupid. He knows you didn't do this."

Peeking at the glowering Were, Logan narrowed her eyes. "I wouldn't bet on the not stupid part myself," she whispered at a volume so low no human could have heard at that distance.

She was rewarded with a deep growl from Connell's direction. *Just like old times.* It almost made her want to smile, but she restrained herself long enough to hug her sister goodbye.

"If you find something, send word. I can get to the island in a few hours."

Gia put her hand on her cheek, and suddenly, Logan felt much younger and smaller than she was. "Trust your instincts and in the Mother's guidance. You're here for a reason. Don't forget that."

With that, the ground underneath them rippled and softened. Logan stepped away to watch the earth open. Gia slowly sank from view, leaving her alone with one pissed-off idiot Were and the weight of the world on her shoulders.

20

Connell watched the Elementals talk across the glen. It was hard to believe that those two small women contained the power of Mother Earth. *Earthquakes and summer storms...*

He regretted his snap judgment of Logan when she admitted feeling a connection to the bit of scrap metal they found. The fragment had to be from a weapon of some kind. Glancing up at the tree trunk where the piece had been lodged, he counted the meters. *At least three.* He stepped up to the tree and turned his back to it, raising his hands over his head as if holding a sword or a spear.

He was close to the right height. In his mind, he pictured the assailant holding the weapon above his head to strike down at Sammy. They would have had to hit the trunk behind him pretty hard to get that shard stuck in the bark.

That someone had to be almost as tall as he was. At most, they were a few inches shorter. He glanced at his mate. She was nearly a foot and a half too small. Not to mention that she didn't need a weapon to inflict the kind of damage that had been done to him. She would use magic.

He was feeling fairly stupid for jumping to conclusions when he heard Logan call him an idiot. Connell chaffed at the idea of his mate thinking so little of him, even if he had been acting like one. Growling in response, he crossed his arms and waited for the Elemental conversation to wrap up. He needed to speak to his mate and clear up this Riley bullshit.

Only half his attention was on them. His mind kept going over the faint scent of surprise he kept detecting among these trees. Then the sound of sand shifting carried to him, and he snapped to attention. Underneath the two women, the dirt was moving like quicksand. The Earth Elemental was sinking, disappearing from view.

Fuck! Was Logan leaving? He crouched and braced himself, ready to spring into the bowels of the earth after them. But Logan stepped away from the shifting sand, and then they were alone.

He heaved a silent sigh of relief.

Logan didn't seem to share his sentiment. Her adorable little nose was wrinkled as if she smelled something bad. They stared at each other for a long moment.

"We should go to the house and check on Sammy," he said, extending his hand, palm up.

Logan glanced at his outstretched hand and smirked. "Get your own ride, douchebag."

She was gone in a blink, a blast of cold air smacking him in the face.

He scanned the skies. "Yeah, that sounds about right..."

Sighing, he started to run.

IT TOOK him a full hour to get back. Forty-five minutes running on foot, and then a quarter hour on his bike. When he got back inside the house, it was late. Most of the lights were off, but his father was waiting for him.

"Is Logan here?" he asked.

Douglas nodded. "She's with the cub."

Nodding, he stopped to take off his jacket. "We found something."

"She told me. It didn't sound familiar."

"No, I didn't recognize the piece," Connell said. "But it's possible they do. The other Elemental agreed and went to go dig up whatever she could on it."

His father leaned against the mudroom door. "Logan didn't mention that, only that Gia held on to it."

"Yes, that Gia woman is looking into it," he said, unconcerned. "Mara says you know her."

"I do."

Connell waited, but his father didn't volunteer more. *Okay, then.*

"I gotta go see Logan," he said, crossing the empty living room to head for the stairs.

"She's not your mate."

Connell hesitated and turned around. He hadn't planned to have this conversation in the form of a fight, but if that was how the chief wanted to play it, so be it.

"Actually, she is." He was ninety-nine percent sure.

Okay, maybe ninety-five.

Douglas sighed and passed a hand over his face. "I'm sorry, son, but she's not. Trust me on this."

Connell's head drew back. He should have expected this reluctance, but his father talking about it out loud was catching him off guard. The chief didn't discuss personal matters with his subordinates, not even his son.

"Father, I have the highest respect for your opinion. As your second, I am ready to serve you in any way that I can, but taking a mate is a private matter. You don't get to weigh in on this."

The issue of getting to choose your own mate was something they'd fought wars over. It was one of the issues his grandfather had lobbied for. Before the packs were united, each pack alpha could dictate who mated with whom—sometimes against the wolf's own natural inclination. When that happened and the alpha didn't relent, he might try to impose his own will over a pair of subordinates to force a union. It was a practice that led to a lot of strife and misery. Allowing wolves to mate according to their own nature had thrown a lot of support his grandfather's way. Any interference with a courtship was now against pack law.

Douglas waved his hand, forestalling further argument. "That's not what I'm doing. I'm trying to explain. I would have warned you, but I didn't think this through. It was my mistake. I should have prepared you for the possibility when you left, but my primary concern was your missing wolf."

Connell leaned against the back of the couch. He crossed his arms. "What are you trying to say?"

Douglas opened and closed his mouth.

This was getting weird. His father was the chief. He was the most confident man Connell knew. He ruled the coalition pack with an iron hand, his quiet authority as solid and as deep as the mountains around them.

"Dad?"

"A true alpha always tries to claim the most powerful female as his mate. It's instinctive, but false. What you're feeling is merely an artifact of what she is," he said.

Ah. Understanding warmed his gut. "This is why you didn't mention knowing the other Elemental—why you didn't send me to find Gia in the first place. She rejected you."

His father bristled. "You assume much—including that I'll allow such disrespect from my second simply because you're my son," he said sharply. He waited a moment before continuing more softly. "However, in time, you'll see I'm right. This business will conclude, one way or another, and the Air Elemental will leave. You'll forget this temporary attraction, and your bond with Riley will reassert itself. After Gia left, things went back to normal for me."

Connell raised his hands. "I don't have a bond with Riley. I have one with Logan, and she feels it too."

His father gave him a look tinged with pity. "Maybe she feels a little something. I think Gia did too, although she never said as much. Most women would be attracted to males like us. But Gia had a mate."

Unnecessary apprehension tightened Connell's chest, thoughts of his mother filling his head. *It's all right. It doesn't matter. He met mom—after—and they loved each other.* He remembered that last part well from his childhood.

His mother had been bright and funny, a vibrant soul. She had balanced out his father's gravity and made them a real family. And his father had adored her. Ellen Maitland hadn't been second best to an Elemental. The parallels between the past and present ended there.

"My situation is different," Connell asserted when he remembered himself. "Logan does have a mate, but it's me."

His father clenched his jaw, his frustration evident. "Once she's gone, you're going to be fine—in a few weeks. Maybe a few months. You and Riley—"

He held up a hand. "I'm glad Mom was still out there somewhere waiting for you. She was the best. But Riley is not Mom."

His father started to interrupt, but Connell shook his head. "The second my wolf was gone, Riley went after Malcolm. She seduced him, but he felt like shit about it, and he confessed it to me. That's why he wasn't around that much while I was away. He was feeling guilty." One corner of his mouth twisted up. "You should know by now that Riley's not the kind to jeopardize her position in the pack by risking being tied to a Were who can't shift."

Silence. Then his father grimaced. "But as your mate, she wouldn't—"

"I told you, Riley's not my mate. I never claimed her. I never even slept with her."

Douglas' eyes widened slightly. "But I thought you two were..."

Connell exhaled, a sound tinged with relief. "No. I guess my instincts were warning me not to tie myself to someone so inherently power hungry," he said with a shrug. "Now I think Malcolm did me a favor, although I didn't feel that way at the time."

His father scowled. "Riley made a huge scene earlier, right before Logan got here—about not trusting the Elemental. At the time, I thought it was justified jealousy," he said in a tone that revealed his distaste for the emotional display.

"It wasn't justified," he said. "Just more of the bullshit I'm glad I don't have to deal with anymore."

His father shrugged. "So your mate isn't Riley. That doesn't mean the Elemental is. There will be another candidate. Maybe even a compatible human."

Man, his father must be grasping at straws to even suggest he take a human mate.

"Dad, I can't explain, mostly because I don't want to, but Logan and I are supposed to be together. I know you may not like hearing that because it means some things might change. I may not be around all the time. But I'll be here when it counts."

"Son, I know your attraction to Logan is strong—"

"It's not mine alone. This isn't a one-sided thing only in my head," he repeated.

Exasperated, his father glared at him, and Connell reluctantly decided to share more than anyone would have wanted a parent to know.

"Look...I didn't want to get into this with you, but Logan and I— we've already happened. I just need to get my wolf back to make it official."

The blank look on his father's face spoke volumes. "What do you mean by that?"

Connell wrinkled his nose. "You're not going to make me spell it out, are you?"

"Oh." Douglas coughed. "I see."

It's about time. He stepped closer and put his hands on his father's shoulders. He hadn't realized that he was taller than he was until this moment.

When did that happen?

"I suppose you could say that she might be playing with me," Connell said, voicing an unacknowledged fear. "All I can say is it doesn't feel that way. Whatever happens, I'm going to try and make this work."

Douglas considered that, stroking his beard with the length of his index finger. "Even if this does go your way, and I'm not convinced it will, you still have to consider your duties here. You're responsible for the safety of the pack. I depend on you, as does everyone else around here. That Logan girl is not the type to be tied down to one place. And that's not just because she's an Elemental."

Chest tight, he nodded. "I know that. I'll figure something out when the time comes."

If it comes.

He could feel the weight of his father's disappointment, but Douglas simply nodded. "I suppose that is all I can ask," he said before walking away.

Well, if that wasn't enough to make him feel like shit, nothing was. Connell waited for a beat, and then started for the stairs. He wanted to see where Logan was sleeping tonight.

She would want to stay close while the cub was still at risk. Of course, that didn't mean he would be able to talk her into sleeping in his room tonight. But at least he could make sure she was comfortable in the bed next to Sammy.

He paused outside the bedroom, surprised to hear Logan talking. After a moment, it became evident that she wasn't speaking to Sammy. The other voice was his sister's, and they were trading war stories.

"You were a UN peacekeeper?" he heard Logan ask with some surprise.

"Yeah," Mara replied. "I volunteered with an all-female unit."

"Human or shifter?"

"All the others were human. Pack females aren't encouraged to fight or become soldiers."

There was a small sound like an approving humph. He thought it came from Logan.

"Did you see any combat?"

"Not that my father knows about. Officially, my squad didn't see any action, but I couldn't sit on my hands during some of those situations. I would sneak out at night after everyone had bunked down for the night and go hunting. It was fun."

Connell smiled to himself. He knew all about Mara's covert

AWOL action, but he was pretty sure he was the only one she'd told. Until now.

Glad that his sister was getting along with Logan, he decided to check back later after a hot shower. He walked to his room at the end of the hall and threw open the door. Riley was sitting on the bed.

Not now. He made a production of shoving the door open wider and gesturing for her to get out.

Riley stood and offered him her neck, a wolf's sign of submission and deepest regret.

He didn't move. "Get the fuck out of my room."

"Connell, I'm trying to show you how sorry I am."

"Seriously, five seconds, or I will show you out—the window," he added flatly.

Riley's blue eyes filled with tears. "Why won't you talk to me? I know I made a huge mistake, but after everything we've been to each other, I think I deserve a little conversation."

He sighed and leaned against the doorjamb. "That's just it. I don't think we ever meant all that much to each other. Otherwise, we would have sealed the deal ages ago."

Riley's face tightened. "That's not my fault! You're the one who wanted to wait."

He shrugged. "We only dated a few months," he said dismissively.

"It was almost a year."

"Really?" he asked, genuinely surprised.

"*Yes,*" she said pointedly.

He stared at the woman he'd expected to marry. When had he stopped feeling anything for her? He couldn't even summon up any anger. All he felt now was a sort of exhausted frustration that he still had to deal with her.

"Look, sorry things didn't work out. But this is over. In fact, it never started, and I think that's for the best," he said.

He didn't feel generous enough to suggest she and Malcolm make a go of it—not when her happiness would come at the expense of his sister's.

Like Mara is ever going to be happy now...

He got a little lost thinking about how few wolves there were out there who could handle someone like his sister. He'd hoped Malcolm would be man enough, but given recent events, it was becoming clear the other wolf preferred someone more submissive.

"Connell, are you even listening to me?"

He snapped to attention. "No," he grumbled. "Why are you still here?"

"God, Connell, is this about her—that *child*?"

He crossed his arms. "You know Logan's hearing is as good as ours, and she won't appreciate being called a child."

"She *is* a child, one with too much power for her own good."

His mouth compressed. "You know, green is not your color."

Riley threw up her hands. "I can't believe you're even considering being with that *thing*."

He growled low in his throat, and Riley gathered her hands to her chest and leaned back. "That's your first warning," he said.

Riley narrowed her eyes. "You can't handle someone that powerful," she hissed spitefully. "You'll regret giving me up when she leaves your ass in the dust."

She stalked past him and slammed the door behind her.

Good riddance.

"Did you bring me up or did she?"

Connell spun around to see Logan standing next to his open window.

God, it was good to see her—especially in his bedroom. "I don't suppose you're here to ask if you can spend the night?" he asked, waggling his brows with a significant nod at his California King.

Logan's death stare was much better than Riley's. "Who brought me up?"

He sighed. "She did. Why?"

"Because I don't need you throwing me in your ex's face to help you end your relationship. Clean up your own mess."

He stepped up to her, a little surprised when she let him put his hands on her shoulders. "Logan, my relationship *is* over."

"Sure it is," she said, her mouth turned down. She walked to the window. "Don't forget. Leave me out of your bullshit, or I'll remove your testicles."

With that unforgettable exit line, she flashed out the window. Following her, he stuck his head outside into the night air.

"Don't do anything rash. You would miss those eventually..." he called after her.

Leaving the window open, he stripped down to take a shower. After being constantly on the go for the last few months, it felt good to be home.

He took his time drying off. By the time he was ready for bed, Logan was passed out in the guest room, curled up in the middle of the bed across from Sammy's. He quietly let himself in and slipped in next to her.

Damn, he thought these things were longer. He used to fit better when he slept here as a cub with his friends. Pulling his legs up closer to Logan, he got comfortable—as comfortable as he was going to get as a man anyway. He would fit in this bed much better if he still had his wolf.

I'll get it back, he assured himself. *And when I do...*

He hoped Logan wasn't allergic to fur.

21

G ia arose from the depths on the beach of T'Kaieri and blinked as the last rays of the sun hit her eyes. She had made it to the island in record time, but not quickly enough to act while the sun was still up. However, that didn't matter. The archives housing their records and artifacts were always pitch black. Torches lit by Elemental fire illuminated the space, even in daylight.

The island was known by many names, but Gia still called it by the one she had learned in her youth. T'Kaieri had been the ancestral home of the Water Elementals since well before Columbus. Her sister Serin was the latest Water to be born there. She had been preceded by Lanai and before that, Kara, who each gave up the mantle voluntarily in accordance with island tradition. It was an unbroken line that stretched back close to a millennia.

Stretching, Gia savored the salt-scented breeze and squinted at the columned streets of the city. The delicate spired buildings rose high above the beach, culminating in a rocky peak known as Siba. The summit housed a temple dedicated to Atabey, which was what the locals called the Mother.

If it weren't for the sunshine and warm, balmy breezes, this place would bear a strong resemblance to a much larger Mont Saint Michel, France, at least from a distance. Up close, the delicate architecture of the spiral turreted buildings and arched colonnades always reminded her of seashells nested in the lush vegetation.

Though the city was divided into districts of concentric rings, there were four major thoroughfares along the cardinal directions. Smaller walking paths could be found equidistant between them, cutting the city into a pie with eight pieces. The path she was waiting at ran all the way up to the Mother's temple on Mount Siba at the center of the island. It continued down the other side, clear across the island. A similar path ran east to west, with an arch at each end marking each entrance.

Gia had always thought the graceful homes and public buildings were too frail to survive the periodic hurricanes this part of the Caribbean was known for. But the Mother never dished out more than the island could take.

Unlike so many other spots in the world, this hidden enclave still felt alive. It was one of those rare places where she could still feel the Mother's embrace—and for a visiting Elemental, that was literal.

The air was full of perfume of either day or night-blooming flowers, depending on when Gia arrived. It was also the ideal temperature. If she were too hot, the breeze cooled her down. If she were cold, the air around her heated until she was warm. It was a small show of favor to one of Her chosen.

The location was classified, but over the centuries, little clues had escaped the tight wall of secrecy surrounding the island—enough to fuel rumors of Atlantis in this part of the world. However, there was no volcanic threat buried in the heart of this place—only layers of ritual and mystery that had the isle locked up tighter than a drum.

Gia felt the welcoming caress of the tropical air, but she didn't relax. Her arrival had been sensed by the wardens, which meant that at this moment, a formal welcoming committee was being assembled in honor of her visit.

She didn't have time for it, but over the years, Gia had learned she had to go through the first few steps before she could reasonably excuse herself. Any attempt to skip the preliminaries either gave offense or generated panic about a possible apocalypse among the populace.

Suppressing a sigh, she squinted at the slow procession assembling on the path above the northern arch, mentally willing them to go faster. Holding her hands behind her back, she counted the number of robes in the party. In her experience, the length of the greeting ceremony was directly proportional to the number of people in modern dress. More robes meant more delay.

She used to think the prolonged meet and greets were a way of keeping her from getting too comfortable here. Gia was Earth, and this was the ancestral home of Water. She imagined it would be jarring for the elders who governed T'Kaieri if another kind of Elemental decided to make their home here. Despite the fact that some outsiders had found a home here over the years, all members of the assembly were related to a Water Elemental by blood. It had seemed only natural that they might feel threatened when she came around.

Much later, Gia had come to realize that the ceremonies and rituals were prolonged especially for her. Diana and Logan both had similar greetings, but in a much abbreviated form. But *she* was the eldest. Therefore, they were showing her the greatest respect by dragging their oldest inhabitants down to the beach to formally welcome her.

Don't forget, it's an honor, she told herself as the motley crew came into view along the beach.

It got a little easier to remember when she spotted John, Serin's uncle, in the crowd alongside the assembly. The title was honorific. He was technically only Jordan's uncle, but most people called him by the title. John was one of the few white men who called T'Kaieri home. He had found the island nearly a century ago and ingratiated himself to the elders. Instead of erasing his memory and sending him on his way, they allowed him to stay. He had eventually married and become a valued member of the community. Years later, he had brought his nephew Jordan here to live with the elder's blessing. A decade ago, the latter had been bonded with Serin.

Though she didn't know Jordan well, Gia did know and like John. She remembered all too well what it had been like before his arrival. His relaxing influence over the elders and warm, avuncular manner smoothed over the inevitable little conflicts that sprang up between Serin and the elders.

Maybe I can get out of this quicker than I thought, she mused as the procession reached the arch. A tall, elegant figure broke away from the crowd and approached.

"Greetings Gia, beloved one of Atabey," Dalasini, Serin's mother, said with a small inclination of her head.

Gia bowed with equal formality. "I thank you for your welcome, Dalasini. You and the other elders honor me with your presence."

As unnecessary as it is, she thought, remembering to smile as Caimen, Serin's father, repeated the greeting, and each elder stepped forward in turn to do the same.

After an interminable amount of time, she came to the end of the line and turned to John. Breaking protocol, he beamed at her and gave her a warm embrace—a move that made most of the elders stiffen. Dalasini's face tightened at the corners of her mouth, and Gia hid her grin before surreptitiously pinching John's arm as she moved away from him.

Caimen came forward to give yet another blessing. Remembering the expression on Logan's face when they parted made the long-winded speech feel interminable, but Gia knew the drill. Several more blessings would be offered before she was invited to the Mother's temple to pray with them. If she didn't do something now, it could be hours before anyone asked her what had brought her to the island.

Keeping her expression serene, she nodded when appropriate while trying her best to catch John's eye. When she managed it, he winked at her, all the while appearing to pay close attention to the words being spoken.

Caimen continued on for another minute before John bent over double with a sudden racking cough. Gia dropped her serene expression and adopted one of concern. She put a hand on his back. "Are you all right, Uncle? May I be of assistance?" she asked.

John's smile gleamed as bright as his bald spot. "Oh, excuse me, my dear. I had a sudden tickle in my throat." He clapped her on the back with just the right amount of chagrin and hapless friendliness. "So poppet, what brings you to the island?"

Behind him, both Caimen and Dalasini frowned, but Gia leapt at the opening.

"I need to get to the archives," she said with a placid nod at the others. "I have a small matter I need to look into for Logan, and I'm afraid time is of the essence."

"Oh, well, we understand you can't sit around all day chewing the fat with us, my dear," John said with his disarming grin aimed at the elders.

Dalasini bowed graciously. "Of course, Gia. Why doesn't John escort you while we continue on to the temple to offer Atabey our prayers?"

Grateful that Dalasini was too well mannered to show her annoyance, Gia accepted the offer. The elders shuffled up the path toward the temple while John fell in step next to her.

"Thanks."

He passed a hand over his rounded belly and laughed. "You're quite welcome, my dear. So what brings you here so late?"

Gia enjoyed visiting T'Kairie during the day. She liked to soak up the sun on the powder-white beach or hike the trails winding around the island. "I really do need to go to the archives."

"Oh," he said, wiping his perspiring forehead with a handkerchief. "I'm surprised. Little Logan doesn't normally need a hand with research."

That much was true. It was an open secret that the winds carried the voices of the dead, and a few others. The Air Elementals had always been predisposed to hear them. The winds weren't all knowing, however, which was easy to forget sometimes.

"She usually doesn't, but the winds are fickle," she reminded him absently, scanning the road ahead for the entrance to the archives.

It was too much to hope that the archivists would have gone home already. The sun had just gone down, and she knew most of them well enough to assume that at least two of them would still be there.

The scholars were a set of well-meaning men and women charged with preserving Elemental history by the Li family line, Logan's distant ancestors. For centuries, they had been the record keepers for their family history. But their ancient history preceded that single family, and so the directive had later been expanded to include all Elemental history. The archive had moved several times until it eventually made its way to the island.

T'Kaieri was founded by the Taino, the indigenous group local to the region during the pre-Columbian era. The population grew from an unexpected source in the following century.

During the colonial period, a steady trickle of gifted slaves escaped from the Bahamian islands. Many had found refuge here. They had intermixed with the local population, marrying among the gentle Taino clans. Nowadays, most of the islanders resembled these forefathers, although a few were smaller in stature, like their Taino ancestors.

It was right after this period of upheaval that the archive made a permanent move here.

"Are you coming down?" she asked John as they arrived at the nondescript door nested at the base of Siba.

"No, my dear. It's not my favorite place. Too damp," John said, taking out a red kerchief and wiping his forehead. "I'll leave you here."

She smiled at him with genuine affection. "Thanks for the assist."

"Anytime, poppet," he said, giving her a warm hug before walking back up the northern path.

The plain wooden door led down a winding stone staircase. At the bottom was another door, a much larger one made of stone. It was supposed to be heavy enough that only an Elemental could move it. However, it was left open these days so the archivists who did not possess supernatural strength could go in and out. Behind the massive door was a subterranean network of caves, each filled with books, maps, and scrolls. There were even carved stone tablets here and there among the more ephemeral records.

And there were weapons—short blades, long swords, spears, and shields. Some had been confiscated from enemies. Others had been wielded by Elementals, but most belonged to Elemental family lines that had died out and would be reborn. Until then, their artifacts were held here in trust.

Organization was rough. At Gia's request, the caves were in chronological order, with the oldest records deeper in the mountain. But within each cave, the jumbled system could only be deciphered by the archivists—and with a little guidance from the Mother, by her and her sisters.

Of course, that guidance was sometimes absent these days. The Mother had grown quieter in the last decades. It was disconcerting, but she had experienced these periods of silence before. They had no choice but to muddle through them as best they could.

Gia didn't run into an archivist until she was in the third chamber. Luckily for her, Noomi was alone.

"Daughter of earth," Noomi, the head archivist greeted her with a formal bow. "May I be of assistance?"

Unlike the junior members of the staff, Noomi was never surprised to see her. Older than she appeared, the head archivist was rounded and motherly. She had a perpetually cheerful and benevolent expression on her face. But her appearance was deceiving—Noomi's mind was a steel trap. She remembered everything she had ever read.

The other archivists always became nervous around her and her sisters. Diana was particularly good at intimidating them, but Gia always tried to put the scholars at ease. She had even granted them interviews so they could record her personal history—the part she was comfortable sharing.

"Hello, Noomi. I've come on an errand for Logan. I need to see records about...well, I'm not sure what I'm looking for. Something relating to the Air Elementals. I'm searching for an artifact made of metal or with a metal piece, possibly a blade."

Noomi nodded, unperturbed by the vague request. Over the years, she had been on the receiving end of many bizarre questions and demands.

"Is there anything you can tell me that would help simplify our search? Any particular century where we should begin?"

"I'm afraid I can't even narrow it down that far. I have a feeling that I've already seen what I'm looking for, and not recently either."

"A record you read during one of your research visits? It's been some time since you did one of those."

Her "research only" visits had stopped before Noomi's tenure. Gia had long since given up reading their history once it sank in that she was busy making it. But in the early days after inheriting, she had spent long periods of time here, determined to know their background as well as she could. Most Elementals did the same to prepare for whatever this job had in store. In recent memory, only Diana had bucked the trend, but Di had never liked being bogged down with a lot of history.

"I don't know when the last one was, but I think it's from a much earlier trip," she said.

"Shall I call the rest of the staff to help you search?"

It was a tempting offer, but in her experience, too many helping hands didn't make this sort of thing easier. "Like I said, I don't even know what I'm looking for. My best shot may be to try and commune with the Mother and ask for her guidance."

Noomi's inclined her head respectfully. "Of course. I can leave you to meditate in private."

"Thank you," she said before the archivist walked away, leaving her alone with thousands of years' worth of records.

Gia tried not to lose heart as she stared at the crammed walls and filled shelves. She *would* pray to the Mother and ask for Her guidance, but she had a very strong suspicion she was going it alone.

22

Logan woke up with Connell's heavy arms wrapped around her.

Great, she thought, refusing to acknowledge that it felt good to wake up this way. She flashed out of bed and glared at the damn Were curled up in the too-small twin bed. He'd taken his shirt off, but he had at least kept his pants on.

Thank the Mother for small favors.

She was going to have to have words with him again. Imagine if someone like the chief or that bitchy ex-girlfriend had come in?

Logan was a soldier, but she liked a *clean* fight. She had not signed up for all this hormone-driven drama. Connell was a fling, nothing more.

At least, that was all he was supposed to be. Somewhere along the line, things had gotten away from her. Pursing her lips, she stared down at him, wondering what the hell she was going to do...

Who says you have to have all the answers now?

She was young, and being young meant one could be stupid about men. She didn't have to know what to do at this very moment. Her focus was, and should be, the case. This other bullshit could wait. If Connell didn't like it, tough.

Pivoting, she turned to Sammy and bent over him. His color was better, and his breathing was deep and even, almost as if he was asleep and not in a coma.

How long would this state last? Did she have to ask the chief to arrange for him to be fed intravenously? He wasn't a chubby kid. He didn't have the fat reserves to go very long without food. Weres burned a lot of calories very quickly.

Exhaling hard, she put a hand on his forehead and was startled when he moved.

"Five more minutes, Yogi," he mumbled and turned over.

Logan snatched back her hand, air exhaling in a whoosh.

Yes! She threw her hands over her head in a victorious V. She turned around, wanting to cheer and shout, but no one else was awake upstairs.

Her impulse was to raise a ruckus and wake everyone, but she restrained herself. She decided to take a break outside and wait for Sammy and Connell to wake up on their own. In the next second, Logan was outside, rematerializing to sit on the porch railing to watch the sunrise.

The cold air felt good filling her lungs. She always liked this hour of the morning. No matter how the night before had gone—if she'd gotten a chance to sleep or not—dawn was special to her. It refreshed her. Cleansed. She felt closer to the Mother at this time, even though she half-suspected that connection was only in her head...

She hadn't heard him, but Logan sensed Douglas before she saw him. He was coming back from the woods, on all fours this time. His second form was massive and slightly terrifying.

His wolf was black as night. For a second, she flashed back to watching *The Neverending Story* on TV. Douglas reminded her of the big bad wolf in the movie, except that his paws were tipped in silver.

Even she, a person who could dematerialize at will, found her fight-or-flight switches being flipped on in the presence of the beast.

Douglas paused at the tree line, those huge, yellow eyes filled with an unnerving intelligence. She nodded at him, and he shook his large head at her in return.

Was that meant to be a nod back? Because if he'd had a rabbit in his jaws, she'd sooner think he was trying to snap its neck.

He disappeared behind one of the outbuildings and returned a few minutes later, fully dressed and on two legs this time. She thought he would pass her and go inside the house, but he stopped next to the stairs and leaned on the railing a few feet away.

"Good hunting?" she asked.

"No."

There was nothing more. After a minute, he pulled out a cigarette from a crumpled pack in his pocket and lit it.

"So you weren't out for a morning meal? Were you looking for the perp?"

He shook his head. "I needed a run. Wolves do that," he said without inflection.

She wanted to say something sarcastic about stating the obvious, but she knew why he was being terse with her.

"You don't have to like me," she said.

He turned to face her, his arms crossed with a face like molded granite. "I don't dislike you."

"But you're worried because Connell *does* like me." She had never been one to beat about the bush.

He looked away. "I'm more concerned that you like him," he said, his inflection unchanged.

Well, that was blunt. But so was she.

"Doesn't mean anything."

This time, he was surprised enough to turn his head in her direction. "Doesn't it?"

She shrugged and decided to be equally candid. "I know about you and Gia and what almost was."

Logan hadn't expected him to crack a smile, but when he did, his resemblance to Connell caught her off guard. "That was before I met Connell's mother," was all he said.

Was he warning her that Connell's infatuation would pass too?

"What was she like?" she asked, curious about the woman who

had caught someone like Douglas—after Gia, the bar would have been set incredibly high.

Douglas' face was uncharacteristically soft as he looked at the distant mountains. "She was...civilizing."

Logan waited for more, but it was like pulling teeth. "When did she pass?"

Douglas' face closed up. "Seven years ago."

She wanted to ask how it had happened, but she didn't want to push her luck. Instead, she picked at her pant leg. "Marco passed too. Sometime in the eighties."

Douglas frowned at her. "Who's Marco?"

Oh. Her sister hadn't told him. "He was Gia's mate. He died protecting a village in South America."

The human mercenaries who had been trying to liberate the population had mistaken Marco for a guerrilla fighter. Gia had been devastated, and Logan thought it was worse because she'd been unable to avenge him. But there had been no enemy. It had been a tragic case of mistaken identity in the heat of battle.

"Gia never mentioned his name."

She pursed her lips and traced a pattern on the railing. "So...are you seeing anyone right now?" He raised an eyebrow. "Gia isn't," she elaborated.

His expression shifted to one of wry amusement. "You're a troublemaker, aren't you? I begin to see why my son is so taken with you. And, no. I don't...date. And I'm not going to start at this stage of life. I would never dishonor my mate's memory that way."

Logan was disappointed. Gia was the most self-contained person she knew, but she wanted her sister to be happy above all things. The Earth Elemental spent too much time alone with her memories.

"That's too bad," she said, flicking a piece of imaginary lint away.

"It's a stupid idea anyway," Douglas said.

Logan scowled at him. "No, it's not."

His mouth quirked up, the first friendly look he'd ever given her. "Gia hasn't aged. I have."

"Not that much," she said dismissively.

"It's enough. That opportunity, if it ever was one, has passed. It's Connell's time now," he said, giving her the side-eye again.

"Meaning?"

He shrugged. "Regardless of what happens, Connell's place is here. He has obligations."

"And if that opportunity had worked out for you back in the day? Would you have followed Gia?"

Douglas rolled his eyes. "You know you're a pain in the ass, right? It's not news to you," he drawled.

Logan sniffed. She was still trying to think of a smart-ass reply when a muddy-green jeep pulled onto the road leading to the house. Straightening, she half-expected a Were to pop out of it to report another stripping. But it was Yogi, and he looked furious.

"Sammy's in a *coma*?" he roared.

"Son, calm down," Douglas said, passing a weary hand over his face.

Yogi pointed an accusing finger. "She put him in a coma! Riley just told me everything."

Of course she did. That one was a bitch coming and going. Making a production of examining her nails, she stayed quiet, waiting for the chief to control his man.

"It was for his own good, so he can mend," Douglas said.

The words were good, but the tone was a trifle flat. *Hmm. He could try a little harder to defend me.*

"And when exactly is he going to wake up?" Yogi yelled.

Logan stopped messing with her nails. "He should be up now," she said ever so casually. "Provided that he meant it when he said five more minutes."

Both wolves turned to her in surprise. Yogi's expression wiped clean before sagging. His eyes started shining, and his face contorted as if he were fighting tears. His annoying, testosterone-fueled behavior dropped, and he was simply a relieved big brother.

"Is he going to be okay?" he asked, voice cracking slightly.

Uncomfortable, she squirmed on the railing. "He's going to live," she hedged.

He would be as well as a Were could be without his wolf.

Douglas seemed to understand what she wasn't saying. "Come on, son. Let's go see him," he said, guiding the younger man with surprising gentleness.

Logan hung back long enough for the family reunion to take place, but she headed upstairs after deciding she couldn't avoid it any longer. Douglas was questioning Sammy about how he felt, feeling him over in a cursory medical exam.

"Do you still not remember anything from when you were attacked?" Douglas asked, his hand stopping to rest on the little boy's back.

Sammy looked small and scared. It probably wasn't helping that it was the chief himself questioning him. "No. I don't remember anything," he whispered.

"Not even a green light?" Connell asked, his face dark.

Sammy shot him a wide-eyed look and shook his head.

By the Mother, couldn't the big bad Weres back off a little? The kid obviously thought he did something wrong to get this kind of attention from his leader and the pack's top enforcer.

The child looked past the men at her with a pleading look. She clapped her hands loudly, making everyone turn to her. "You must be starving, kiddo! I am too. Let's go find some grub."

Sammy beamed at her and hopped out of bed, too young to realize he should excuse himself when in the presence of his pack's alphas. Racing over to her, he took her hand. Surprised, she looked down at him before shrugging and turning to walk out the door, leaving the men behind. She *was* hungry.

"Should we follow them?" Yogi asked, his naturally loud voice following them.

"I could eat," Connell said, exiting the room and trailing them down the stairs.

Twenty minutes later, Logan was wolfing down eggs, sausage, and a stack of pancakes she couldn't see over. Halfway down the stack, she bothered to glance up, only to find the table full of male Weres staring at her.

She paused, fork hovering. "What?"

Connell and Douglas exchanged amused glances.

"We've never seen anyone eat more than us," Sammy whispered.

"Is that right?" she asked, surprised.

After a beat, Logan shrugged. It was good for them to lose to a girl every once in a while.

23

G ia sneezed violently, the dust from so many old books getting the better of her. She may have been Earth, but she wasn't immune to the little human irritations.

Rubbing her nose absently she added a book to the heap next to her. Piles of leather bound volumes surrounded her at the large stone table reserved for visitors. Noomi and the other archivists all had their own private nooks hidden away in the stacks, but each of the major chambers had a communal table for tasks like hers.

She had been researching for hours. At first, she had been worried she'd be searching for a needle in a haystack, and she wasn't wrong. However, she soon realized that the haystack was made of needles, pins, maces, and the occasional sword.

Despite Noomi's suggestion to start with the indexes of artifact catalogs, there was still hundreds of books and scrolls to scan...and so far, there had been no hint from the Mother on where to look.

Ignoring the gnawing disquiet in the pit of her stomach over the Mother's continued silence, Gia doggedly pulled record after record. She had vastly underestimated the number of weapons associated with Air Elementals, those that they fought with or had taken possession of in the course of their duties. The latter was a complication that had the potential to skyrocket the number of potential candidates.

Though Connell and Logan's reaction suggested it was a weapon that belonged to someone of Logan's family line, Gia couldn't eliminate the other possibilities. She could be looking for a sword or spear that had switched allegiances after an Elemental had killed its original owner. Instances like those were uncommon, but not so rare that she could afford to ignore them.

Her list of possibilities was currently at a dozen weapons. Some were less likely based on the fragment Logan had found, but there were many entries in the archives that were only written descriptions with no accompanying sketch. Too many of the archivists in years past had no artistic skills. Gia was going to have to send all the descriptions to Logan and hope that one resonated with her. She was nowhere near finishing her list.

After a few minutes, she got up to replace one heavy leather volume on the shelf behind her. Standing on her tiptoes, she slipped it back in place before grabbing another. Removing it caused the precarious stack to shift and bump into the little pile next to it, dislodging a rolled-up cylinder—dropping it on her head.

"Ow," she muttered, picking up the offending item and rubbing at the sore spot on the back of her skull.

The culprit was one of the many scrolls stuck into random crevices all over the archive. Unfortunately for her head, this one was wound around a brass bar, with heavy, ornamental knobs at each end.

Sighing, she was about to stick it back up on the shelf before thinking better of it. She had been waiting for a sign. Maybe this was it. Unrolling the scroll with care, she frowned before smiling. The text was in Latin, but the actual record was a translation of the original Mandarin.

All Elementals were gifted with languages. It was part of their inheritance, but the archivists only knew the languages they studied, so most had chosen to keep their records in Latin since the early

Renaissance. This particular scroll was a listing of the great battles fought by Feng Po Po, one of Logan's most famous ancestors.

A small doodle on the margin caught her attention. It was a hastily drawn picture of a spear or staff with an elaborate dragon headpiece. The fierce-looking creature was wound around the top of the staff, a line of raised scales running down its back.

Gia held the scroll at arm's length and squinted. If this doodle was accurate, there was a small chance one of those scales could be the spike Logan had found. Maybe the Mother had been trying to tell her something by nearly concussing her. Of course, she could be reading too much into a random coincidence. There were at least seven other weapons that were equally valid possibilities.

Walking over to the table, she added the scroll to the pile. Feng Po Po was an Elemental of great renown, even among others of their kind. If the doodle were a weapon associated with her, there would be mention of it elsewhere, and perhaps a more detailed drawing. In the meantime, she would send descriptions of what she had to her sister. They might get lucky...or she might be here searching for weeks.

24

L ogan had been hoping to get back out to the woods after breakfast, but her plans were disrupted by the fact she sprouted a four-foot shadow.

Sammy followed her wherever she went, trailing her like a puppy. Even Connell and Yogi were ignored in favor of her, a situation neither man had experienced before, judging from their nonplussed reaction.

She could have taken to the currents to escape, but Logan found it hard to leave Sammy. Though he was up and smiling now, he had been close to death the day before. Her lingering sense of obligation to him was heightened by the sparkling bits of her aura intermingled with his own. She could feel the tug on her heartstrings as they walked all over the chief's house and outside around the nearby buildings.

Logan was hoping to tire Sammy out, but it didn't seem to matter that he had just risen from his sickbed. The little boy was bouncing off the walls and climbing all over her, his energy boundless.

Yogi and Connell were no help either. They sat back and watched her and the kid from the couch, sipping at home-brew beers while Sammy did a credible imitation of a whirling dervish.

Would it be kosher to dose him with something so he'd go down? *Nah.* The chief would have a problem if she drugged a still-recovering cub.

Maybe I can feed him a lot of turkey. All that tryptophan might knock him out. She was wondering where she might get a fully cooked thirty-pound bird when she felt the tug along the aether, signaling a message from Gia.

Peeling Sammy off her back, she handed him to an amused Connell.

"Take this. Give him a gallon of warm milk or something and put him to bed," she ordered. "He shouldn't be taxing himself this hard yet. I have to take a message."

Connell passed Sammy to his brother like he was a hot potato in order to follow her. "What message?"

Logan walked through the mudroom doors and out to the porch before answering. "That one," she said, pointing to the symbols forming in the dirt.

A long line was assembling themselves before their very eyes. They stretched out along one side of the house, the shallow grooves deepening in the hard-packed earth until they were clear and defined.

Connell came up behind her and whistled before remembering he was an alpha Were. "That's kind of cool, I guess," he mumbled, trying to downplay how awesome Gia's skills were.

Logan grinned. "It's totally badass, and you know it," she said, kneeling in front of one of the pictures before dismissing it.

"What are these?" he asked, leaning over a badly formed representation of a mace.

She didn't blame him for being unsure. Some of the pictures were pretty rough, but that wasn't Gia's fault. Her sister could transmit what was in her mind's eye faithfully. If the pictures were bad, it was because they were done poorly to begin with.

"This is our list of suspected weapons. Or a part of it," she amended, examining the mace carefully before moving on down the line.

She took the spike out of her pocket and held it in front of the next drawing.

"I don't think that's it," Connell said, his nose wrinkled.

"No shit, Sherlock," she grumbled while revolving the spike above the likely protruding bits of each drawing, trying to fit the fragment into place without success.

"What about this one?" he asked, standing at the far end of the line.

"Stop backseat driving," she ordered with a scowl before moving to the next one.

"But it's *this one*," he insisted, pointing down.

Digging in her heels, she ignored him while she steadily worked her way down the line. By the time she got to the last drawing, he was openly glowering at her. She nudged him away from the drawing with her hip. Connell folded his arms and backed away with an eye roll while she looked down and made the connection.

The depiction of the dragon headpiece was rough, but it still seemed as if the little creature was looking right at her.

"I told you so."

"Shut up, you gorgeous bastard," she muttered above his deep-throated chuckle. "This is off," she said, turning to him.

His smug expression fell. "So it's not it?"

"Oh, it's the right one," she said, her stomach knotting. "But this sketch is shitty. The tail is wound the wrong way."

"*Ah*," he said, a wealth of meaning behind that one syllable. "So you recognize this dragon-spear thing?"

Sucking in a deep breath, she nodded. "I have to make a call."

"Are you going to do your schizo talking at nothing thing again?"

She took exception to that. It wasn't schizo. "I'm not calling one of the girls. I need my phone," she said, feeling her pockets before remembering it was in her pack.

Logan wanted privacy for her call so she flashed up to the roof of the chief's house after grabbing her things from the sickroom. It was a pointless gesture, however, as Connell effortlessly climbed up there after her like the agile jerk he was.

"I like to watch the stars from up here," he informed her, stretching out like a lazy Roman emperor waiting for a servant to feed him grapes. He leaned closer. "By the way, the next time you decide to visit my bedroom for any reason, you better plan on staying a bit longer..."

His voice dripped with sexual innuendo, but with the exception of a sudden heightening of her color, she ignored him. She mumbled something noncommittal and fished her phone from the side pocket of her bag.

"Who are you calling? A weapons specialist? Some professor?"

Logan ignored him and hit the top listing on her favorites list. It rang a few times while Connell reached for her pack and started poking through it.

Smacking his hand only resulted in another one of those sexy grins. Meanwhile, the person with all the answers finally picked up on the other end.

"Mom, I need your help."

25

C onnell's head whipped around when Logan said *Mom*. He sat up straight, unapologetically eavesdropping.

"I need you to do me a favor," she continued. "Can you go to the hallway, to the silk scroll of Feng Po Po? No, the other one —the one with the staff. Can you take a picture of it and send it to me?"

Fascinated and surprised that Logan's mother was still alive, he focused on her end of the conversation, despite her obvious annoyance at having him there.

"No, don't use the big camera," Logan said in a tone of barely controlled patience. "Take a picture with your phone."

She tapped her fingernails on her thigh. "Because that way you don't have to download the picture from the SD card. You can send it as a text. No. No. Just hold your phone up to the painting and tap on the camera app...It's the picture of the camera in the corner. Now tap on it once. Did it open? Good. Now tap on it again and send it to me. There's that little box with an arrow on it. Use that. My phone number's already in there. Yes. Perfect."

His grin was so wide it was threatening to split his lip wide open. Logan sounded like every child with a technophobic parent, the ones over a certain age who could never remember how to check their email.

He could picture Logan's mother now, a sweet, grey-haired lady who drank lots of tea out of those tiny cups they used at Chinese restaurants. He couldn't wait to meet her. If she wasn't too frail, they could invite her out to the compound for a relaxing weekend in the mountains.

"Mom, this is really blurry. I need to see the details of her staff better. Can you try again? And this time, can you tap on the screen so the camera focuses better? Zoom out with your fingers to get a close up. Okay, good..."

An alert sounded. Logan removed the phone from her ear and looked at her screen. "This is good enough, Mom. Yes, I'll come home as soon as I wrap up this case. I have to go now. Give my love to Aunt Mai." Logan rolled her eyes. "Of course, I love you too."

She finished by making a loud kissing noise he found charming —and would be imitating to taunt her at every opportunity.

"I hope you kiss me goodbye like that when I call you," he said, leaning up on his elbows. "So when do I get to meet your mom?"

Logan laughed. "You're seriously more concerned about meeting my mom than seeing the weapon that rendered you impotent?"

Ouch. "I'm not *impotent.*"

She muttered something about not being able to get his wolf up, and he huffed and snatched her phone out of her hand. "So this is it?"

The photo was of a classic Chinese silk painting. It looked like something straight out of a museum. Logan's mom had this hanging in her house?

The figure depicted a fierce-looking woman in full battle dress. "I've seen ancient depictions of warriors in similar poses, but none of a female before," he said, fascinated. "Is this some long-lost ancestor?"

"Yes, she's the founder of my family line. And you've probably seen many females in this kind of painting and not known it."

Hmm. The stylized figure could have passed for male if he didn't know any better. He supposed the reverse was true—many of the male figures could be women. Weren't Chinese lines matrilineal? There must be hordes of notable women hidden in their history, especially among the Supernaturals.

"That's true," he admitted, zooming in on the staff the warrior woman was holding. The ornate dragon head was depicted in much better detail than the drawing that appeared in the dirt by the porch.

It looked more like a sea serpent than a dragon as he knew it from TV shows and movies. The little creature stared at him malevolently from the top of the staff, its jewel-green eyes unblinking and cold. He half expected the thing to start hissing at him.

"If the serpent on the caduceus staff was evil, it would look like this," he said with a frown.

Logan snatched the phone out of his hand. "It is not evil. It's majestic and noble," she lectured.

"Noble?"

He made a face at the picture. Nope. If he saw something like that in the barn, he'd go for the shovel so he could cut its head off. The headpiece wasn't very big either. How could that thing strip a wolf?

"Do you know how it works?" he asked her.

"Not a clue. I always thought the staff was just a bo weapon, and that the head was ornamental. And I've memorized every story about Feng Po Po's battles. Some of the legends even mention the staff, but in a general way—a *"she struck out with her staff and smote her enemy"* kind of thing. No actual details and no mention of stripping an enemy of their magic."

"Fuck," he said, grunting. "So even though we know what it is, you don't know how it works?"

She shrugged, tucking her hair back in a big bun. "We have to find the staff first. There's not a lot known about it."

We. Warmth shot through him. "Any ideas on how to do that?" he asked, keeping it casual. At the very least, she wasn't mad at him anymore.

"Give me a minute. Who are those people?"

Connell sat up and craned his neck. A few cars had pulled up in front of the house. Some more wolves had gathered to see Sammy now that he was up.

"More of Sammy's family. The one in the blue jacket is Bishop, his dad."

Logan looked up from her phone. "I should talk to him."

Connell shrugged dismissively. "Don't bother. I already did, at his house. He doesn't know anything, but I pity the poor fucker who messed with his kid. Dad was worried he was going to start in on the Averys again, but that didn't happen."

"Who are the Averys?

"A shifter family upstate. Bishop opposed them joining the clan during unification. Lots of Hatfield and McCoy like history between his family and theirs, but other than driving to their town and driving around he left them alone."

"Do you think they're involved?"

"Ten or twenty years ago, I might have. They used to be pretty insular, but these days they interact a lot more. Some of them have even married outside their clan. After checking them out, Bishop went back scouring the woods to try to track any strangers in the area."

"So if he gave the green light the Averys are okay?"

He shrugged. "Something like that. And I still think it's a witch. This is some sort of black magic shit. Truthfully, if Bishop finds the bastard before me, I won't mind that much because the asshole will die screaming."

"Charming," Logan muttered absently. "Can you check and see if he's found something new?"

"I can, but I think he'd be moving faster if he had." Bishop and the others had walked into the house unhurriedly. They had probably just come to check on Sammy. "What are you going to do?" he asked.

Logan stood up on the roof. "I have an idea, now that I know what we're dealing with."

She scanned the sky. The wind picked up and swirled around her, whipping her hair in a circular motion. It was like a living thing, surrounding and caressing her in a way that was almost sensual.

Or I just think that because I'm horny as fuck. Connell smirked. He always would be around her.

The wind unwrapped itself from around Logan's lithe body and moved away. It may have been his imagination, but he could almost see a ripple of that Logan-scented air rushing away.

"What was that?"

"A message."

He waited for more. Eventually, Logan pursed her lips and continued. "I was confirming the weapon for Gia, so she can narrow her research to that one. We may have more information on it buried in the archives."

"What archives?"

Logan reached down, indicating he should get up. He took her hand and let her help him stand, the move effortless for her. "I'll tell you all about it later. I have to go check something out. I'll be back in an hour or so."

Connell tensed. "Where are you going?"

"To our safe house," she said. "It's not far. I need to look something up."

He frowned. "Can't you just ask your wind friends for the answer?"

Her smile was crooked. "I wish it was that simple."

Wasn't it? "How is it complicated?"

Logan took a deep breath and exhaled, as if trying to find the words to explain her relationship to the air spirits. "You know how some kids have imaginary friends?"

"Yeah."

"Well, I had those voices as mine."

So she heard them even before she became an Elemental. "And so they told you stuff. It must have been hard to keep a secret around you."

"It did annoy my parents that I always knew where they hid my birthday presents—especially when one of the voices swore up and down they had bought me a pony... and they hadn't."

Connell laughed.

"It's funny now, but when they told me to jump off the roof because I could fly, it wasn't all that hilarious."

He frowned. "But you can fly."

"I couldn't back then."

His head drew back. "Well, fuck. So the voices can't be trusted."

"Some of them can, some of the time. It's a bitch deciding which and when. Especially since most of them fade over time. Just when I think I've gotten one figured out, it grows quiet. And they rarely return once they go silent. New ones appear in cycles I can't identify. They are useful, but only to a point."

"So they haven't whispered the name of our enemy in your ear yet?" he asked, growing serious.

"They've been whispering names non-stop, including yours, your father and sister, and Mary fucking Poppins. The few voices I would trust on this matter are quiet. I don't think they can see things clearly when they're not near me. Gia thinks they feed off our energy and become strong enough to focus in our vicinity. But some distance away, and they lose that focus and become distracted. I'm not sure if that's right, but it's a better explanation than some others I've heard."

All right, so the wind talkers weren't reliable. "I still don't think you should go anywhere on your own." His reluctance to let her leave was instinctive, but the reasons why it was justified were starting to multiply.

It was no coincidence his search had led him to Logan. There were three other Elementals out there, but he had found *her*, tracking her and bringing her to his home.

And now they had identified the weapon responsible for stripping him. And lo and behold, it was something tied to her. Not Gia or one of the other two Elementals. It was Logan, his mate.

What if he and the pack had never been a target? What if this was about her? What if it had been all along?

Discomfited, he scanned around them, half-expecting the

chimney to have sprouted eyes. The shadows behind the trees at the forest line seemed deeper and the chill in the air was a little colder. But there was no way anyone could see them up on the roof.

"It's fine," she assured him. "No one knows where the safe house is except for my sisters and me."

"And their mates, right?" he asked, glowering. What if one of his counterparts was the asshole behind this?

"Jordan and Alec are all right. This isn't one of them, so you can stand down," Logan said.

Belatedly, he realized he was crowding her, unconsciously trying to occupy the space around her—not just next to her, but above her as well.

"Then how did the weapon get here? Someone you trust could have lifted it from one of your safe houses."

Logan shook her head. "Something like this wouldn't have been out in the open at one of our places. It's a historical artifact. It would have been in the archive or with the family it descended from— unless the line died out. In which case, the thing could have gone out into the world and been picked up by God knows who."

"So it's not from your family line? Then why do you have a picture of it at your mom's house?"

"I am related to Feng Po Po. But she lived hundreds and hundreds of years ago. The staff might have been passed on to another branch of my family, one that isn't around anymore. Even Elementals don't always have a direct line to all these artifacts. They get inherited the same way everything else does. We do pick them up when we find them, but the families they belong to are allowed to keep their arti- facts—so long as they're not using them to do harm."

Connell digested that in silence. He still had a bad feeling about this, and no matter how strong and smart Logan was, he wasn't going to stop trying to protect her.

"And you're sure about the other mates?"

Logan rolled her eyes. "Jordan and Serin have been together forever. He's from her community. As for Alec, he worships the ground Diana walks on. Besides, they're nowhere near here and..." She trailed off.

"And what?"

Logan muttered something and looked away.

"And *what*?"

Logan gave him a loose one-shouldered shrug. "I said Alec is a pretty good guy, for a vampire..."

Connell's eyes widened. "*A vampire?*" he shouted.

His sprite gave him the evil eye. "Stop screaming like a fishwife. He's *fine*. Alec's a professor, and he loves my sister. And trust me—he wouldn't step a toe out of line around her. He'd be toast if he did."

Connell was so thrown by her naïveté that he was almost dizzy. "Logan, you can't trust any bloodsucker, no matter what he does for a living."

"Says the werewolf," she shot back. "And I mean it. Alec is an all right dude for a vamp. Not to mention he is in Australia with his mate right now."

Did she say toast earlier? "Diana is the Fire Elemental?"

Logan grinned. "Ironic, isn't it?" Her smiled dropped away. "You know, I could have been halfway to the safe house by now."

He closed his eyes, giving in. "Give me your phone," he said, snatching it away without waiting for her to hand it to him.

Punching in his number, he gave himself a call. "If you're not back in an hour, I'm coming after you. Call me when you get there."

With an air of resigned patience, she took the phone back before dematerializing before his eyes. He could feel her presence dancing away in the wind and sighed heavily. Fishing his own phone out of his pocket, he saved Logan's number under the contact listing *Mine*.

26

When he went downstairs, he found a subdued group of wolves. They were scattered around watching Sammy and another cub who had come to visit play in the living room.

He looked around for Bishop, only to be told that he'd already left to keep his search going in the woods. Nothing had been found so far. No one asked him for an update, so he didn't give one—not in front of everyone.

Connell wasn't ready for everyone to know they'd identified the weapon or that it was one that had belonged to a legendary Elemental. There was only one person he could trust, aside from his father, who wouldn't fly off the handle and accuse Logan of being behind the attacks.

Mara was leaning against the back wall, away from the others. She too was watching the children play, but it was obvious her mind was elsewhere.

She didn't see him until he was right in front of her. With one of those silent communications innate to siblings, he gestured for them to find a more private place to talk.

"You'd think everyone would be a little happier to see Sammy up and around," he observed once they were outside on the porch.

Mara didn't answer right away. She was still staring at the tree line when she answered. "I think the pack is trying to come to terms with a cub who can't shift. No one quite knows what to do."

Pivoting, she turned to face him. "And they are worried about what to do about you. How can you be the pack's enforcer if you don't get your wolf back?"

It was a question he'd been avoiding asking himself. "There's always Malcolm," he said quietly.

Her face darkened, and Connell ached with sympathy. Malcolm moving up in the hierarchy would be excruciating for Mara now— even more than it already was. The pack's enforcer was second only to the chief, and he was always around. Not to mention that Mara couldn't move away from home until she took a mate—not unless their dad bought that she'd gone on another "mercy mission" with the UN.

"He isn't as well liked as you are," she pointed out. "You've always been more popular, the star athlete and a war hero to boot. And being the chief's son bought you a lot of goodwill. Malcolm doesn't have that kind of built-in support. Other wolves will challenge him to get that number-two spot. It's inevitable."

Connell hadn't thought of it before, but she was right. Their father was the hero who had unified the packs and stopped decades of constant bloodshed. It was only natural that he and Mara had inadvertently absorbed some of his popularity. "It's too bad you can't serve as enforcer." He sighed.

His sister rolled her eyes. "Yeah, right."

"I'm serious," he said. "If you were enforcer, no male would challenge you—they would just try to mate with you."

Mara's mouth curled. "*Ugh.*"

"It's true," he said with a laugh.

The pack's sexist double standard would work in her favor. A male was hard wired to protect the females in the pack. Plus, if someone put some thumbscrews to him, he would admit that Mara was kind of pretty. The only reason she had such a lousy love life was because she was too alpha for most of the Weres in these parts.

Plus, only a rogue male would challenge a female. But the likelihood of that happening was low so long as his father was still around. In the meantime, Mara would take apart anyone who threatened them. As a fighter, she was ruthless, even more so than he was. But few people were aware of that...

The sad truth was that as a woman, Mara couldn't be the pack enforcer. Her position in the pack would be determined by her mate's status. If her future mate was a beta or lower, it wouldn't matter that her innate nature was alpha. By pack law, she would be whatever her husband was. It wasn't fair, but some traditions were too deeply engrained to change.

If only his likely successor hadn't been such an idiot..."Where is Malcolm? Didn't he come back with Bishop?"

After Connell's search party had found the site of Sammy's attack, Malcolm had gone back out with the others to help Bishop hunt down the culprit. But they were rotating out regularly and he'd expected the Were to check in before now.

"No, I haven't seen him since he came in with you."

"So...did you two talk?" he pried.

"Briefly."

"And did you guys patch things up?"

Mara glared at him. "There was nothing between us to patch up. And I can't believe you've already forgiven him. He *slept* with your almost mate."

Connell shrugged with wry acceptance. "I think he did me a favor," he said, but he immediately wanted to punch himself in the face when Mara blinked rapidly and looked away.

Way to put your paw in your mouth. Connell sighed, trying to find the right words to fix this awful situation for her. In the long run, Mara was better off forgiving Malcolm. He didn't want her ending up with some weak-ass beta.

Poor stupid, horny Malcolm. He'd screwed the pooch on this one. *Literally.*

"What about Logan?" Mara asked, changing the subject. "Where's she gone off to?"

Connell could see he was going to have to give his sister more time. "Did you see those symbols in the dirt?" he asked.

They were still there, but indistinct now as the wind slowly erased them.

"Yeah, everyone saw them," she replied. "Bishop was excited that there might be a break in the case, but Dad told him not to get his hopes up. The weapon could have been any one of those depicted or something else entirely. A spell even."

"Well..." He took a look around to make sure they were alone. "It's not a spell. It's definitely one of those weapons. Logan recognized it."

"How?"

"I'll let you know soon. She went to check something out. I think we're getting closer."

Mara sighed. "I hope so, although it doesn't feel like we are."

"Knowing what's responsible is a step forward," he pointed out.

"But it doesn't tell us how to find the asshole behind this."

"Yeah, I know. But chasing our tails in the woods isn't going to do it either. I think we need to call back the search teams and regroup."

"Gonna share that with Dad?" she asked.

"I was about to. Want to join me?"

Mara shook her head. "I think I'll stay out here for a bit."

"Are you sure?" he asked, concerned at her subdued response. He was used to his sister swearing up a storm. This quiet and distant version of Mara was disconcerting.

She must really be torn up about Malcolm. If only he'd realized how deep her feelings went before this whole mess started. He could have given Malcolm a push to ask her out back when it would have made a difference...

Leaving his sister to gather herself, he went inside to update the chief.

The meeting was tense. Once he got Douglas alone in his sound-proofed office, Connell had shared everything he knew about the Elemental weapon and its connection to Logan. His father hadn't come out and accused her of any wrongdoing, but he'd agreed it was a damning coincidence.

"I don't think we should tell Bishop or the others about the weapon's history until Logan comes back, and we find the damn thing," Connell said.

"And how does Logan plan on doing that?" his father asked.

"I'm not sure," he admitted. "But she is nearby checking on something, so I think she has a plan."

"We'll see. When do you expect to hear back from her?"

"Now," a loud, cheery voice said.

Both wolves snapped to attention, leaping to their feet, canines bared. A deep growl emanated from both their throats before they realized who had spoken.

At the window, Logan rolled her eyes.

"Babe, don't do that," Connell barked.

"How did you get in here?" the chief asked, his neck corded. He relaxed it with some effort.

Logan's mouth curled as if the answer was obvious. "You left the window open."

She took something out of her bag. It was a small, obsidian arrowhead.

"What's that?" Connell asked.

"Something I like—for focus. I found a ritual I think will help. It's supposed to help you find something you've lost."

"But you didn't lose the staff," he pointed out.

"If I'm right, it shouldn't matter," Logan said, the outline of her svelte body highlighted by the sunny day. "It's of my bloodline. Regardless of who has it now, it should want me more."

His father frowned. "You make it sound like this staff is somehow alive."

Logan took a few steps and perched on the office's long, oak desk. "I realize your kind doesn't really go into the magical artifact thing, but it *is* almost like that. When an object gets strong enough through use and history, it can take on a mind of its own."

"What if you're wrong about it wanting to be with you?" Connell asked. "What if the evil little dragon headpiece has decided to change sides and stay with the bastard pulling this crap?"

Logan bit her lip. For a second, she looked young and undecided. But it was only a moment before she rolled her shoulders, her usual cocky swagger firmly in place. "I'm betting that after being crafted for an Elemental and spending years at her side, it won't. It'll want to be with me."

She sounded confident, but there was a tiny hint of doubt in her voice, one he was betting his father had missed. However, Connell was starting to know his sprite's moods, and he recognized that carefully concealed uncertainty. He saw it in the mirror enough to be familiar with it.

"All right, well, let's do this," his father said, reaching for his phone.

Suddenly, Logan was at his side, her hand staying his. "What are you doing?" she asked.

"I was going to call in the others out searching. Bishop and Malcolm at least should be here."

Logan shook her head. "Hold off on that," she said, belatedly adding a *please* when his father raised a heavy black brow at her.

"Any reason why you don't want them around?" Connell asked.

Logan was quiet.

"Babe."

She scowled. "Don't call me that." Crossing her arms, she exhaled hard. "All right, I haven't done this particular ritual before. I don't particularly want to do it now either... And I don't want an audience."

"Why?" he asked.

Because she thought she would fail? He studied her expression. No, that wasn't it...

Logan looked at him, one corner of her mouth turned down. "You'll see," she said darkly.

27

They were out in the yard in front of the house, a few dozen meters from the tree line. Logan had drawn some elaborate symbols in the dirt, not unlike those pictograms and pictures that had appeared by the porch earlier.

The symbols formed a rough circle, and his sprite was in the center. When she held out her arms, she looked like she was in the middle of a sundial.

The day was very bright outside, but there was a cold wind pinkening Logan's cheeks. It contrasted nicely with the black of her leather jacket.

"What is she doing now?" Mara asked.

Despite her request not to have an audience, Logan had gone out of her way to find his sister to give her one of those exaggerated "get your ass over here" gestures before going outside.

"I'm not sure," he admitted as the sprite gesticulated in an odd, staccato rhythm.

The buzz in the wind was starting to get louder the more Logan did...whatever she was doing. Which now appeared to be talking to herself or maybe...chanting?

He couldn't hear anything, but the wind started rushing in his ears. This time, he didn't need to be touching Logan to hear the voices. The damned whispering set his teeth on edge.

"Do you hear that?" he asked Mara when the ebb and flow of the noise hit a particularly loud crescendo.

Mara glanced all around them. "Hear what?"

"Never mind."

His father was the only one of them who didn't look confused or curious. He watched Logan impassively. Maybe he'd seen Gia do something similar back in the day.

How long would this go on? Connell hated having to sit back and watch while someone else did all the work. Logan had already scolded him once for breaching her circle. He hated waiting around like an idiot, his thumb up his butt—metaphorically, of course.

Connell closed his eyes, deciding to try to pick out an individual voice from the background buzz. Maybe he could learn something that way.

His sister nudged him. "What were you going to say—no shit!"

The surprise in Mara's voice made his eyes snap open, his head whipping back around to the circle. Logan was holding the obsidian arrowhead, which suddenly looked very pointy and sharp, to her open hand. With a tightening of her facial muscles, she stabbed herself, scoring the sharp tip across her palm.

A burst of adrenaline carried him to her, but Logan's eyes flicked up at him, telling him to stop. "Don't breach the circle," she ordered.

"What the hell are you doing?" he asked.

"Whatever I have to do to find the staff," she said before taking the arrowhead with her bloody hand and cutting the other one wide open.

"Fuck, Logan, *stop*," he shouted at her.

The blood was pouring from the cuts in a steady stream. Logan looked nauseated, but her voice was steady when she spoke next.

"It's done. Calm down, Connell," she soothed.

Closing her hands into fists, she moved her bleeding hands over the symbols she had drawn. She passed her fists over them until each symbol had at least one drop of blood on it. When she had finished the last one, the wind roared, the sound growing louder before climaxing with a loud pop.

Then there was silence. No wind, no leaves rustling. All the background sounds of the nearby forest were gone, the birds quiet.

Connell scowled at the sudden stillness. "Did you have to cut yourself so deep?"

The flow of the blood wasn't slowing.

"Shh," she scolded.

Muscles tight, he started to look around for something to wrap around Logan's hands when the damnedest thing happened.

Before his disbelieving eyes, the blood stopped falling to the ground. It was like gravity had stopped working. The dark drops hung like jewels suspended in mid-air. And then... they began to climb.

The droplets rose back up to the height of Logan's hands, separating into a fine mist. It looked like the cloud was pouring out of the cuts, a vapor of red rising from her palms.

Freaked out, he pulled off his shirt. He was about to breach the circle to press the cloth to Logan's wounds when the cuts started to close on their own.

Mara appeared at his side, her eyes like saucers. "Far-fucking-out!"

"Not the words I would choose," he snapped, tugging his shirt back on.

Inside the circle, Logan heaved a sigh of relief. She turned to smile at him. Relieved, his shoulders dropped. Until she blew him a kiss—because that wasn't what she did. It just looked like it.

The red mist had been hanging there, denying the laws of physics, but when Logan blew over her palm, it fanned out, floating with purpose now. The cloud moved around him, parting in the middle to pass on either side before continuing past them into the trees.

Logan hopped out of the circle and ran after the cloud. Right before reaching the tree line, she turned to look at them, exasperated.

"Well, come on!"

Next to him, his father laughed. Mara grinned at him. A hoarse laugh rose up from his throat.

And then, the chase was on.

THE MIST POURED OVER HILLS, shifting and twisting around trees. It didn't bother with the easiest path, moving haphazardly one minute and with obvious intent the next. It would have been difficult for a human to keep up, but Logan and the others didn't have a problem.

Connell ran fast, even as a human. He kept pace with her while the two wolves ran behind. Mara and the chief had shifted to their four-legged forms. They could have easily overtaken them, but there was no point.

The cloud wasn't trying to outrun them. It was searching, taking one route, and then another, occasionally backtracking or circling over a spot aimlessly before resuming its course again.

They pounded after the blood cloud for a solid twenty minutes. It was high above them near the middle of the tree line when it topped a rise and abruptly stopped. Logan frowned and hurried up the hill. The blood cloud hadn't stopped to circle over the weapon as it was designed to. Instead, it had flattened out, pressing against a barrier she couldn't see.

"What the hell is that?" Mara asked.

Logan turned to her and blinked rapidly. Connell's sister was standing right behind her, stark naked. So was the chief. Cheeks on fire, she pointedly looked back up at the trapped cloud.

Next to her, Connell snickered. "Wolves can't magic their clothes back on," he informed her before whipping off his shirt and handing it to Mara.

His sister, really? Couldn't he give his father something to wear?

Rolling her eyes to plead with the Mother for patience, she turned back to the obstruction, ignoring the nudity of the Weres behind her.

Connell walked up to the top of the ridge and reached out. His hand stopped short as it came into contact with the barrier, and Logan snatched it back.

"Don't do that. It could be booby-trapped."

He shrugged off her concern. "It's almost solid," he said, looking down at his fingers. "And kind of gooey."

Glowering at him, Logan took his hands and blasted them with a harsh rush of air. The smallest traces of magical residue blew off and dissipated into the aether.

"Let me handle this," she scolded.

Reaching out she extended her hands, but she didn't touch the barrier. It wasn't visible to her naked eye, but when she directed air at the unseen force, the air spread over the surface, giving her an idea of the size and circumference of the invisible wall.

The obstruction was dome-shaped, but irregular on the side closest to them. It was almost like a huge, misshapen bowl had been dropped in the middle of the woods. And Connell was right. The barrier had some give to it. The force of the wind warped its surface, like when a child blew on a soap bubble without breaking it.

Air, however, could work its way through some of the most solid of barriers. Narrowing her eyes, she applied a little more force, directing the wind like a saw blade at the space just in front of them.

The blast blew back her hair in streamers behind her, but that was nothing compared to the noise. The sound of the wind increased in pitch until it was a whistling shriek that vibrated her eardrums.

"*Fuck,* Logan," Connell swore, slapping his hands over his ears.

Logan wrinkled her nose and checked behind her—focusing on Mara. She was doing the same thing.

"Sorry," she muttered. "This shouldn't take long."

Redoubling her efforts, she forced a gap in the barrier. Air rushed in, widening the rift like surf pouring through the hull of a boat. Using a booted foot, Logan kicked the edges wider until the whole dome cracked and burned up, the energy contained in the shell spontaneously combusting when it gave.

"What's that smell?" Douglas asked from behind her.

"Burning force-field," she said, checking the reflexive impulse to look at him when he spoke.

Connell noticed her averted gaze and was still smirking at her when she stepped over the ridge. She made her way around some trees halfway down the slope, trailed by the Weres.

The smug expression on Connell's face wiped clean when he looked over her head.

At first, Logan didn't notice the body. She had been so focused on finding the staff of Feng Po Po that she almost missed the fact it had been driven clean through a man.

"Shit," she swore, hurrying down to the body.

It was a Were. That much she could tell from his size and build. He was lying in the middle of a small, cleared space at the bottom of the ridge, the wind ruffling his golden-blond hair. His eyes seemed to be staring sightlessly at the dragon winking down at him from the top of the staff—the one embedded in his chest.

Connell and his family fanned around her and the body.

"Anyone you know?" she asked, frowning down at the victim. He'd been quite handsome in life. And he looked familiar.

There was a pointed silence. Logan quickly realized something was wrong and glanced up at the wolves in question. Their faces were grave, shock and dismay in every line. But there was something more in Mara's eyes that made her turn away quickly.

Connell cleared his throat. "It's Malcolm, my father's third."

28

Gia hauled another book off the shelf and sneezed at the dust that followed it. Ever since Logan confirmed that the weapon involved in the Maitland case was indeed Feng Po Po's staff, she had been pulling all the records she could find on that famed Elemental.

"Noomi," she called out. "Did you find that index?"

The head historian had returned to the archive complex a short while ago. The rest of her staff had as well, but they were staying out of Gia's way, letting Noomi be the one to interact with her.

Gia liked to think she was friendly and approachable, but the head archivist appeared to be the only one comfortable looking her in the eye. Trying to be respectful of the staff's sensibilities, Gia let the others go about their business, but occasionally, Noomi drafted one of them to pull the records she needed as they tracked them down.

Noomi popped her head around the corner. "One moment, Daughter of Earth."

Gia smiled and put the heavy volume on the table. Even when harassed, the head archivist was unfailingly polite.

She opened the book and started turning the pages. There had been several mentions of the staff in their records, but so far, she had found little that would help Logan. It had taken her half an hour to find this particular volume. It was supposed to include a story from Feng Po Po's last years as an Elemental in Asia.

Gia had wanted to find this book because it was supposed to be the Air Elemental's famous stripping of the Korean Crown Prince Sado. The story was a legendary tragedy. The witch in question had been the favored son of the prominent family until he'd gone mad. His magic had made him dangerous and unpredictable. Fearing for the safety of the other members of her family, the matriarch had turned to their kind for help. Feng Po Po had stripped the witch, but not before he had killed hundreds of servants in his household.

Gia was hoping the account would confirm her suspicions. She and the others now had the ability to take away magical ability using only their talent, but that hadn't always been the case. Long ago, that had been done with long, arduous rituals—and tools designed for the task.

All such devices had been destroyed long ago—or at least, they should have been. Now that they could perform a stripping without any kind of tool, those objects presented a danger to the Supernatural community. It would have been difficult for anyone other than an Elemental to wield one, let alone use it correctly. But, if she was being honest, a skilled witch could have figured out how to use one given enough time.

A few minutes later, Gia found the story she was looking for, but again, there was no helpful information that confirmed the staff was the instrument used in the stripping.

Sighing, she rocked back in the chair. There were a number of possibilities to consider. If it was indeed the staff they were looking for—and Logan's hunch was good enough for her—then it shouldn't have been around anymore. It would have been destroyed in the purge of the other objects like it—*if* its dual nature had been recognized. But she, like many others, assumed it had been a weapon and nothing more.

What if the archivists and other Elementals at the time hadn't realized the staff performed double duty back in the day? The purge of those tools would have occurred long after Feng Po Po's death. In the meantime, the staff would have been passed on to other Elementals in her line or her family if none were chosen.

It was even possible that some could have wielded the staff, unaware that it was more than it appeared.

The possibility also existed that some eager archivist had known of its second ability, but left the staff off the rolls of artifacts earmarked for destruction simply for its historical value. They might not have considered that someone outside of an Elemental line might get their hands on it, or if they did, that they could learn how to use it.

That was why Gia had set the present day archivists to work. The scrupulous record keeping of recent generations meant they kept an index cross-referencing Elementals and their exploits. Each volume Gia appeared in was listed in an index. So was Logan, and her other sisters. And thanks to Noomi's need to improve the efficiency of their organization, the staff had steadily been working backward in time to include their predecessors.

Technically, the indexing work hadn't reached the time of Feng Po Po, but since she had been such an imposing figure in their history, they knew enough of where her records were to make a start.

Noomi huffed around the corner, holding a pile of books pressed to her round belly. "Here we are!"

Gia looked at the stack in dismay as Noomi dropped them on the table. It was huge.

"Don't worry. We've bookmarked the relevant pages."

"Thank you," Gia said gratefully, taking the nearest book and going through it, examining each record marked with a piece of parchment.

After a few pages, she noticed the repetition of a certain number. It was scribbled next to two stories in which the staff featured prominently. The number was repeated a third time on a more official entry that had a sketch of the staff in one of the larger indexes.

"Noomi, what is this number?" she asked, pointing to the entry.

Noomi, who had been opening the other books for her and laying them out, squinted at the page. "Oh, that. It's from our old system."

"Our system?"

"Yes, these first two digits are the room, these two are the cabinet, and the last is the shelf number."

"Wait, do you mean *in* the archive?"

"Yes, that is the designation from the artifact catalog."

Gia's head was spinning—and that had not happened in a long time. "So that means the staff was in the collection at some point?" she asked in surprise. "Before it moved to the island?"

Noomi shook her head. "No, the system was modified after the move. The numbers were different. These correspond to our collection as it is today."

"So it was here in these rooms?" Gia frowned. "How long ago?"

Naomi frowned at the numbers. "Well, to have these particular numbers, it would have had to be here during the last major reorganization."

What?

"That wasn't that long ago," she observed, disquiet spreading through her like a cold wind.

"It was in 1897, to be precise."

That meant the staff was still here when she'd become an Elemental. When had it gone into circulation afterward? And why hadn't she been told?

29

L ogan didn't know what to say. They were back at the chief's house, and it was *tense*.

She was currently hiding in the office while the wolves snapped just outside the door.

It had seemed like a good idea to get out of the way when the body arrived. It had been carried in a litter and laid out in the middle of the living room. Weres had been pouring in ever since—all of them very large and hostile. And she didn't blame them for feeling that way.

Losing the ability to shift was one thing. The death of the chief's third was another. This was an act of war. Only they hadn't found their enemy yet, so they were looking at her with retribution in their eyes.

It hadn't helped that when he saw her, Sammy had taken one look at the staff she'd been holding and started screaming his head off. He didn't know what it did, and after being questioned, it was obvious he still couldn't remember his attack, but he did recognize the staff.

She had ducked into the office after that. She didn't believe Connell or his father blamed her. That was generous given where the staff had been found, but the rage that had filled Mara's eyes had made her flinch.

Logan used to think she was a people person. She'd never had the issues being around them that Diana did anyway. But this situation was extremely uncomfortable. These messy, emotional situations were new to her. Deep down, Mara probably didn't blame her, but that didn't mean Logan wouldn't be an excellent scapegoat.

I hope she doesn't want to fight me. She had grown fond of Connell's sister in a short time and getting into a physical confrontation with her would be a mess. She would be torn between not wanting to humiliate Mara on the field of battle, while making it clear that an Elemental couldn't be bested so easily. Any suggestion that she wasn't as badass and lethal as her predecessors, and Logan would have her hands full with wannabe challengers itching to take down one of her kind.

Sighing, Logan hopped on the desk to wait, the staff held tightly in her hand. Drawing her legs up, she sat cross-legged and examined the weapon. The length was made from steel forged in Elemental fire, instead of wood, with no carvings or symbols of any kind. It was a little long for her. Feng Po Po had been at least four inches taller.

Figures. Everyone was taller.

With a flick of her wrist, she swung the staff sideways. There was a distinct whistle as it sliced through the air. She could feel something—a connection unlike any other she'd ever felt with an inanimate object. The bo felt right in her hands. But the true magic was the headpiece, in the little dragon Connell found so malevolent.

It didn't look that way to her. It was less ornate than she had thought, although it was a beautiful specimen for its time. What she found most interesting was the gaping mouth, as if the little creature was about to breathe fire on her.

Her eyes snapped up as the door opened. She had been expecting Connell or the chief for some time, but it wasn't them. Her visitor was Yogi. Muscles tightening, she got ready to spring up from the desk in case he decided to jump her.

"You can relax. I'm here to make sure no one bothers you."

She raised a brow. "So you don't think I drove this thing through your friend's chest?"

The end of the bo wasn't sharp, but Logan had the strength it would have taken to force it through the ribcage of the Were. So would another wolf—but only a very strong one. *Like Connell or the chief...*

Well, it wasn't one of them. And she didn't know enough of the others to be able to point fingers.

"I don't believe it," Yogi said. "But I might have if you hadn't saved Sammy."

"That doesn't mean I didn't do it," she couldn't resist pointing out.

"You wouldn't have bothered to save him if you were the one behind this shit."

He had a point, although a more devious thinker might have done the same in order to throw them off. She appreciated that it didn't occur to him. Wolves were refreshingly direct that way.

"How is Mara?" she asked, still wondering if the female Were was going to challenge her.

Yogi looked at her sideways. "So you know about her and Malcolm?" He shrugged, not waiting for an answer. "She seems okay, considering. Pissed off like we all are. She might have fantasized about doing him in a few times after that Riley situation, but she didn't want him dead. At least, I don't think she did..."

"*Oh.*" Had Mara been involved with Malcolm when he slept with Connell's ex?

"Stop gossiping about my sister," Connell interjected, coming in from the hallway and closing the door. "Mara has enough to worry about right now."

"*Does* she blame me?" The suspense was killing her.

"No, imp, she doesn't. That's just Mara. Her primary reaction to grief is anger. She knows you didn't kill him and has said so to more than one person out there."

That was good. But Logan felt terrible for Mara, even if she didn't quite understand what had been happening between her and the dead man.

"Okay," she said, turning the staff over one more time.

"Any luck figuring out what the hell it does?" Connell asked.

Logan fingered the open mouth of the little beast. "I have a few ideas." She took her phone out to examine the photo of the painting her mother had sent once more.

"This painting is a copy of a masterpiece by Gu Kaizhi," she said, holding out the screen so the men could see. "The original was destroyed years ago, but this copy has been handed down in my family for generations. I think the original may have looked a little different. Do you see her fighting stance and these squiggles?"

She pointed to a few lines in front of the small dragon's head. "I think the original stance might have had her pointing the head in front of her like this," she said, holding the staff out to demonstrate.

"Who cares?" Yogi asked with a frown.

"I do," she said, flicking him an irritated glance. "If the head was facing out then the squiggles would have served a purpose. In this version, she is in a traditional fighting stance for the period when the copy was made. I suspect it was altered to make it fit. It's a small adjustment, but now the dragon head is pointing down at the ground."

"I still don't get why the change is significant," Connell said.

Logan held up the staff. "If it was pointing up like I think it was, then those squiggles that look random actually represent something coming out of the dragon's mouth. If that was the case, then it means Feng Po Po somehow channeled her talent, her chi, through it."

Yogi stepped closer, his eyes wide. "You mean that little statue actually breathes fire?"

"No. Feng Po Po was an Air Elemental like me. So it would breathe wind."

Yogi no longer looked impressed. "That's not as cool."

Connell scowled at him, exasperated. "I don't give a shit how cool it is. What I want to know is what good that will do us."

Logan rolled her shoulders. "Well, normally, it wouldn't do us any good. Not unless you want another wolf stripped. But..."

"But what?"

"Well, since this is an instrument designed to channel magic, there's a chance I might be able to force it to run the other way."

"How?" Connell asked, crossing his arms.

She held up the headpiece. "It's a conduit, right? I direct *my* magic in and force it through the body of the dragon and out its mouth. Well, I'm wondering if I can call the shifter energy from the aether—provided it hasn't dissipated by now—and pour that *out* the mouth of the dragon instead."

"You can do that? Do you even need the staff for that?" he asked.

"When I strip talent, the magic bleeds off into the aether with the air currents. If I called it back, I wouldn't be able to focus it or channel it."

"But you might with this?"

"Well, maybe," she answered honestly. "I can try, but there's no guarantee it will work."

"Because it might be gone already?"

She nodded. "If it dissipated, it probably happened right away. But there's a chance it stuck together and is still floating around out there or can be called back into a cohesive force. We won't know until we do this."

"We should try, guarantees or no," Yogi said. "I don't want Sammy to grow up without his wolf. It's bad enough being the runt of the litter."

Connell nodded in agreement. "What do you need?"

Logan thought about it. Technically, she didn't *need* this, but she wanted it.

"Can everyone leave?"

30

L ogan had been asked to wait until after the funeral to perform her experiment. In truth, she had been grateful to postpone it. Once she got the go-ahead, the complexity of what she proposed began to feel daunting.

Pushing her misgivings out of her mind, she went up to Mara as the chief and Connell built a fire in the clearing. Everyone was here tonight. Even Sammy, who was waiting with his family on the other side of the clearing.

They were only a mile or so into the forest, not far from the compound's main buildings. Every wolf in a hundred-mile radius was there. And not just the males this time. The women had finally been allowed out of their houses. Little girls dotted the group along with the little boys.

Aware that most eyes were on her, she stepped into the space next to Mara, who was standing some distance away from the others.

"I'm sorry," she whispered.

"Thanks," Mara said. Her green eyes were flat and fixed on the pyre currently smoldering in the damp night air.

Logan turned back to the fire. She had never realized how much wood was needed to burn a body. The logs had been chopped from the trees around them by several young male Weres. Then they had been piled into a tall rectangle in the middle of the cleared space. Malcolm's body had been covered in a black shroud and placed on top of it.

"He texted me."

Surprised, she turned back to Mara. "What did it say? Did it mention what he was doing before..."

The Were looked down at her. "Before someone turned him into a kabob?" Logan winced, and Mara's lip curled. "Sorry. No, it was personal."

Oh.

"It said *I'm sorry. Please give me another chance.*"

Crap on a cracker.

"So you two were a couple?" Logan asked as quietly as she could.

Mara didn't seem to care if they were overheard. "No. But there was...an expectation."

"I see." She racked her brain for something comforting to share. What would Gia or Serin say at a time like this?

"I wasn't going to forgive him," Mara whispered.

"*Err.*"

"Riley's a bitch," Mara continued in that same low tone. "And yes, I'm a bigger one, but in a different way. I never wanted her with my brother. When I found out Malcolm slept with her, I lost all respect for him. Any half-formed ideas I had about him, about us, went out the window. But I should have forgiven him, I guess—except I'm still mad at him."

Logan looked down, acutely uncomfortable. "Just because someone dies, it doesn't mean they weren't flawed," she said in a low voice. "I know there's an unspoken rule about speaking ill of the dead, but the dead weren't perfect. And there's no law that says you have to forgive all their sins just because they're gone."

She glanced at their audience and edged closer to Mara. "I'm still angry at my father for dying. And I loved him. He was a great dad. But I still feel that same rush of anger at him for getting himself killed. It was a car accident. To me, he was a superhero, and he shouldn't have died in such a normal, stupid way."

She had never told anyone that, not even her mother.

Mara focused on her. "I'm sorry."

Logan shrugged. "My point is that you're allowed to feel conflicted about the dead. They weren't saints, and neither are you."

A hint of a smile appeared on Mara's face for a moment, but a log on the pyre shifted, and they both turned their attention back to the fire.

"I wish Diana was here." This would be over if her Fire Elemental sister was in charge of the blaze.

Mara didn't answer. Her eyes were distant, and Logan decided to stay quiet for the rest of the burning. She studiously avoided meeting the other wolves' eyes, deciding that in this case, discretion was the better part of valor. Not that anyone was looking to start something. Not with Connell and the chief so close.

After tending to the flames, Connell came to stand next to her and Mara, a grim, silent sentinel with his arms crossed. The chief stood a little away, next to Sammy and his father.

Eventually, the excruciating service was over. Every wolf stayed till the last bit of the body was consumed, and then they started to take their leave. By the time the last stragglers departed, the moon was high in the sky.

Logan suppressed a shudder and dematerialized to the top of the tree behind her. She had hidden the staff in the top branches before the funeral had started. At her request, only Connell and Sammy's family were going to be present for what happened next.

Reaching up, she fingered the staff and looked down. There appeared to be a slight disagreement among the few remaining wolves.

"I don't want anyone to be out in the woods by themselves," Douglas was saying.

"You're being ridiculous. No one is going to catch me off guard," a larger older man said. Logan thought it was Sammy's father.

"I have to find the monster who did this to my boy," the man continued.

Yup, that was Bishop. Douglas leaned in and said something else, but the guy put his hands up. "I won't go alone."

"Yogi's staying with Sammy," Connell pointed out.

Bishop waved off their concern. "I'll take someone else. Several someones."

Logan waited, but they weren't able to talk Bishop out of leaving. Once he was gone, she dropped down to the forest floor with the staff in hand. Douglas gestured. As a group, the wolves fanned out and started walking back to the main house. They headed to the clearing in front of the porch where a much smaller and less tragic bonfire was built.

Logan wanted to be outside for this.

"Any reason why you didn't want the rest of the pack around?" Douglas asked as she drew a few runes in the dirt.

She inclined her head and held up the staff. "I don't think it's a good idea to show more people how to use this thing—if I succeed, that is."

The chief narrowed his eyes at her. "My people won't betray your trust."

Logan didn't have time for a last-minute pissing match. "Rumors can spread faster than you can spit. Connell said you heard about me stripping the Burgess witch immediately after. There's no need to give anyone a detailed description of this staff."

"Won't you destroy it afterward?" he asked.

Sighing, she held it up, admiring the craftsmanship. "Only after we restore the ability to shift." She didn't bother to add her doubts about whether they would succeed.

Connell finished checking out the perimeter and joined her next to the circle she had drawn on the ground.

"You better not be cutting yourself up again," he growled.

She frowned. "It was necessary."

"Well, I don't like seeing you bleed. Judging from your expression when you were slicing yourself up, neither do you. You're squeamish about blood, aren't you?"

"I'm fine when it's someone else's," she snapped. "And it usually is."

Connell humphed. She bit her lip to keep from arguing with him more because, judging from his expression, Douglas was trying not to laugh.

Gesturing to Sammy, she motioned for him to join her in the circle. Yogi was right behind him.

"There's no danger to him, right?" Yogi asked.

Logan shrugged. "Probably not."

Yogi glowered and stepped up to the circle's edge. "*Probably?*"

"Hey, you're the one who wanted me to do this," she snapped. "In theory, it's a simple transfer of energy, but I haven't done this before. No one has. So you have to be aware of the risks. This isn't one-hundred-perfect safe."

"Which is why I still say I should go first," Connell pointed out.

Logan was tired of arguing this point. "I know, but I have a better chance of success with Sammy since his attack was more recent. There's a higher chance his shifter magic is still intact and floating around in the aether. But if I try and fail with you, I won't know if it's because the ritual is wrong or too much time has passed."

There was also the issue of size. Connell's magic would have been proportional to him—his body mass, age, and alpha status. So the energy she was trying to channel would have been more potent with him. Sammy was only a cub, so in theory, it should be easier for him.

Not that this was going to be easy. If she didn't control the intensity of the energy and the rate of the transfer, Sammy could be blown sky-high. So could she. However, she chose not to mention those cold, hard facts. She'd stop the ritual if she felt the child was in imminent danger.

Of course, the decision wasn't hers...

Logan knelt to Sammy's level. "Kiddo, you don't have to do this. You can grow up to be a perfectly normal man. You'll be just as smart and special as you are right now."

"No, I want my wolf back," he said quickly before looking down at the ground. "The other boys act different around me now," he added in a lower voice.

"Okay, then," she said, putting her hand on the back of his head.

She had been half-hoping he would say he was fine the way he was. *Like that had been realistic.*

"In that case, let's get started," she said in a loud, clear voice. She straightened up and looked around, pointing the staff at his brother. "Yogi, back off and get outside the circle. And don't smudge those runes."

She positioned Sammy a few steps in front of her on the left side of the circle. Her blood pounded in her ears as she took her place on the right and held the bo up. Peeking out of the side of her eye, she took one last look at Connell and the others before breathing deeply and calling for the magic.

It was different from using her air talent. Calling the winds was second nature to her by now. Like breathing. She didn't have to think about it. But this was something else.

The weight in her stomach increased as she searched for the specific signature of shifter energy in the aether. The words were similar to the spell she used to strip the Burgess witches, but she'd modified it extensively. There, she'd cast the magic out and away. Now, she was trying to coax it near—pleading for it to come to her.

The spirits on the wind heard and mocked her efforts. One of them, a nasty bogeyman-like male she had secretly nicknamed Gollum, whispered swear words in both English and Mandarin. Pointedly ignoring him, she focused on her chant, keeping her voice low so the words would be unclear.

It wasn't that she was worried about the ritual being copied by the wolves here. This wasn't their kind of magic, but Elementals were secretive by nature when it came to the spells they used. They were safer that way.

She was well into the second verse when Gollum shouted in her ear. "You're going to fail, you stupid fucking cunt!"

Logan flinched. "Son of a bitch," she swore, breaking off mid-chant.

In the distance, she could hear Gollum laughing, his delight in derailing her obvious.

"Everything okay?" Connell asked, his mouth turned down in concern.

Shifting her weight, she tightened her hold on the staff with a determined grip. "It's fine," she said from behind gritted teeth.

It had been some time since an air spirit had managed to unnerve her that way.

Connell shifted his weight impatiently, but she tore her eyes away from his tall, tense form. It was a good thing he could only hear the spirits if he was touching her. Ignoring the dead douchebag continuing to shout in the background, she refocused on her task, getting through the first, second, and third verses without cracking again. When nothing happened, she started over again. Thankfully, Gollum got bored and subsided into the background hum of the other spirits.

Her sweep was systematic. Logan would direct her calls out to the aether, turning periodically to face each cardinal direction before beginning the cycle again.

She had just become convinced that Gollum was right when the magic came hard and fast. It struck the staff like a lightning rod, running through it and her with a blast stronger than any bolt from the sky.

Oh, fuck.

Logan had miscalculated. There was too much energy to channel directly into Sammy's little body. In a split-second decision, she did the only thing she could think of. She ran the energy through her body before passing it on to the little boy—efficiently frying her aura in the process.

Pain exploded in her head and her vision whitened out before clearing. When she could see again, it was through squinted eyes. Sammy was lying on the ground in front of her.

She held on long enough to make sure his chest was still moving up and down before letting go. The ground rushed up to meet her.

31

Ow. Pain raced through her body as she regained consciousness. Logan cracked an eyelid, but even that hurt.

There was nothing but white above her. *Crapulence.* Had she died? Had the Mother called her home?

"Logan, thank God!"

Connell's anxious face appeared above her, and her body rolled into his as he sat next to her. They were on a bed in an unfamiliar room. His weight was enough to displace her, the staff she held tightly in her hand knocking into his knee.

"Maybe you'll let that go now," he said gruffly. "I couldn't get it out of your hand when you were unconscious. Neither could my dad. It was the damnedest thing, but your grip was supernaturally tight."

No wonder her hand ached. With a wince, Logan lifted the bo staff straight above her. For a second, she thought her hand was fused to the bo. It took far too much effort to force her fingers to relax, but she finally did. Connell took the staff from her and propped it next to the bed, the dragon head winking down at her.

"Did it work?" she croaked, her voice raspy and tight.

"I don't know. Maybe. My father says Sammy's energy is different now, but he hasn't shifted yet. He was out for a few minutes, too, but he woke up as soon as we got him inside. Dad said he should wait a little longer before trying to change."

"Is that all it's been? A few minutes?"

"No. You've been out for hours."

"*What?*"

Logan sat up with a grimace, despite Connell's effort to hold her down. She ached from head to toe, but she wasn't about to stay in bed a minute longer.

"Hours?" she asked in disbelief.

"Yeah." His face grew dark. "The longest damn hours of my life. Don't ever fucking scare me like that again," he growled, pulling her into his arms in a hard, inflexible embrace.

"Okay," Logan said, patting him awkwardly on the back. "Did you forget the part where we have to try again to restore your wolf?"

Connell leaned back to meet her eyes. "Fuck it. I don't want it back if it's going to kill you."

"In case you failed to notice, I'm not dead."

"You could have been." He scowled. "And if it was that hard to get Sammy's wolf back, then I don't want you to try for mine."

"Well, I didn't say I wanted to do it right this minute, did I? And really, I'm fine now." She started to get up, but Connell rolled on top of her. "*Hey.*"

"Did you notice you're in my room?" he asked silkily.

Logan took a look around again. She hadn't recognized it at first, although the size of the bed should have tipped her off. "So?"

"And did you forget what I told you I would do to you if I got you back here?"

Oh. All of sudden, she had no desire to get up and back to work. Relaxing, she let her body melt against his. "I don't suppose everyone has gone to bed?" she asked.

"As a matter of fact, they have. You slept till dawn."

"Hmm. Well, in that case..."

She wrapped her arms around his neck, deciding she wasn't that sore after all.

32

L ogan was studiously avoiding looking at Connell's family at breakfast the next morning. She was kicking herself for falling into bed with him again, and she couldn't believe she had done so under his father's roof. Her only excuse for her weakness was her recent brush with death...

Not to mention those ten-pack abs.

Sex with Connell had been even better this time, and she had lost herself in his arms. However, she was aware of how sensitive a Were's hearing was, so she'd made an effort to do so quietly.

Unfortunately, Connell hadn't bothered with discretion. Or he hadn't cared that he was waking everyone on their floor of the house. She'd wanted to kill him at the time, but she hadn't been feeling up to it.

Even now, she was feeling a little shaky in the aftermath of that blast to her aura. Her nerves were normally rock solid, but she felt jittery and uncertain, although she would have chewed her own leg off before admitting it.

Connell had slept in, but he'd been up most of the night keeping watch over her when she'd gotten zapped. He needed the rest. So she went downstairs alone and ate quickly, hoping to get out of there before the rest of the pack descended on the house.

Her plan was to return to the safe house for more research. Hopefully, with a little modification, she could repeat the ritual to get Connell's wolf back without getting knocked on her butt again. But first, she needed to refuel. She helped herself to more pancakes.

Mara sat across the table from her. From time to time, she gave Logan a speculative look, but she kept pretty quiet.

She's thinking of Malcolm.

Sammy provided a brief distraction. The little boy blew into the dining room to wolf down breakfast. He could barely sit still long enough to gulp a glass of milk before running outside, bouncing up and down the entire way. When the chief went outside to check on him, Logan relaxed.

"Do you want kids?" Mara asked.

Logan choked on a large bit of breakfast sausage. The pack enjoyed a lot of meat with every meal. "Err. I guess. Someday."

"Connell wants them. A whole litter," Mara continued in a matter-of-fact tone.

"*Okay.*"

"You're too young to be thinking of having kids, aren't you?"

Logan nodded, widening her eyes for emphasis.

"I guess that's okay. Connell is still young for a Were. Not as young as you, but he has time."

God, this was uncomfortable. "Look, I know a lot has happened. To you. To your pack. Even between Connell and me. But that doesn't mean we're..."

She trailed off, unsure what to say. She knew what Connell would want her to say, but Logan didn't want to make any claims either way. Wolves put a lot of stock in verbal declarations.

"I want to be an aunt," Mara declared firmly.

"Um..."

Mara was staring at her expectantly when a great shout went up outside. It was Douglas, and he was yelling Logan's name.

She was out the door in a flash. She didn't even bother to run, just dematerialized and threw herself out the nearest window so fast she made herself dizzy.

Regaining her legs, she ran up to Douglas, who was standing a little away with a group of male Weres and cubs. Yogi was there, his eyes trained on something behind the wall of men.

Mara ran out of the house behind her, catching up as Logan pushed past the Weres blocking her view.

There in the middle of a shredded pile of children's clothing was a small, blue-and-gold *dragon*.

Yogi spun Logan backward with a large hand. "How do we turn him back?" he cried.

"How do we turn who back?" she asked, the answer coming to her before she had finished her sentence.

The kid's clothes. She had seen that shirt this morning. This was Sammy, and he *was* a shifter again. Just not a wolf.

"Holy crap on a cracker," she muttered before looking up at the men.

A ring of shocked gazes stared back at her.

She coughed and cleared her throat before turning back to the little dragon, who was preening and swishing his new spiked tail. "Well...this is awkward."

33

By the Mother, they were going to kill her.

"What the fuck do you mean by it is more nurture than nature?" Yogi yelled.

"Calm down, son," Douglas said for the third time.

"It's not her fault," Connell pointed out. He'd shot out of bed when the yelling started. "We *asked* her to do this."

Yogi had been ranting at her for a solid ten minutes—ever since they'd persuaded Sammy to stop flexing his wings and swishing his spined tail in favor of having some ice cream.

That last had been Mara's idea. She knew the kid pretty well. Only the offer of three scoops of rocky road had gotten Sammy's attention. Otherwise, it was doubtful he would have given up playing in his dragon form. He seemed thrilled with the new status quo and kept trying to set the shrubbery on fire.

It hadn't helped that Logan had yelped, and then *laughed* when the little dragon had succeeded in breathing a weak flame. Once the bush he'd set on fire was charcoal, he'd shifted back to his seven-year-old self.

"It has to be that damn dragon staff of yours," Yogi continued. "It turned him into one of them!"

Logan shook her head. "It's not a magical dragon creation device," she said sarcastically. "The headpiece at the top is purely ornamental. Even if Sammy focused and somehow imprinted on it during the ritual, it shouldn't have been enough to override your natural wolf programming."

"What the hell does that mean? We're not programmed," Connell protested, his head drawing back.

She raised her shoulders and made little circles with her hands. "Well... actually...you kind of are."

"*What?*"

"Well, you know that whole shifting-into-wolves thing is more a cultural practice than anything else, right?"

Even the chief stared at her blankly.

Logan shuffled on her feet. "Okay, so it's like this. There aren't that many types of Supes out there. You have your Fae, your vamps, and your witches."

Douglas passed a hand over his face. "Go on," he said impatiently. "Faster, if you please."

"I'm simply trying to be clear here," Logan said, exasperated. "There are those species of Supes. And then there are shifters. There are a lot of different kinds of shifters...in practice. But the reality is, you're all...just shifters."

"Well, I can't turn into a fucking dragon," Yogi spat. "Or a goat. Or a fucking bunny rabbit. We're *werewolves.*"

Logan nodded. "I know you're wolves. Don't expect to suddenly be able to shift into something else if you try. The wolf meme is strong. They all are."

Even Connell was starting to give her a frustrated glare. "Fuck, Logan, being a werewolf is not some fucking fad."

"I didn't say it was. It is, however, more along the lines of a very *strongly held conviction.*"

More disbelieving looks. She turned to the chief. "You know how some ideas are so strong that we hold onto them as an inviolable truth, and then we meet another culture or society and find out they don't believe in that truth the way we do, and it seems almost incomprehensible to us?"

"It's how most wars get started," he said flatly, looking down at her with get-on-with-it expression.

"Well, werewolves are very much like those truths. The concept of a man—or woman," she said, breaking off to glance at Mara, "changing into a wolf is an idea so strong, and so compelling, that it's been passed down in your blood."

"So we *are* wolves by nature," Connell said.

"In a way...but there's this thing human scientists have described recently that sort of explains what I mean. Has anyone heard of epigenetics?"

"What the fuck are you talking about now?" Yogi asked, his volume raising.

Logan wiggled her hands, searching for the right words. "Epigenetic traits are changes in your cells caused by the environment that aren't necessarily hard coded into your DNA. They happen at a level above that. Sometimes, they're inherited by the next generation, but sometimes they aren't."

"So what?" Yogi spat.

It was her turn to start losing her patience. "*So* being a wolf is something that is usually inherited. It's a powerful trope. One that is so strong it's become the foundation of an entire society. But it's *not* hard coded into your DNA."

That was met with complete silence.

"All right," Douglas said after a long while. "What you're saying is that Sammy's signals have been scrambled, and now he's settled on another...trope."

The last word was said with distaste.

"Basically," Logan conceded with a nod. It was a tiny bit more complicated than that, but there was no point in dissecting the nuances.

"Then can we change him back? Reprogram him again?"

"Um...I don't know."

34

"This is *your* fault," Salome yelled at her older brother. "His walls have been covered with dragons ever since you let him watch *Game of Thrones* with you!"

The siblings had been yelling at each other for quite a while now —ever since Salome had driven up to the front door, her four-wheel drive SUV skidding in the mud.

Yogi winced, but he didn't back down. "How was I supposed to know he'd be able to choose to be a fucking *dragon*?"

"He was too little to be watching that show at all. *I told you that!* Now he's gone and decided to be a freaking reptile!"

Logan wanted to point out that a conscious decision hadn't been involved, but she had already tried to reason with the Weres. It was like spitting into the wind. She'd stopped wasting her time and was now trying to come up with a plan B after the chief had made it clear they couldn't leave Sammy the way he was.

"I still don't see why you can't let the kid be," Logan muttered to Connell, who was sitting next to her on the couch watching Salome tear her brother a new one.

And Salome had seemed so sweet. She fingered the head of the staff. "Dragons are pretty cool."

Connell smirked, but his tone was as uncompromising as the chief's had been. "We can't raise a dragon. Sammy's still a little kid with next to no impulse control. You saw him breathing fire. He could burn the whole forest down. And it's been pretty dry this year."

"Fine." She sighed, rolling her shoulders. "I guess you don't want me to try the ritual on you now."

Connell turned his amazing green eyes to her. "Not if it's going to fry your tiny body," he admonished.

Her lips firmed. "I'll find a way to prevent that."

"Well, when you do, we can think about it. I guess I could handle shifting into a dragon," he mused. "It's better than nothing."

His smooth tone didn't fool her. Even he knew dragons were badass. It was a shame she had to burst his bubble.

"I don't think it's likely to happen with you. You've been a wolf too long. And you obviously like it. Apparently, Sammy happened to like dragons a bit more."

He turned to face her more fully. "Is there anything in those books you went to consult at your safe house? Some way to fix this?"

Logan shook her head. "It was a miracle we were able to find a way to restore any shifter ability at all. And the texts we keep copies of locally aren't specialized or specific to shifters. If there is a way out of this, I won't find it at the safe house."

She looked around, but the other Weres were still engrossed in their argument. "Your only chance, if there is any, would be found in the archives on T'Kaieri."

"What's T'Kaieri?"

"Someplace you aren't allowed to go. It's where Gia is now, looking up the staff in our archives."

"Why can't I go?" he said, a hairsbreadth from pouting.

"First off, you want a quick solution, so I'll have to fly there. T'Kaieri is heavily shielded by protective spells and enchantments. It's an island, the home of Water Elementals, and there is absolutely no way for you to get there without me."

Connell looked pained, but his voice was firm. "Then I'll fly with you," he said grudgingly.

"It's not a quick trip. It would be hours. Plus, once we got there, you wouldn't be allowed inside the archive itself. There are some pretty strict rules about it. Most of the members of the T'Kaierian community don't have access."

"Fine," he said, giving up. "How long would you be gone for?"

She shrugged. "A day or two. The archives are dense. Also, there's no guarantee I'll find anything that can help."

Connell looked like he wanted to argue with her some more, but he miraculously held his tongue and gave her a short nod. They talked a little more about the island before he gestured to the staff still in her hand.

"Are you going to take that with you?" he asked.

"It belongs in the archive," she said, holding the staff closer. "It's the safest place for it."

"Well, don't leave it there. Not yet."

"I wasn't planning on it. I'm just saying the staff will be safer there long term. Until the time comes to destroy it."

Connell frowned. "It belongs to your ancestor. Do you really want to destroy it?"

Reluctantly, she nodded. "It should have been taken apart already. Now that we can strip with spells alone, it's not needed. And you, of all people, know how dangerous it is."

He leaned back. "All right. Try to hurry back. I'll keep an eye on things here."

"Don't do anything stupid," Logan said waspishly.

She was reluctant to leave him given Malcolm's recent death. The Were had been almost as big and strong as Connell, and someone had taken him down.

"I didn't get to be the chief's enforcer because I happened to be his son. I had to fight for the position," he said with an irritated scowl.

"I know that. Just watch your back," she said in a low voice.

Connell's shoulders relaxed as he gave her a soft, understanding glance. "I will."

Logan turned back to the squabbling siblings. They'd been going at it long enough to drive the chief away. "Do you think I can take off now? Yogi will assume I've abandoned you all to your dragon-y fate."

"He won't think that," he assured her. "I'll explain. Although, I don't even think either one of them will notice that you're gone."

Before she could move, he pulled her forward for a hard kiss. "Forty-eight hours and no more. If you take longer than that, I'm coming after you again. And believe me, it doesn't matter how many spells are hiding that place, I *will* find you."

Logan blinked, but she didn't say anything before dematerializing. Technically, what he was threatening was impossible...except she believed him.

35

A s the Air Elemental, Logan traveled at speeds her sisters weren't capable of. She'd always considered herself fortunate, but now it seemed even she was too slow.

What I wouldn't give for a Star Trek transporter, she thought, reaching the shores of T'Kaieri late that evening. Wondering if it was too late to meet Gia, she skipped the requisite meeting at the gate and landed at the door to the archives.

The council wouldn't look too kindly on her skipping the usual meet and greet—and she didn't kid herself that the Elders didn't know she was here. Most of them were well versed in the craft. But being the youngest of her sisters gave her a little license to act like a punk sometimes. Logan had no compunction of playing that card when she needed to.

She ran down the steps, hopping down the last four and landing lightly on her feet in front of the huge Colonization mural with the staff clutched in her hand.

"Gia," she called out, hoping her sister was still down here and not at the house reserved for their use.

"Logan, is that you?" the Earth Elemental called out.

"Yeah," she called out, following her sister's voice through the warren of rooms.

"Get your tiny butt over here!"

Logan pursed her lips. She found Gia in a back room, in front of tall cabinet. "My butt is *not* tiny," she protested.

She didn't have Serin or Gia's figure, but her butt was just fine, thank you very much. And Connell didn't seem to mind that her curves were on the small side.

"Of course not, sweetie," Gia said distractedly. She looked over at her, relief flickering across her expression. "Oh, good, you brought it," she said, reaching out for the staff.

Logan handed it over. Gia lifted it and put it into the cabinet on the third shelf on a green baize cover. The dragon head nestled snugly into an indentation at one end.

"Weird. It almost looks like it was made for it," Logan observed.

Gia sighed, staring at the staff. "It was. Which means we have a big problem."

"You have no idea," Logan rushed out. "Sammy's a dragon!"

She turned to Logan, eyes wide. "He's what?"

"An honest-to-God baby dragon. Breathes fire and everything."

"*Oh.*" Her mouth lax, she gestured to the staff. "Did you..."

"Yes."

"And he's..."

"A dragon."

"How...interesting."

"Is that all you can say?" Logan asked.

Gia's sense of humor overtook her surprise. "Douglas must be beside himself." She giggled.

"They're all shitting bricks. Douglas and Connell are worried he'll huff and puff and burn their houses down. And I don't blame them. I don't suppose you know how to fix it?"

Gia exhaled. "Sorry, doll, you are in uncharted territory now."

"I was afraid you were going to say that." Logan grumbled and surveyed the full shelves around them. "Guess I have to hit the books after all. I don't suppose I can haul Noomi's butt out of bed and get her crew down here?"

"I'm sure they'll come if you wish, but I need to talk to you about this first," she said, reaching out and taking the staff off the green cover. "This shelf was made for Feng Po Po's staff. In fact, the entire cabinet's dimensions were determined by its length. The archivists wanted to display it properly."

Logan rocked back on her heels. "Oh. Well, shit. When did it go back out into the world?"

"I'm not sure, but it was recently."

Her brain started to fuzz with static. "How recently?"

Gia shook her head and looked down at the staff in her hands. "As far as I can tell, it's within the last five or ten years."

She stared at her sister blankly. "That doesn't make any sense. Did it go to one of my relatives in China?"

Only a blood relation could have taken it. And it would have to have been before she inherited. Otherwise, it would have automatically been given to her as both Feng Po Po's blood descendent and an Elemental in service. No one else would have had a stronger claim.

Her sister's face darkened. "No. I have no idea how it got out of here. There's no annotation in the record for it beyond the inventory at the turn of the century. But I've questioned the archivists and some of them have seen it more recently than that, although no one is sure when the last time was."

Realization dawned. "So it was stolen?" she asked, stunned.

"It's worse than that."

"What could be worse?"

Gia winced. "I don't think this is the only artifact missing."

"*What?*"

"Do you remember that knife that stabbed Diana? The one with extraterrestrial metal?"

Logan was starting to get dizzy. "Don't tell me it's missing too?"

"No, it's here. And it has been since I returned it, after Sage Burgess' death. But according to the records, it's been here for the last century since it was confiscated from a dark Fae in the Adirondacks."

"*Shit.* I need to sit down."

"There's more."

Logan's stomach was twisting into knots. Gia's tone was low and even. She was trying too hard to sound calm.

"Something tells me I don't want to hear this."

"And I don't want to say it," Gia said before taking a deep breath. "But it seems the only person who's accessed both these artifacts in the last few decades is Serin."

Logan reached out and smacked Gia on the arm. "I told you not to tell me!"

36

"I refuse to believe Serin had anything to do with this." Logan was adamant.

It was true she hadn't known the Water Elemental as long as Gia had, but the fact her oldest sister was even entertaining the suspicion was crazy.

"I don't think she did either. But some things aren't adding up. These two items aren't the only ones missing. And the only person the archivists remember asking about them is Serin."

Logan was immediately incensed. "Then it was one of *them*. They must be lying, and they're trying to shift the blame."

"I've considered that, but I think they're telling the truth. Granted, I don't have Diana's built-in lie detector or your spirits to ask for intel, but they strike me as being truthful. Plus, the archivists haven't left the island in decades. How would they smuggle not one, but multiple, artifacts off T'Kaieri when they never leave?"

"They must have managed somehow. It makes more sense than Serin doing it. She's spent her life tracking down bad guys and bringing their weapons here for storage or destruction."

Gia nodded, "I know, but there is something else. I think some of the other weapons, like the blade used to stab Diana, were supposed to be melted down. Almost all the others are items Serin confiscated personally. The staff is an exception, but given what the latter is capable of, the thief must've found it too tempting."

"Well, that proves it wasn't Serin. She can strip powers with a spell like we can. She wouldn't need the staff. And she hasn't been lurking in the woods of Colorado to torment Connell's pack."

"Again, I don't think she's the one behind it. But I've sent her multiple messages in the last few hours trying to get her here, and I haven't heard anything."

"That's not unusual," Logan pointed out. "She's probably in the middle of a case. Do you know how many things are gone?"

"So far, at least half a dozen confirmed, not counting the staff."

"Shit!"

"We need to talk to Serin."

Logan's stomach roiled. "You can't believe she's involved."

"No, but she might know something. You have to admit she's not been herself lately. That stuff about Jordan and her general unhappiness..."

"C'mon. That is hardly an airtight case," she protested.

"No, it's not," Gia admitted. "But she has been acting strangely. Maybe she knows something."

"She would have shared something like *this*," Logan shouted.

Gia held up a hand. "Unless she isn't aware she knows something."

"What?"

"I don't know." Gia raised her voice abruptly, betraying her frustration. "I'm simply following where the evidence leads. Like I said, we need to talk to her. Diana, as well, for that matter. They both need to know what's going on."

"All right. Where are the archivists? As far as I'm concerned, they're our prime suspects."

"Noomi is here. And I've known her since she was born. I trust her. The other two are at their homes. I sent word to the Elders already. None of them will be allowed off the island."

"So the Elders are aware of the situation?"

"I had to tell them something, but they don't know the full extent of the damage."

Logan took a good look around them. Each shelf in the room was crammed full of books or scrolls. Totems and statues were mixed in with them. Not every weapon was obvious, like a sword or the staff. There were hundreds, perhaps thousands, of magical artifacts in their collection. With the right skill set, a determined practitioner could use any of them for something nefarious.

And those were the ones that were supposed to be here. If Gia was right, there were even more that could be unaccounted for because they were supposed to have been destroyed long ago.

"What a shitstorm," she muttered, covering her eyes.

37

Connell watched Sammy play outside from an upstairs window. His father had decided he should stay at their house rather than being sent home in his condition.

It was a good idea. Now that Sammy was a shifter again, he could be in danger of being struck down and robbed of his second form twice. Not to mention the fire danger...

"Any word from Logan yet?" his father asked, joining him at the window.

"Not yet. But she warned me she'd have to leave the island before she could get in touch. Phones don't work there."

He'd shared what little he knew about the place with his father and Mara. The chief had been intrigued. Mara hadn't cared. She was very quiet these days.

"We're missing something," Douglas said, his gaze on Sammy. "There's an explanation hidden in all this mess."

Connell rolled his shoulders. "We make piss-poor detectives."

That kind of thing was against their nature. Werewolves tended to be a very straightforward group. Challenges were made, and fights were common. Everything was out in the open. It was hard to keep secrets in their community. Even their enemies came at them in direct frontal assaults. All this sneaky subterfuge was bullshit.

"I feel like there's something out of my reach," his father said. "There's some detail that's been in front of me the whole time, but I can't see its significance."

"I know exactly what you mean," Connell murmured. He broke off, something occurring to him. "Logan once said something right at the beginning when she was questioning me about that night I lost my wolf. She asked if I sensed anything new in my vicinity when I was attacked."

"You didn't right after it happened, when it was still fresh. Unless you remember a new detail now. Do you?"

"No. But then she asked if something familiar was present that should not have been there at that moment."

Douglas narrowed his eyes. "And you remember what that is?"

"Not yet. But there's this idea I keep circling around—not from the attack, but ever since we got back. Like it's not something present so much as missing. I just can't put my finger on it," he said, running a hand roughly through his hair. "I want to go back to where Malcolm was found and take a look around. Maybe it'll come to me."

His father, whose face did a good imitation of being carved in stone, cracked. He looked at Connell with uncharacteristic concern. "I don't want you going alone. Malcolm wasn't your equal in a fair fight, but that was before you lost your wolf. And whoever is behind this has no honor. They could be lying in wait for a second chance at you."

"I'll take a few of the guys from my old squad," he promised. "Mara and Yogi should stay behind to keep an eye on things here."

His father hesitated before nodding. "As long as you watch your back."

Connell paused at the head of the stairs. "I always do."

38

It had taken some convincing to get his sister to stay behind at the house. His announcement that he was returning to the site of the third attack had broken through the cool, icy shell she'd wrapped around herself since Malcolm's death.

Mara hadn't wanted him to go without her. But after assuring her he wasn't going alone, he'd talked her into staying to watch over Sammy and the others.

His sister was the dirtiest fighter in the pack. If the threat came to their doorstep, he wanted Mara there, even if his father still refused to acknowledge her skill.

It took a little longer to get to that spot in the woods than he'd wanted because his two most trusted lieutenants, Derrick and Leeland, had both been at home. But he'd called, and they had come. Now they were all there in that cold, quiet spot where Malcolm had died.

"What are we looking for?" Derrick asked while he and Leeland walked the perimeter where the concealment dome had met the forest floor.

Both wolves had served in his elite Special Forces unit. He trusted them implicitly—even more so than Malcolm, who had coveted

Connell's position as second, although he'd never done anything about it.

"I'm not sure," he admitted. "Something that should be here and isn't," he added in a lower voice.

Neither of the other wolves questioned him. They were too well trained. Instead, they fanned out, sweeping the area for clues.

He pivoted on his heel, his eyes gravitating to the spot where they had found Malcolm. The image of him lying on the forest floor, the staff driven through his chest, was burned into his brain.

Would Malcolm have challenged him if he'd lived? Before he lost his wolf, it would never have happened. Connell had been tested. Malcolm knew he couldn't beat him.

Mara had been right to some extent. Being the chief's son had kept the number of contenders down, but Connell had fought viciously to become his father's second. Each time, he had been the clear victor. But if he failed to get his wolf back, he would be expected to step down. And with Malcolm dead, there wasn't a clear successor. The fight to establish the next in line was going to get messy.

Pushing his concern to the back of his mind, he refocused on his task, bending close to the ground where the body had been found.

It was probably pointless to come all the way out here, but he couldn't get rid of the nagging feeling he had missed something. This seemed like the best place to start. Connell carefully scented the air, grateful his sense of smell was still intact. But aside from the fading trace of death and blood, there wasn't much.

Except. There it was again. The faint smell of surprise. Malcolm's surprise. It was Sammy's attack all over again. Malcolm had been surprised, and that was it. A split second of fear, and then death had come quickly. The barrier spell had prevented them from smelling those strong feelings, but now that it was down, that tang of negative emotion clung to this place.

Malcolm had seen someone. He'd been shocked by whoever it was. And then he'd died. There was no way around it. Malcolm had been killed by someone he knew. It wasn't an outsider after all. It was one of their own.

Derrick and Leeland were talking in a low tone at the periphery of his vision. For a second, he watched them, suspicion clouding his thoughts.

Stop it. These men had served with him. This situation was making him paranoid. They were good men, and as far as he was concerned, above suspicion.

Connell watched approvingly as the other two walked the diameter of the bubble spell. Maybe they would find something since his mind was clearly elsewhere.

What am I missing?

There was something clamoring for his attention at the edge of his memory. Deep down, he knew who was responsible.

What the hell is it? What did I not see?

Though it was cold out today, the breeze was suddenly warm, whipping around him in a rush that felt almost deliberate—like it was trying to prod him into remembering what he'd forgotten. The scent of the other two men, salty pine mixed with musk, carried to him.

"Oh shit," he gasped aloud. "His scent. His scent was gone. *It was missing.*"

He spun around to the two men, intending to shout across the clearing. They had to get back to his house right away. He knew who the enemy was.

But it was too late. When the attack came, it was out of nowhere.

39

Logan was holed up in the corner of the Egyptian room in the archives, dourly flipping through the piles of research Noomi had pulled for her on werewolves.

Though she was still suspicious of the archivists, she agreed with Gia that Noomi was probably okay. Painfully proper and circumspect, Noomi had never stepped a toe out of line for as long as Logan had known her.

Noomi worked her entire life to achieve the position of head archivist, and when it came right down to it, Logan didn't think she would do anything to jeopardize her job. And Noomi seemed genuinely appalled that such a thing had happened on her watch. She'd offered to resign her post—practically prostrating herself at Gia's feet. But right now, they needed her, so Gia had put her to work.

"Here are some more accounts of the Anubis form," Noomi said, coming into the room with a stack of scrolls she couldn't see over clutched in her arms.

Logan hopped up from the table to help her when a few of the cylindrical cases slid to the floor. "I think I have enough for now," she told the archivist for the second time as they arranged the scrolls on the table next to her to-be-read pile.

Noomi turned to her with eyes that shined too brightly. Logan suspected she was on the verge of tears, and that she had been since she learned of the thefts. "Are you sure?" she asked hesitantly. "Because there are several more accounts from the time of the Pharaoh Khayu that may be significant."

It had been the head archivist's suggestion that Logan research the Anubis form of Egyptian Weres because they were the only shifters they knew of that could alternate multiple forms.

Like the werewolves of Connell's pack, Egyptian Weres could turn into four-legged wolves, but they could also hold a second form where only their head shifted. Their body remained human. It was an evolutionary synapomorphy—a trait characteristic and unique to the Weres of that region.

No other shifters could do anything like it, which was why Noomi thought it might help to read more about it. The situation wasn't quite what Logan was dealing with back in Colorado, but it was a place to start.

"Seriously, I have enough to read for now," she said, shooing Noomi away before the pile got any bigger.

"All right," the head archivist called out, backing of out the room, bobbing her head respectfully.

That respect was just for show. "Why don't I start a second pile in the other room?" Noomi asked when she was at the doorway.

She was gone before Logan could disagree. Huffing a hard breath to blow the hair out of her eyes, she climbed back on the table and forced herself to pick up another volume.

Gia was also still here, but she couldn't help research a solution at the moment. She had her hands full keeping the Elders at bay. The group of old-timers had descended on them hours ago, which was why Logan was hiding in the back storage room. She didn't have time for the endless debate and politely phrased recriminations that were currently flying around in the central chamber.

They still hadn't heard from Serin. Logan kept telling herself that meant nothing...but she was starting to worry.

Diana, on the other hand, had contacted them a little while ago.

And she was spitting mad. Logan didn't blame her. If an evil witch had stabbed *her* in the gut with a magical blade, and then she'd found out said knife was supposed to be dust—destroyed by your own people—she'd be pissed too.

Logan only hoped Diana hadn't blown up and burned something important down when she found out—although Di did a good job controlling her temper these days. Alec helped with that. He had a way with her.

Both of them were en route to the island. They'd flown out of Cairns a few hours ago and would stop in the Bahamas to switch to a seaplane. T'Kairie was too small for an airport and had no natural harbor. A seaplane was the quickest way for a non-Elemental to travel, and Diana didn't want to leave Alec behind.

He would pitch a fit if she tried.

Alec had been champing at the bit to get inside the archives for some time now, but the Elders had been reluctant to allow a vampire on the premises—even one mated to an Elemental. But the Elders couldn't put him off anymore. Not if he was escorted here by his mate.

Logan sat up, the lightbulb in her head flashing like neon. She could put Alec to work doing this research! He was a renowned scholar. She knew he would love to help if it meant he could riffle though the stacks with impunity. Plus, his vampire speed extended to his reading ability. Alec could blow through all these scrolls and books in a fraction of the time it would take her.

Connell would object if he knew a bloodsucker was pitching in to help his pack out, but what he didn't know wouldn't hurt him... For that matter, he also didn't need to know that Alec had *already* helped her modify the ritual for the shifter energy transfer. They had sent messages through Diana about it. With any luck, she wouldn't burn herself out again if she followed his advice.

Logan was about to call out to Noomi to broach the subject of Alec helping out when pain exploded in her chest. Her vision was swamped with red, and she screamed aloud. Her shriek of pain echoed off the walls, reverberating back to her, seeming to magnify the agony ripping through her. Clutching her stomach, she rolled off the table, literally trying to hold herself together.

Gia came at a dead run. Naomi peeked from behind her with wide, frightened eyes.

"Logan! What's wrong? What is it?" Gia asked.

Logan struggled to stand, putting a shaky hand on her stomach, which was twisted into one huge knot. She could barely breathe. "It's Connell. I don't know. *Fuck.* Something's wrong with him."

It felt like she was being torn in two. Almost limping, she headed for the door as fast as she could. "I have to go!" she yelled.

Gia ran after her. "Logan, I just heard from Serin. *Jordan is missing.*"

She stopped short, spinning around to face her sister. "What?"

"He's gone. Serin can't find a trace of him anywhere. She's frantic. She thinks he's dead."

Logan shook her head. "No! She would have felt it."

Like I'm feeling Connell now. By the Mother, was he dying? The pain of that thought nearly knocked her to her knees, but she forced herself to stay on her feet.

"I know," Gia quickly agreed, the wounded light in her eyes catalyzing to anger. "I think he's hiding."

Gia had felt the pain she was feeling once herself. She would know that this agony was unmistakable.

There was only one way Jordan could hide from them—using a witch's spell. Rage bubbled up her throat. She clutched at Gia's arm, her grip so tight it would have severely hurt anyone else.

"It's him! He's behind the missing weapons. Go find him. You find him and *make him pay.*"

She staggered back to the doorway, struggling with her panic and fear. With a herculean effort of will, she closed it up until she was cold through and through. But she was able to function again. "I have to go to Connell."

She dematerialized.

"I can go with you," Gia called after her. But Logan didn't stop. She had to move *now*. Even at her top speed, Colorado was hours away.

It might already be too late.

40

C onnell stared down at the hole in his shirt in disbelief.

A bullet? Really? The surprise of being struck down with a prosaic weapon froze him in his tracks...until the second gunshot hit him.

Reacting too late, Connell threw himself to the side behind the partial cover of a small boulder. Pain belatedly exploded in his chest. Clutching his hands to his front, he pulled his head down, trying to keep his most vital areas out of the line of fire.

A roar went up behind him. Twisting, he tried to catch sight of Leeland and Derrick. One of them must have been seriously wounded to make that sound. He shouldn't have brought anyone with him. It had been stupid, and it might have cost his friends their lives.

They were being attacked with human weaponry. He had never dreamed a Were would do something so underhanded. Even rogues came at you face to face.

This was his fault. He should have known something like this might happen. Their enemy had used witchcraft to hide himself— why would he be above a cowardly attack with a gun? Now they were pinned down, taking fire from a machine gun hidden behind the cover of some shrubbery on the far side of the clearing.

Blood was pouring out of his chest. It was quick and warm, but growing cooler by the second. His natural healing ability, already decimated by the loss of his wolf, wasn't working. He struggled to take a breath.

He wanted to call out to the others, to tell them who their enemy was, but all that came out of his mouth was an alarming rattle.

"Connell, get down," Derrick yelled from somewhere to the left of him.

Squinting through a haze of grey, he saw the green of Derrick's plaid shirt pressed against the trunk of a large tree.

Good. At least Derrick was still alive.

The shots came faster and faster until it was almost a barrage. The gun had to be an automatic weapon of some kind—most likely a Kalashnikov. And the hail of bullets seemed to be focused on him.

One blast sounded next to his ear. Chunks of rock flew, striking his left ear and cutting his cheek open. Much more of this and the small boulder he was hiding behind would be blasted to smithereens. Muscles screaming, he sat and rolled over to the left, trying to stay behind his cover.

His vision was starting to darken when a dark blur veered toward him from the right. It was Leeland, his dark grey fur flying up to Connell like a wave of darkness. Sharp jaws snapped at his shirt, tugging him left in an unmistakable message to *move.*

He wanted to protest. How could he get to the trees in this shape?

The tug came again, and he forced himself forward in a controlled fall. Leeland came around him, getting between him and the rock. Half-pulling, half-nudging, he covered Connell from the right—a moving barricade between him and the hail of bullets.

"No," he managed to whisper when he realized what Leeland was doing. He couldn't allow his man to be a living shield.

But Leeland's jaw gripped and pulled him forward inexorably. Forcing his legs to move, Connell crawled toward the trees, a trail of bright red blood staining the ground in his wake.

A hard thump knocked the wolf's flank into him. Leeland's front legs collapsed, and his whine abruptly cut off.

No. Please, don't! He couldn't allow his friend to sacrifice himself for him.

Connell pushed the fur weakly, trying to herd his man into the trees, but Leeland wouldn't go. His shaggy head turned to him, and he snapped at Connell's shirt, adjusting his grip. He resumed pulling, forcing Connell along.

It was the thought of Logan that made him keep crawling, but he only made it a few more feet before Leeland collapsed. Unable to go further, Connell fell over on his back, his bloody chest filling his view before he turned to stare at the sky.

At least he was outdoors. He would always feel closer to Logan in open air.

Connell put his hand on his brother wolf's fur, his vision dimming. *I'm not going to see her again.*

Hard hands bit at his shoulders, but he barely felt them. Both he and Leeland were moving. He was pinned between Derrick and Leeland as the former dragged both of them behind the cover of the trees.

His mouth opened and closed several times. He needed Derrick to warn his father.

"Tell...scent."

That was all he managed before everything went dark.

41

"How the fuck did this happen?" Mara demanded.

No one answered.

For once, her father didn't chastise her for her language. They were both standing over Connell's hospital bed. He'd been rushed there after Derrick had called them for help. They'd been ambushed in the woods, pinned down by automatic gunfire—a human weapon, not magic.

The bullets had been impregnated with silver. Connell had taken three slugs, two to the chest and one that passed through his upper arm. He'd managed to get down behind a boulder, but it had been too small to provide complete cover.

Leeland had been killed. He'd shielded Connell, who had been his superior officer in the Army. The younger wolf had taken multiple hits before a bullet to the head ended his life. Derrick had been hit too, but not before he'd gotten Connell behind a tree using their Ranger brother's body as a shield.

The bullets had still been flying when the call for help came. Mara had heard them over the line. Then the world had exploded. His father had shifted and bayed, howling for his top lieutenants to come to him. Mara had run after him and the others.

Minutes later, everyone had poured into that clearing in the woods, but the culprit was long gone. Spent shells were found scattered on a patch of ground above the clearing. Two sets of fresh boot prints had been uncovered a few feet away, but they abruptly disappeared. There was no scent trail to follow. The search was over before it began.

Emergency surgery at their private hospital had brought Connell back from the brink. Because they were the largest pack of shifters in the country, they had resources that other groups lacked. In this case, that included a small clinic outfitted with a surgical suite. Of course, no one had ever been treated for a bullet wound there. Kiera, the pack doctor, had surgical training, but they'd only ever used those skills for more commonplace injuries—fingers being sewn back on due to carpentry accidents or C-sections during difficult births. These were things their shifter healing ability didn't help with.

Kiera hadn't wanted to do the surgery. She had taken one look at Connell and panicked. Only the chief's calm, but implacable, demand had gotten the small, dark Were into surgical scrubs. Kiera had extracted the two bullets from his chest and had done her best to repair the damage. But Connell's healing ability wasn't taking over.

Her father had tried to help his body mend by borrowing some of the pack's energy and surrounding Connell with it. But without his wolf, her brother hadn't been able to absorb it.

He was still unconscious now, some of her blood running in his veins. He'd lost so much of it that he'd needed a transfusion, and they were the same blood type.

Derrick was sitting nearby in a chair, his arm in a sling. Stirring, he turned to the window, which had been left open. He moved up and reached for the sill with his good hand, but she snapped at him.

"Leave it open."

"But shouldn't we keep it closed? There are germs and shit flying around," he pointed out.

"Leave it," Mara ordered.

Her father nodded. "She'll be here soon."

42

L ogan was a comet streaking in the sky. She had never moved so fast, and with good reason.

She wasn't supposed to reorder the major air currents. The jet stream ran in a predictable pattern for a reason. What she was doing was forbidden. But she didn't care.

Logan had manipulated the flow of the jet stream to carry her back to Colorado. If the Mother wanted to punish her for messing with the natural order of things, She could sideline her and choose another Air Elemental—*after* Logan got back to Connell.

He wasn't dead yet. She could feel the connection between them still intact. It was like a silvery thread tying their auras together. When she tugged on it, there was a vibration along the aether.

But he was hurt, grievously so. And he could still die. She didn't know how she knew that, but the knowledge was there, burning a hole in her brain.

The blurred scenery beneath her changed, filling with a sea of green and brown that could only be pine trees. She honed in on a low, concrete building nestled in the woods in the small town ten miles from the chief's compound.

This was the right place. A crowd of wolves of every shape

and description was milling around outside. They had even started a few bonfires. Some were passing around food and drinks—and they were showing every sign of settling in for a long stay. Logan felt like weeping when she realized it was a vigil.

And the tears did fall when she plunged into Connell's room, materializing next to him on the bed.

Reaching out, she touched his beautiful face. He was so still and cold, but his aura was still there. It hadn't bled off into the aether. He was still holding on—barely.

Mara appeared in her line of sight, next to Connell's head. Logan looked at her ravaged face.

"What happened?" Her voice was thin and thready.

"He was shot. So were two others. Leeland died."

Confusion swamped her. "Shot with a *gun*?"

Mara nodded. "We couldn't track the asshole. The scent disappeared."

"The scent!"

Logan whipped her head around. A tall, attractive wolf with his arm in a sling was standing in the doorway next to Douglas. "He wanted to tell you something about a scent."

"What was it, Derrick?" the chief asked.

The Were shrugged helplessly. "I think he realized something right before we were ambushed. His last words before passing out were *tell scent*. But I don't know what he meant. The scent trail of the attackers died at the scene. It wasn't masked with something stronger. It was just gone."

"Witch's spell," Logan said, turning back to Connell. "Why isn't he healing? He still has some of his gifts."

"Not the ability to heal. Not in this form. There's too much trauma," Douglas rasped from behind her. "If he could shift, it might be different. But he can't heal trapped in one form. It's in the act of transitioning that our wounds mend."

"Well, can't you tap into the pack's energy to heal him yourself? Can't a chief do that?"

Douglas shook his head sadly. "He's too far from us now. If there's no wolf, he's not pack."

Her stomach twisted, a heavy ball of lead somewhere in the center of it. Logan turned to Douglas, but a glimpse of his face made her quickly turn away again. The chief had aged ten years in a few hours.

For a second, the world titled wildly. Had Douglas accepted the loss of his son? Logan searched Connell's face. The light in his aura was very weak, and it was growing dimmer, blinking in and out like the last flames of a spent fire. He wasn't going to make it. Any minute now, he was going to slip away.

No, no, no. Logan couldn't accept that. She had just found him, and she wasn't about to let him go. "Let's give it back to him."

"What?" Douglas asked blankly.

"His wolf. He needs it to heal—specifically, he needs to shift. Let's give his wolf back to him."

"He's too weak."

"And he's going to stay that way unless we restore him." She was sure.

Douglas frowned. "I'm not sure he can survive the blast in his condition. You almost didn't the first time."

Logan shook her head and turned to face them. "I was fine. I needed to reboot is all. Granted, there were some issues—problems that are bigger this time around. Sammy was small, and Connell possessed a full-grown shifter's energy."

"So you can't do it," Mara said, the nascent hope in her eyes stuttering and dying.

Logan held up a hand. "The blast would be bigger," she admitted. "But there might be a way. Now that I've done it once, I think can control the energy transfer better. And I have to modify the ritual to use a filter."

"What kind of filter?" Douglas asked.

This was not going to go over well, but Alec had been clear about this point.

"It has to be another werewolf. I can diminish the force by

running it through someone with a similar signature. The energy would be less harmful to them. But whoever it is will suffer. There might be permanent damage."

Given enough time, she might have found a way to soften the blow to the volunteer, but they couldn't afford to wait. Someone was going to have to put their life on the line for Connell.

She stared at them, wondering if the chief would let Mara volunteer or if he would insist on doing it himself. Maybe she should suggest they draw straws.

"I'll do it," Derrick volunteered in a rush.

Logan turned to him in surprise.

"Connell has stuck his neck out for me multiple times," he explained. "Any man in our unit would do it. I can go round them up if you want. They're all outside."

Mara twisted to glare at him. "No, you're already hurt, and the others all have families to look after. I should do it."

"No." Douglas shook his head. "It should be me."

And she had been worried about getting one volunteer. "I don't care which one of you does it," Logan protested.

"I'm his twin, the closest to him genetically. It should be me," Mara insisted.

"But you're female," Derrick said. Mara blasted him with a glare that could kill, and he held up his good hand. "I just mean that you're very different from Connell in a fundamental way. Any of our team members would be a better fit. We're all large men, all alphas."

"*No*," Douglas announced with an air of inflexible finality.

He came to stand next to Logan at the head of the bed. "It will be me. Being the pack's chief affords me a certain amount of protection from black magic. I know this isn't the same, but I still have the best chance of coming out of this alive. And you two," he turned to point at the other wolves, "will keep hunting for the asshole responsible for this mess if this goes sideways."

"Dad—"

"This discussion is over." He turned to Logan. "What do you need?"

"Charcoal or chalk. Something to draw with. Can we move this bed to the center of the room?"

They were ready in a matter of minutes. Logan busied herself drawing the runes, altering the ones representing the path the energy should travel. This time, it was going to take a detour—right through Douglas' body.

Logan took one last look at Connell, moving to hold his hand. It was icy and lifeless in hers. *Mother, if you can hear me, please, help me. Please!*

Trying to hide a tremor, she took a deep breath and closed her eyes. She had to be calm for this. Connell would die if she screwed this up.

"Are you ready?" Mara asked anxiously.

"Yes."

Logan wiped the charcoal dust from her fingers on her pants. Her palms were sweaty, but her heartbeat was steady. *Focus.*

Shifting, she moved to the foot of Connell's bed. The chief was in between them. It grew very cold around them. The wind picked up, coming through the open window and making a circuit around the room. For a second, the babble of voices came with it, but it was abruptly silenced.

Begin, a voice in her head said. For a second, she imagined it was the Mother herself, but it wasn't. It sounded like the same spirit that had helped her find the shard from the dragon staff, the one that sounded like her Nai Nai. Logan spared a second to thank her.

She started the chant in her mind, letting it spill over her lips at the second verse. The wind carried her words through Douglas. They wrapped around Connell, caressing him the way Logan wanted to.

She felt the energy coming. It didn't blindside her this time, but it was still strong enough to knock her to her knees.

Out of the corner of her eye, she saw Mara move toward her, presumably to help her up, but Derrick stopped her. Logan had warned them not to cross the barrier of the circle or risk interrupting the ceremony—and possibly blasting them all to hell.

Logan staggered to her knees. She hadn't passed the shifter

energy to Douglas yet. If possible, she was going to get them all out of this alive.

Collecting the current within herself, she was startled to see the surface of her aura start to heat and bubble.

Panicking, she pushed the energy out toward the chief, trying her best to keep some of it with her. But the stream leapt toward him eagerly, hitting Douglas like a brick wall. He grunted but kept his feet.

Shit. The shifter energy wasn't cooperating with her attempt to slow the transfer down. It recognized the chief's signature and rushed toward him—a torrent of power that couldn't wait to leave her incompatible body and settle in a shifter. Gritting her teeth, she used the winds to hold it back—her heart dropping when she saw the same sizzle in the chief's aura as her own.

Logan fought to adjust the stream, keeping her chant going rhythmically. The energy tore at her aura as it went, and her vision dimmed. Pain began to consume her until it was beyond her ability to register it. A broken gurgle escaped her, and she tasted blood. Breaking off in between verses, she spat on the floor before she choked on it. Ignoring the alarming amount of blood, she refocused on her chant.

Her pain didn't matter. She needed to finish. Connell, who was partially blocked by his father's bulk, moved on the bed, and she knew it was working. Then her view of him started to obscure as her aura became visible to the naked eye, an unearthly light appearing in the cracks.

Okay, *faster*, before she killed herself by burning off her own aura. Loosening her hold, she let the power run out of her. The remaining energy moved around Douglas like a boulder in a raging river and settled to fill the void in Connell.

By the time it was done, she was on her hands and knees. She couldn't see anything but a field of white flecked with grey streaks. Blinking, she realized she was staring at the scuffmarks on the tiled floor.

"Logan?" Mara's hands appeared in her field of view. She was hauled to her feet.

Logan let Mara carry her past the chief, who was lying on the floor. Her muscles screamed with tension until he groaned, to her everlasting relief.

Derrick hustled to Douglas while Mara propped her up in front of Connell's head. "Is he okay? Will he be able to shift?" she asked.

Logan squinted at the dark blur that was Connell. Her eyes watered, but she could still recognize her own handiwork.

Crap. She'd done it again. Big bits of her mate's red-and-gold aura were interwoven with hers. It was far more extensive than what had happened with Sammy. While the child's aura had briefly sported a Band-Aid-sized bit of her silvery-blue aura, this was like several giant skin grafts.

Logan looked down at herself, relieved to see her own aura was intact. It was a bit frayed, the net of shimmering threads more widely distributed than she remembered, but she was fine. She sent a quick prayer of thanks to the Mother for seeing her through this.

"I think so," she rasped eventually, wiping her mouth. There was definitely something like a shifter signature to Connell's energy again.

"Oh crap," Mara said, spinning her around. She pressed something to Logan's mouth and under her nose.

"What's that?" Logan blinked, reaching up instinctively to pull away whatever it was.

"Leave it. *Fuck.* Blood is coming out of your ears too. Here, hold this to your nose."

Mara nudged her, urging her to sit next to Connell. Logan took the cloth from her while Mara accepted another from Derrick and started to wipe around her ears.

"I think it worked," Logan repeated, her voice muffled behind the towel.

"Well, now I hope my brother doesn't wake up soon, because if he sees you bleeding like this, he'll kill us."

Other wolves started to filter through the door. Derrick and a few other strapping Weres picked up Douglas off the floor.

"Is he okay?" Logan asked, holding her middle. Her entire body felt as if it had been stung by a horde of wasps.

Derrick shot her a worried look. "He's breathing. Does *his* energy thingy look okay?"

"Uh...yeah, kind of." She probably should have made an effort to sound more sure of herself, but the flaring threads in Douglas' aura were wigging her out.

She squinted at him. His aura was sporting a few holes here and there, but he was the *Canus Primus*. They were already knitting closed.

Mara straightened, her head held high. "He's still breathing. And he's the chief. He'll recover," she declared firmly before starting to bark orders at the growing group of men.

Derrick nodded deferentially, and he and the others scrambled to carry out her orders. Soon, the chief was laid out in a bed next to Connell. One short, dark female Were came around the bed to check their vitals. In another minute, she was attaching an IV to Douglas' thickly muscled arm.

Logan leaned back and watched the wolves mill around while Mara directed everyone from the head of Connell's bed, her arms crossed.

Interesting. Mara's authority was apparently alpha enough to fill the temporary vacuum. The burly soldier Weres didn't even seem to notice they were taking orders from a woman.

Connell moved again, and Logan forgot about their audience. She crawled up higher on the bed, lying next to him. Reaching out, she put her hand on his chest, reassured by the regular rhythm under her fingers. His pulse was still a little weak, but it was steady.

Mara leaned over him too, testing his temperature with a hand to the forehead.

"What do you think he meant by *tell scent*?" Logan asked.

"I don't know." Mara shrugged. "Maybe he thought we could

follow the culprits after the attack. But it wasn't possible. Their scent had vanished."

Logan cocked her head to the side. A thought occurred to her. "What about the smell of the gun? I've never used one before, but don't they smell like smoke and gunpowder? Or gun oil?"

Mara stopped to think about it before replying. "I don't think we can use that to narrow it down. Most male wolves have served in some branch of the military at one point or another. They all have guns, although most don't use them much at home except for target practice."

"Do you even need practice? Don't your superior reflexes and eyesight make you all natural marksman?

"That doesn't mean every man around here doesn't try to prove his masculinity by shooting at cans and bottles. What's your point?"

"My point is that they don't do it that often. They don't need to," she huffed. "Especially now with the shit hitting the fan. So we track the smell of freshly fired gun."

"But there was no trace of a spent firearm in the woods either."

"Yeah, I know," Logan said. "I think that's because the assholes are using a spell to mask themselves like before. It moved and shielded them as they left."

Mara frowned. "Is that possible? Wouldn't it have to be fixed in one place like that weird bubble dome we found?"

"Unfortunately, no. One of my sisters ran into a spell kind of like this recently. It masked a person's aura as well as their scent and heat," she admitted.

In fact, the similarity was troubling. The witches who had crafted that spell were dead or had been stripped, but they had been selling their hexes and charms for a while before Diana took them out. Could she be dealing with the same fucking spell?

Acknowledging the possibility, Logan had the disquieting sensation she was still missing something.

"If that's true, we'll never be able to track them," Mara growled.

"Which is why we track the gun," Logan said, beginning to get excited.

"I told you, everyone here has a gun. This is America. Even some of the females in the pack carry a gun."

"*Oh, really.* Does Wendy werewolf tote a recently fired machine gun in her purse?" she asked caustically.

Mara scowled at her. "You're forgetting the gun scent was masked too."

"And it will be so long as the enemy is holding them. But once they put them down, that protection will move off—the spell will follow the body of the gunman."

Mara shifted her weight. "I still don't know how we can use this. Are we supposed to run around the entire fucking state trying to catch the scent of a recently fired gun?"

"We're looking for *two* recently fired machine guns. And my guess is they'll be stored with a cache of other weapons."

It made sense that if there were two machine guns, there would be many more.

"Even my nose isn't that good," Mara said, shaking her head. "The scent will fade before too long."

"That's why you're going to do it from the air with me." *At super-sonic speeds.*

Dismay filled Mara's face. "Um, Logan, are you sure you can take me up too? I know you were able to take Connell up, but..." She trailed off.

"There's only one way to be certain," Logan said impulsively. She held out her hand.

"If you're sure..." Mara still looked uncertain but instinct told Logan to do it.

Connell was hers, and Mara was a part of him, his twin. *This will work.* It had to. She was going to end this now. Grabbing Mara's hand, she took to the air, the startled exclamations of several wolves following in their wake.

43

Connell cracked an eyelid and winced. The sun was in his eyes, blinding him.

"He's waking up." The flare of light moved away, and he realized someone had been shining a penlight in his eyes.

His father appeared at his side. Derrick and Charles, another member of his Special Forces unit, were holding him up. The chief looked like hell. "Son, are you all right?"

No. He felt like shit. "I'll live. But you look like you got hit with a train," he said, his voice dry and cracked.

He tried to get up, but Kiera, their local doctor, tsked and pushed him back down.

"Ow," he complained when the skin on his stomach stretched underneath a thick layer of bandages.

"I think you've got a chance at shifting now," Douglas said, squinting at him. "You feel like pack again."

"What?" Connell was startled.

His father accepted a cane from Kiera. "Your woman did the ritual. If you're feeling up to it, you should try to shift. It should help knit those bullet holes together."

Bullet holes? What bullet holes?

Derrick read the confusion on his face. "Don't you remember the ambush?"

The echoing report of a gun firing filled his head, and he tensed. The memories started flooding back. He knew who had done this. The threat pushed buttons in his psyche. Without meaning to, he shifted.

A dizzying rush of vertigo swept over him. Blinking, Connell realized he was staring down at his own paws. Like his father, he was a black wolf, with dappled, silver paws.

Shit, he hadn't meant to shift yet.

The howl that ripped from his throat was involuntary. It was a mingled sound of frustration and pain, combined with an unmistakable war cry. Every man in the room stood at attention. They knew the sound well.

Connell whined. Fuck, his chest hurt. But his father had been right. The wounds on his chest were a little smaller than they had been a moment before. But he had things to say, and, for that, he needed a mouth.

Tensing, Connell prepared to shift back.

"*No,*" his father burst out. "Stay like that for a while. You can't rush this, or you'll set yourself back."

Shaking his muzzle vigorously, he focused. It hurt like a motherfucker, but he was able to change back. As a man, he fell back on the bed, gasping and sweaty.

"What the hell, Connell?" his father scolded.

"It was Bishop," he gasped, struggling to sit up. "Bishop shot at us."

The background murmur of the other wolves in the room died out.

"No. You're confused." Douglas shook his head. "His boy was one of the one's attacked."

"It was him." Charles moved to help him when he tried to stand. "She reminded me that something was missing," Connell continued, wincing as he got to his feet.

"Who?" someone asked.

"Logan. She asked me if there was something at the attack that shouldn't have been there. It got me thinking that something was actually *missing*. It didn't come to me until much later, but Bishop's scent is gone. It has been for a while."

"No," his father said. "We would have noticed something like that."

"Except we always talked to him at his house or outside. We were so focused on new threats, we didn't notice his scent was missing when we were out of doors. Inside his house, his scent is all over the place, but it's old, and *we didn't notice*."

His father stared at him, unconvinced.

"I'm telling you he did this. Sammy and Malcolm were surprised. When they were attacked, there was the scent of surprise but not fear —not in Malcolm's case—because the attack was out of the blue, and it was carried out by someone he knew and trusted."

"But there was Sammy too. Bishop wouldn't do that to his own son." His father was adamant.

"Unless he thought it would be a good way to throw suspicion off himself. And I didn't die. He was probably sure Sammy wouldn't either. But by the time he got around to Malcolm, he knew he had to start covering his tracks better. Or maybe Malcolm was on to him or saw something we didn't."

"I still don't believe it."

Derrick looked from one of them to the other. "Why don't we go check out his house? We can see for ourselves if he has his scent masked or not."

Connell nodded vigorously and scanned the room. "Wait— where's Logan?"

"She took off with your sister a few hours ago."

Fuck me. "We've got to get to the Kane's house now. Logan doesn't know what she's up against."

Was she bulletproof? He had no idea. He hadn't been to the Kane house in ages. Bishop could have heavy artillery disguised in his backyard.

"Why would she go there? She doesn't know what you just told us," Derrick pointed out.

"Doesn't matter. I bet she's already tracked all this shit to him. If we want a piece of him, we have to hurry."

CONNELL HADN'T BEEN KIDDING. Being formless *did* hurt like a motherfucker. Mara was ashamed to admit she'd spent the first few minutes howling her head off until Logan sternly told her to shut up.

They had been at it long enough that she grew numb and no longer noticed how much pain she was in. Once she did, she began to enjoy the ride. It was like running in the woods—with a jet strapped to her back.

Mara had always loved running flat out, racing Connell. Her sleeker, more aerodynamic form ensured she usually won despite his larger muscles.

Here?

Logan's voice in her head was very unnerving. They had paused over a farmhouse. Mara waited until her head stopped spinning.

You don't have a head, Logan reminded her.

But I have a sense of smell? And I can see? Elemental magic doesn't make sense, she thought, wondering vaguely how to avoid having every thought heard. There seemed to be no distinction between thinking and speaking.

Focus, Mara. Logan sounded as impatient and cocky as she did in real life, whereas her own inner voice was distant and oddly tinny.

No, she replied after a moment. There was no hint of burnt powder here.

Her ride didn't answer, choosing instead to streak to the next house. Mara wanted to squeeze her eyes shut, but since she didn't have eyelids, she was forced to watch the ground moving at light speed underneath her.

They rocked abruptly, and Mara wanted to claw at something. The speed was cool, but stopping was absolute shit.

What about this place?

Um, I don't know, she said. *There's something...*

Logan dropped altitude in a dizzying rush, and they circled over the rambling two-story farmhouse. It took her a second to recognize it.

This is Bishop Kane's house, she told Logan.

It had to be a mistake. But the distinctive scent of gunpowder and burnt oil was strong over the shed next to the house. *He must have been out hunting*, Mara thought, confusion swamping her. It could be the smell of a rifle.

More like several rifles, Logan chided. *Besides, don't wolves prefer to hunt on four legs?*

Before Mara could brace herself, they were plunging to the ground. Her body came together with a pop, and she immediately bent over to retch. Bile splashed on the ground while she steadied herself against a tree. She held on to the trunk by her nails until she recovered.

Mara raised her head in time to see Logan stalking to the door of the Kane's storage shed. She busted the very sturdy lock with one blow and threw the doors open. For a moment, she stood there before shooting a grim look over her shoulder.

Still reeling from the effects of Elemental air travel, Mara staggered to the door. Inside was a huge cache of weapons. Handguns and rifles hung neatly on shelves next to machine guns of every type and description. There was also a shelf of grenades next to another one of land mines. Most were Claymores, but a few were anti-personnel mines meant for under-the-ground burial. There was even a fucking rocket launcher.

"Damn it to seven hells," Mara swore. "What if he mined the woods?"

Wolves running at top speed might not notice the metallic and chemical smell of a mine until it was too late—especially the cubs who had never been trained to notice such things.

Logan walked into the shed and reached for two of the Kalashnikov guns on the back shelf. She smelled them and scowled before holding them out to Mara.

Her stomach had twisted in one huge knot, but she bent over to sniff the barrel of the gun anyway. Not that she needed to. It was clear that the Kalashnikov had been fired recently—within the last six hours.

"There must be some explanation," she insisted. "Bishop is my father's best friend. His own son was attacked and stripped. *He's Connell's godfather.*"

"Then he must have attacked Sammy to deflect attention from himself," Logan said implacably. "And if he's willing to do that, then why would he hesitate to kill someone else's child?"

The world spun in an unsteady circle. "Oh God, I think I'm going to be sick again."

The Elemental whirled around on her. "I shouldn't have to tell you this, but you're going to have to nut up," Logan snapped. "We have to find him *now*."

Mara passed a hand over her eyes. "*Fine.* I think he's here. That's his truck over there," she said, turning to point at a Ford XLT in the driveway.

She was still pointing when Yogi came around the corner of the house. He looked tired, but he smiled when he saw them.

"Hey, I thought I heard voices. I was just about to leave for the hospital. What are you doing here?"

"Do you know what's in here?" Mara asked in disbelief.

"Dad keeps the shed locked in case of thieves. He uses it for his hunting rif..." Yogi's voice trailed off, and his eyes widened when he saw the veritable arsenal crammed into the small shed.

"What the hell is going on?" he asked, voice strangled.

"It's been your father all this time," she told him, her jaw so tight she could barely form the words.

"What are you talking about?"

"I'm talking about your dad shooting my brother. He killed Malcolm and Leeland! Bishop was even willing to sacrifice your own brother!"

"No." Yogi shook his head, his face closing up. "You're wrong. He wouldn't do that."

"Then how do you explain all of this stuff? These two guns are the exact same kind used on Connell and his friends."

"Maybe he knew already," Logan said, her eyes narrowed at the young Were.

"*What?*" Yogi narrowed his eyes at them. "I would never hurt Connell, and I would kill anyone who threatened my family."

Mara turned to Logan. "All I smell is confusion. I don't think he knew."

"*My dad didn't do this,*" Yogi insisted harshly, the cords in his neck standing up in stark relief.

Logan's head cocked to the side. "Two men are running. Come on, they're getting away."

Mara scrambled after Logan. The Air Elemental was streaking to the front of the house. Bishop and another man were running full tilt to the truck in the drive.

Bishop had just opened the door when Logan disappeared before her eyes. A gust of wind slammed the door shut, hard. Then Logan was there again, in front of the truck this time. Her fist came down, slamming into it with supernatural strength. Crushing metal shrieked and groaned as she drove a deep furrow in the hood, completely decimating the engine block.

Bishop and the other Were, whom she recognized as one of the Gibson brothers, spun around and ran for the other vehicle in the drive, an SUV. They were a few yards away when a cyclone appeared out of nowhere. It picked up the heavy vehicle and tossed it like a toy. The SUV landed on its roof next to the house.

"That was my car," Yogi yelled. "Everyone needs to stop acting like lunatics! This is all a misunderstanding."

He ran ahead, but Mara reached out and snagged his shirt collar. He landed on his ass next to her. "If he isn't the one, why did he run?" she yelled at him.

"There's been a mistake. Don't let her kill him!" He strained against her hold and struggled to his feet.

A flash of bright light took them by surprise.

Her sensitive retinas were burning. Blinking madly, it took Mara several seconds for her vision to clear. Each one felt like an eternity. When she could see again, it was just in time to witness Bishop lobbing another road flare at Logan. Only... it wasn't a flare.

A bright blue ball of light hit the tree next to Logan, exploding with a blinding flash. Mara squeezed her eyes shut. Holy shit. Those were spell balls! Bishop had gotten those from a witch.

"This is fucking insane," Yogi breathed. He looked wrecked, confirming to her that he hadn't known what was going on. "We have to stop this!"

He turned to her, grabbing her arm, but she shook it off. Without warning, she hauled off and struck out with her fist, sucker punching him in the face. Yogi crumpled to the floor.

"I'm sorry, but I can't let you interfere," she apologized to his motionless form.

He didn't answer. Swallowing hard, she wiped sweat from her face before running to join Logan.

The Gibson brother had disappeared, but Bishop was crouched in front of a boulder, fending off Logan by hurling vials at her from a bag she hadn't noticed at first. They ignited in midair, turning into fiery comets you couldn't look directly at.

Logan dodged the balls easily, whipping in one direction, and then another. She disappeared and reappeared closer to him, but had to duck because his Were reflexes let him throw with deadly accuracy.

As quick as she was, the Air Elemental couldn't avoid all the projectiles. As she watched, one of the vials hit her full in the chest. Logan looked down at the bubbling black mass covering her left shoulder and breast. It sizzled, and Mara smelled burning flesh before Logan passed a hand over it. The wind blew the dark goo off her, leaving a patch of red, raw skin visible on either side of her tank top strap.

Mara was going to ask if she was okay, but the words got stuck in her throat when a dark shape streaked toward them. The Gibson brother hadn't left. He leaped toward Logan, his fangs bared and aimed at her throat.

Faster than her eyes could follow, Logan batted the Gibson shithead off her. He landed on the floor on his back, but he twisted around with a vicious snarl.

Mara reacted. She didn't have time to shift, but she had spent years training to fight in human form with Connell.

Stepping forward, she protected Logan's flank. Gibson snarled at her and feinted right, trying to trick her into leaving Logan exposed. Mara didn't fall for it. She threw her arms out, catching him in midleap. Then she was consumed, struggling with a snarling, snapping ball of teeth and razor-sharp claws. In the background, she heard loud booming noises and an unearthly shrieking she belatedly realized was the wind.

Mara stifled a cry as one of those claws raked across her stomach. Spinning viciously, she gritted her teeth and punched with all her strength. She only succeeded in rocking Gibson's head back. His muzzle dripped with blood, but he squirmed and snapped, missing her jugular by an inch.

She threw him off. He landed hard on the ground but jumped right back up again, snarling. Undaunted and furious, she growled back. When he leapt at her, she had a plan.

The Gibson brother was strong. He didn't need much of a running start to get airborne. His powerfully muscled hind legs bunched, and he was halfway to her throat before she could blink.

As soon as he was close enough, Mara slammed her hands down over his muzzle, forcing it closed. Pulling him closer, she hugged him to her, so close his claws couldn't shred her.

Mara closed her eyes and held tight, squeezing with every ounce of strength she had. Her muscles screamed and her ribs groaned, but she kept trying to crush him until her biceps locked. Ignoring the painful burning, she kept going until the snapping tree branch sound of breaking bone filled the air.

Gibson's high-pitched whine was abruptly cut off when she dropped him on the ground. He tried to crawl away from her, but she hauled him back. Stepping over him, she took hold of his head and twisted. His neck snapped, and the asshole finally stopped moving.

She inhaled deeply and winced. Breathing was painful. She might have bruised or cracked a few ribs with that move. Pausing for a second, she kicked the murderous shitpile of fur that used to be a Gibson brother—Matt. She recognized him now.

Spinning on her heel Mara turned to find Logan facing Bishop. He was still pressed against the boulder, but now he was surrounded by debris. Rocks and fallen logs littered the space in between the two of them. Logan raised her arm, and another much bigger log whistled through the air. It followed the motion of her hands, hurtling toward Bishop like a ballistic missile.

Sure that she was about to see Bishop, who'd she'd always thought of as an uncle, smashed to a paste, Mara had to force her eyes to stay open. She had to see this though for Sammy and her brother.

But the log stopped short, rebounding on a barrier she could see for a split second when the log made contact before glancing off.

The iridescent oily glow of the bubble protection faded as soon as the log stopped touching it. Bishop was crouching in front of the boulder, his hands up to shield his face. When the log was deflected, he put his hands down and looked at her and Logan, a half-mad light in his eyes.

The asshole laughed. "He said this thing was good, but this is beyond anything I ever imagined." He straightened, letting loose another deep chuckle that made her blood boil.

"Let me kill him," she hissed at Logan.

"Except you *can't*," Bishop shouted. The smirk on his face made her want to smash his face in.

"Why in the world are you doing this?" she asked, her composure cracking unexpectedly.

Bishop had been her father's best friend for years. He had taught her how to ride a bike and bought her dolls when her father had given her baseball mitts and toy cars.

He shook his head. "Your father should have listened to me...

about so many things. The goddamned fucking Averys and Malcolm being his third. Yogi would have won the challenge for third if he'd been given a little more time to prepare."

What the *fuck* kind of answer was that? Those pissant complaints couldn't be the reason for all of this! "But what about Sammy? Your own son. How could you do that to him?"

"He didn't die! The staff doesn't kill—not unless you want it to. I just needed a smaller test subject to perfect my technique. I didn't think he was going to get so sick. Your brother didn't. And after, I was going to put the wolf back. Or someone else's. That's the beauty of the staff. You can just pluck and take, mix and match."

"Actually, that's not how the staff works at all," Logan said. "Not even close, and definitely not if a non-Elemental is wielding it." She paused and turned to Mara. "Can you smell him?"

Mara shook herself, letting go of her anger long enough to think. She was standing downwind from Bishop and hadn't even noticed. "No, I don't," she whispered.

"His aura is red and blue, normal for a Were. There's no stain of murder."

How was that possible? He had *killed* Malcolm.

"Don't talk about me like I'm not here," Bishop shouted, his face contorting. "I won't let you ignore me!"

"Except you are here..." Logan muttered as if she were talking to herself. "You have no scent, but you give off heat and have an aura. Not like the nothing man, but so similar."

"What the hell are you talking about now?" Mara asked, her voice louder than she intended.

"He's protected," Logan clarified, turning to her. "A barrier enchantment stronger than any I've ever seen. We can't touch him."

Across the way, Bishop cackled. "And so I've won?" More laughter doubled him back over again.

I used to love that laugh, Mara thought in disgust. It was a deep, rich baritone, rather similar to her father's. Red-hot rage bubbled up her throat.

"What the fuck are you going to do?" she yelled. "Wait us out? Are you going stand there all fucking day until you starve?"

That wasn't good enough. This man had tried to kill her brother, had torn the pack apart. His betrayal cut her to the bone, and it would destroy her father.

"I guess so," Bishop said nonplussed, his amusement dropping away. He turned to the crushed, incapacitated cars. "Or I can start running into the woods and just keep going..."

He looked down at the bag in his hand. "These spells were supposed to kill you both. The number-one rule was leave no witnesses behind. Guess I'll have to settle for just killing Mara."

The handgun was in his hand, his finger on the trigger faster than Mara could blink. She threw herself to the side, registering Logan in front of her a split second before she hit the ground, the wind a deafening roar in her sensitive ears.

Mara twisted onto her back, her mouth falling open when she saw what the Air Elemental was doing.

Logan was protecting her front, a huge cyclone emanating from her hands. Bullets changed trajectory, separating and flying past on either side of them—except one. Somehow, she had missed it. It struck Logan, grazing her skin and leaving a deep furrow in her upper arm.

She tsked and looked down at the wound. "Not normal bullets, are they?"

Bishop gave Logan a hapless shrug Mara would have found charming under other circumstances. Then he raised the gun and fired again. The thin click was followed by another and another. Heaving a sigh of relief that the gun was empty, Mara got to her feet.

"There's more where that came from," Bishop said with a shrug. He gestured to the shed. "The good news is, if you can bleed, you can die. So don't mind me, I'm going to grab a few more magazines. It's not like you can do anything to stop me."

He pushed himself away from the boulder and started walking in the direction of the shed. Furious, Mara lunged at him, but Logan checked her momentum with one hand. The Elemental's head cocked to the side, her face colder than any Arctic peak.

"It's still my turn."

Her eyes... They were a glacial blue with no irises. A shiver ran down Mara's spine. Suddenly, she was more afraid of Logan than of anything Bishop could do.

A blast of air whipped her hard in the face, almost knocking her to the ground. Eyes watering, she could no longer see Logan, but she could hear her. The wind hurtled away from her with a shriek that threatened to burst her eardrums.

In her mind's eye, it was no longer Logan, but the dragon at the top of that fucking staff leaping in pursuit. The vicious beast had been given life in the wind, and it was savaging the barrier protecting Bishop. It hit the surface over and over again like a cobra striking.

With the wind focused away from her, Mara was able to turn around and watch the assault by partially shielding her eyes. Each time Logan pounded the surface, she could see the glowing surface of the shell for a split second.

Bishop kept trying to bat her away like she was some sort of kamikaze bird he could wave off. But the attack was relentless. After a minute, she couldn't even see Bishop in the flurry. It was as if Logan had made the wind solid—a battering ram made of Mother Nature's primordial rage and power.

Eyes burning, Mara watched the onslaught with fisted hands. There was a crack, almost like shattering glass. Whipping her head back, she saw Logan standing over Bishop, who was now sitting on the ground. Between them was the thin layer of the barrier, a thread-like network visible to the naked eye because Logan's hands were touching it.

"Won't do any good," Bishop wheezed. "It's supposed to withstand a nuclear blast..."

He didn't seem as confident now. Unnoticed by the two, Mara sidled closer.

"That doesn't really matter, does it?" Logan asked him softly. She stroked the bubble with an almost loving gesture.

"I don't understand," Mara whispered, moving behind them.

Logan turned to her, those winter-blue eyes meeting her green ones. "Then watch. You will."

The leaking hiss like air escaping a tire didn't even register at first. Not until Bishop was red in the face. His eyes looked bloodshot, and his chest was moving in a shallow rise and fall... He was suffocating. Logan was drawing the air out from the cracks in the shield.

The rage burning in Mara started to cool. Reaching out, she put her hands on Logan, but she stopped short of pulling her away.

Wolves were fighters. Even their worst enemy didn't deserve this. Weres should die on their feet.

But Mara didn't say so. As long as she was unable to wrap her hands around the fucker's throat, she had to let Logan finish.

Trembling, she bit her tongue and waited, wide-eyed, for it to be over. She stood vigil until Bishop slumped over. She would have kept standing there forever if Logan hadn't bent to snatch the bag he held —the barrier was gone.

Logan turned his pockets inside out and opened his shirt. There was a charm of some kind hanging from his neck. She broke the leather strap with a flick of her wrist and threw that in the bag as well.

"Is he dead?" her father asked from somewhere behind them.

Mara whirled around. The chief had arrived. Just behind him was her brother, being propped up by Derrick and another Were named Max. Connell's shirt was open over a chest wrapped in bandages. In the distance, other cars were approaching, pulling off the road in a steady stream, parking anywhere they could.

"No," Logan said distantly, her attention on the contents of the bag she had confiscated.

"He's not?" Mara asked in surprise.

"Weres police their own," Logan said flatly, turning around, her eyes still in that freaky pupil-less state.

When she saw Connell, the cold, forbidding expression disappeared, and her eyes shifted back to their normal light brown shade. "Connell, you should be in the *hospital*," she shouted.

She marched up to him, finger wagging, presumably to read him the riot act. Connell ignored the scolding digit, using his good arm to cup the back of her head and pull her in for a long kiss.

Logan waited a few beats before self-consciously pushing him away. "*Hospital*," she hissed.

Connell looked over her head. Derrick and the others were pulling Bishop to his feet.

"After," he said softly.

It looked like she was going to argue, but she nodded. "I have to search his house."

"What about his son?" someone asked.

Yogi was starting to come around too. A few soldiers had helped him up, but they held onto him by both arms. Mara shook her head at the same time as Logan.

"His children weren't a part of it," she said.

"And who's that?" Derrick asked, pointing to the Gibson brother she had killed.

Mara told them, her attention fixed on Logan.

The Elemental had stopped in front of Yogi. She spoke to him in a low tone. Yogi shook his head, but she put a hand on his arm. "You don't want to watch," she whispered.

There was an excruciating minute of silence as Yogi stared at his father.

Bishop was on his feet, head lolling. The end wouldn't come until he was fully aware and able to defend himself.

Yogi shook his head again, his palm out in a broken gesture that could have been disbelief or grief. Then he turned away, letting Logan lead him away.

44

Nearly an hour passed before Connell crossed the threshold of Bishop's house. He entered through the kitchen. Yogi was sitting at the wooden kitchen table, a mug of tea in front of him. He was staring sightlessly at the side of the refrigerator, his eyes disturbingly blank.

"Hey, man," Connell said quietly.

Yogi looked up at him. "Oh. Hey." He looked around and seemed startled to see the tea in front of him. Mechanically, he picked it up and took a sip. "It's cold."

"Maybe you should make yourself another one," Connell said. His friend's disconnected expression was starting to unnerve him.

"I didn't make it."

Connell reached out and took the mug. He popped it into the microwave for a minute before putting it back in front of him. Unsure what to do, he excused himself and went to find Logan. Maybe she would know what to do with Yogi.

He found her in the dining room. Scattered across the table was an assortment of weapons, vials, jars, and statuettes. For a second, the image of her dancing on top of the table in that house in Provence flashed across his mind, and he smiled softly.

"Are you one of those tea-cures-whatever-ails-you kind of people?" he asked.

Logan looked up at him and shrugged. "It's what my aunt Mai does whenever my mom or I are upset. I also called your dad's house. The number was on the refrigerator."

"What for?"

"I was looking for Salome. Yogi should be with his family right now."

What's left of it, he thought with a pang in his chest.

"Is it over?" she asked.

"Yes." Bishop was dead.

Logan narrowed her eyes at him. "It better not have been you. You're in no shape for that."

"No, it wasn't me. I wanted to. Well, no, that's not right. I didn't want someone else to have to do it, but some of my ribs are still cracked. It was Mara. Dad...well, he just couldn't, so she did it for him. One lunge and it was over."

He thought about Bishop in those last moments, surrounded by a circle of Weres who had passed judgment on him. "I think he meant to stand there and take it, but he moved at the last. He tried to defend himself. But he was too slow for her."

It had been bloody, but over quickly. No one would ever doubt Mara's lethal skills again.

"Did he say anything more about why he did it?"

Connell's lip curled. "It wasn't much of an explanation."

"What did he say?"

"He grumbled about the Averys and a few others we didn't realize he had issues with—including Malcolm and me. Apparently, he really hated that his son had been passed over to be third, even though Yogi didn't care. Yogi never took the challenge to be third seriously. He only made it in the first place to please him."

He broke off and rubbed his forehead with the heel of his palm. "And he said..."

"What?"

"Bishop said that it's better to be a king of a pile of rubble than buried under it."

Logan scowled. "I don't like the sound of that," she said.

"Neither do I."

"What is all this?" he asked, gesturing to the table.

"Contraband."

He picked up a knife. It was a combat-issue Seal Pup with a serrated edge. "Are they all magical?"

She nodded.

"Why would anyone bespell a tactical knife?"

"I assume they wanted to adapt it for ritual use, the same as this antique dagger," she said, indicating a dull-looking blade with an ornately carved hilt.

Moving to the left, she picked up a mason jar from a small box. "This is the most significant thing here."

"A jam jar?" he asked, leaning over to take a sniff.

"That's what it *was*. Now it's a receptacle to hold magic. I think it was meant to store your wolf. Yours or Sammy's. But Bishop failed to capture it." She paused, setting the glass jar down on the table. "There are two others here."

She held up the box. Two jars were nestled inside, but there were four spaces.

The implication of that sunk in. "So one is missing."

"Yeah, I assume it's the one he used for Malcolm's wolf."

Connell sat down heavily on one of the dining room chairs. "So he succeeded," he rasped.

"I guess third time's a charm," she grumbled. "He seemed to think he could put wolves back as well as take them away. Maybe he thought he could put Malcolm's wolf into Sammy, but it's not here."

"Any idea where is it?"

Logan lips compressed, her eyes growing distant. "Not in this house. It's possible he traded it for the rest of this stuff. And maybe a lot more that we haven't found yet." She paused. "Did he ever challenge your father for leadership?"

"Yeah, but it wasn't a real challenge."

She frowned. "Because your father was too strong?"

He shook his head. "No, I mean Bishop didn't try to draw blood. It was just for show. We do stuff like that sometimes, when we don't agree with the alpha's decisions and want everyone to know it. Bishop was protesting letting the Averys into the pack."

"So it was more like having his objection noted? Did he fight your dad on other issues?"

He nodded. "But so do a lot of people. Wolves like to argue. It wasn't anything out of the ordinary for a pack this size. I...I just don't get what he was trying to accomplish with that staff."

"I may have some ideas... In my opinion, Bishop was just getting started. I think he was planning to take a lot more wolves, and then start mixing and matching them as he saw fit."

"How the fuck would that help him?"

Logan cocked her head, staring into space. "What if he thought he could put your wolf in Yogi or your dad's in himself? The strongest, more dominant wolf always wins a challenge right? Then he'd be chief and he could do whatever the hell he wanted. The possibilities are endless when you think you have an all-powerful magic staff at your disposal to right all your imagined wrongs."

"Fuck," he growled, planting his hands flat in front of him.

"It's worse than that."

Connell's head snapped up. Logan sounded a little scared, and suddenly, that was the worst thing that had happened all day.

"What is it?"

Logan sighed. "Bishop was using a spell to hide in plain sight. My sister Diana ran into a similar one not so long ago. From the stuff left in some of these vials, I think this spell was based on that one."

Connell fingered the tactical knife. "Makes sense. We know someone else involved gave him all this stuff. So now we know who it is. That's good news."

"It would be, but there's a problem. Those witches are already dead."

He grunted, relieved. "So Bishop got this spell from them before they died."

Logan shook her head. "This spell is more advanced. You couldn't smell Bishop, but that was the only flaw. I could see an aura when I looked at him. It just wasn't his. But if you saw those witches Diana and I fought in the street, you could *see* them, but that was all. They had no smell, no heat, and *no aura*."

"Well, that doesn't mean it wasn't them," he pointed out. "They could have easily sold a more advanced version to Bishop."

Logan crossed her arms and looked down at the table, her eyes passing over all the things on its surface. "I don't know. If they had a more advanced version, I think they would have used it on themselves."

Damn, his head was starting to hurt. "Okay, let me see if I understand this. Your theory is that there is some mysterious third party hiding in the shadows. Someone who was in league with the witches you ran into before and with Bishop now."

"Yes. And that someone has access to T'Kairie. That list is short."

Good. Now they were getting somewhere. "Who's on it?" he asked, trying not to sound too homicidal.

He needed to know because he was going to hunt down everyone on that list and question them *personally*. And it was better if Logan wasn't aware of his intentions—unfortunately, his tone didn't fool her.

"Don't worry about it," she said, giving him a narrow-eyed look.

He switched tactics. "Logan, we need to work together on this."

"No, what *you* need to do is go back to the hospital. I'm going to take this back to the others. My sisters should all be gathered at the archives by now. We need to figure out how bad this is."

"Let me go with you."

Logan closed your eyes. "Connell, I don't know what will happen to you in the currents with those injuries. You almost died." She came around the table and put her arms around his neck. "Please stay here and get better. I will come back as soon as I can."

Connell tugged hard and pulled her into his lap—and he immediately regretted it. Her elbow hit his chest, and he hissed aloud.

Wincing, Logan got off his lap gingerly. She pushed some things aside and sat on the table in front of him instead.

"Okay. I'll stay here. *For now*," he conceded from between gritted teeth. His bullet holes hadn't completely healed by shifting, and he didn't want to retry that fucked up Harry Potter thing just yet. "But when you get back, we're having that long talk about our relationship I told you about. And we *are* in a relationship."

Her mouth opened as if she wanted to object, but she didn't say anything. "*Logan*," he warned.

The little eye roll told him he'd won. "*Fine*. We are in...a...relationship."

About time. Her reluctance to admit it made him smile, but nothing worth having was easy. "Thank you," he said with a satisfied smile.

"I wouldn't thank me yet," she muttered in a little aside before giving him a wicked grin.

Evil little minx. "Behave yourself while you're gone," he ordered.

"And you don't do anything stupid while I'm gone," she countered.

The moment of levity passed. "Am I saying good-bye already?" he asked softly.

She shook her head. "No, it will be later. I have to search the woods for more of this crap. I won't be leaving for a while yet. In the meantime, do I have to go outside and hot-wire a car to get you back to the hospital?"

"Oh, you mean one of the cars you flipped over?"

She pushed her hair over her shoulder. "There is no need for sarcasm."

"You know, that SUV was Yogi's."

"I'll flip it back, okay?" she drawled.

He reached out for her hand. "I'm sure some of the guys are still waiting outside. One of them can drive me, and Yogi too, if Salome doesn't pick him up. But we're going back to my dad's house. I don't need to be in the hospital anymore."

"Connell—"

He grabbed one of her outstretched hands. "Really, imp, I'm on the mend now that I can shift again. And if I need anything, I'll call Kiely, our resident doctor."

Logan squinted at him, examining every inch of his aura. "All right. Get your butt in bed. I'll come say goodbye once I'm done."

"Are you sure you don't want to *share* the bed for a while before you go?"

Logan looked at the ceiling as if pleading for patience. "You have actual *holes* in you, and you're still a dog..."

He grinned unrepentantly. "Never doubt I have my priorities in order."

45

The sun had set when Logan walked up the stairs to the second floor of the chief's house. Her feet felt like lead.

It had taken her hours to search the woods near the Kane home. A few search spells had cut that down considerably, but she'd retraced her steps and covered every inch twice to ensure she hadn't missed anything.

But there hadn't been anything outside of what she'd found in his house and shed. He must have been supremely confident to believe no one would suspect him.

Despite Connell, Logan was glad she had to leave for a while. The atmosphere around here was heavy. She wasn't as bad as Diana when it came to dealing with emotions, but she had no idea what to do or say to the people Bishop had betrayed.

Connell appeared to have bounced back, but it was obvious that underneath his cocky brashness, he was as hurt and bewildered as everyone else.

Logan turned the corner in the hallway, hoping she had hidden the stash of magical contraband well enough. There was some bad mojo sticking to most of those objects. She hadn't wanted to bring them into the chief's house, so she'd tied the bag to the tallest branch of the highest tree in the vicinity. She would pick it up on her way to T'Kairie.

She had said goodbye to the chief and Mara, telling them she would be back soon, and explaining that she had left an insanely skilled scholar, Alec, researching solutions for Sammy's little problem. With any luck, he already had a solution waiting for her on the island.

Connell's bedroom door was open, and when she saw why, she was no longer tired. Riley was sitting on his bed, watching him sleep.

"If you don't get off that bed, I'm going to toss you out the window." She was in no mood to play games. It had been a hard fucking day.

"Actually, I was waiting for you," Riley said quietly. The towering blonde took a deep breath and stood, holding out a hand to indicate they should speak in the hallway.

Logan sighed and backed up so Riley could exit the bedroom. She reached for the door, watching Connell sleep for a moment before closing it.

Riley stood there for a very long minute without saying anything. Expecting her to start on a "you don't belong with Connell conversation," Logan crossed her arms and waited.

"Bishop is my uncle."

Oh, okay, not about Connell. She straightened. "And?"

"And I was in their house a lot. I used to babysit Sammy for a little extra cash. I never saw Bishop do anything...you know, evil, but he went out at night every once in a while. I used to wonder where he was going. He always said he was going for a run, but then he'd take his car. For a while, I thought he had a secret girlfriend. The one time Salome came home from school early, I decided to meet up with some friends at a bar a few towns over."

Logan's ears prickled. Could it be that the evil Amazon had a lead for her? "Did you see something?"

Riley handed her a piece of paper. "I saw Bishop at the same bar a little later that night. He was holed up in the corner with some man. One who wasn't a Were. I know all the male Weres around here."

Logan bit her tongue so the scathing remark she wanted to make wouldn't spill out. She opened the piece of paper. It described a blue sedan and had a license plate number. "This is the vehicle of the man he was meeting?"

Riley nodded. "Yeah. I don't even know why I wrote it down, except that I thought it was weird."

"How was it weird?"

The blonde behemoth waved her hand. "The sneaking and lying about it, and to top it off, the meeting took place at a human bar. Bishop always avoided outsiders and used to discourage Yogi and Sal from making friends with humans. That's why I figured something was up—because otherwise, there's no way he would have been caught dead at that place. But I never imagined this..."

Riley's eyes grew distant, her mouth slackening slightly.

Logan shifted her weight, surprised to feel sympathy for her annoying predecessor. "I'll follow up on this," she promised.

Riley took one last look at the closed door, a jumble of emotions in her eyes. She left without saying anything else.

Logan held up the piece of paper and took out her phone. She texted the information to her contact at the DMV, a fae goblin who owed her a favor.

Based on the model of the car, it was probably a rental, but there might be a trail to follow. She put the phone away and opened the door to Connell's bedroom to wake him for a quick goodbye.

At least, it was supposed to be quick... It was well after midnight when she finally left for T'Kairie.

46

Three weeks later, Logan landed in front of the chief's house with a thump. Her landings were normally a little softer, but she was in a hurry. She only had a little while to prepare the group for 'the solution'.

A lot of Weres were milling around the main compound today. A few surprised her by waving in a friendly fashion, although most gave her that stoic male nod that used to annoy the hell out of her.

She found the chief and Mara in the barn. They were surrounded by a bunch of teens in fighting stances. To her surprise, there were girls mixed in with the boys.

When one of the girls, a fierce-looking black Were with her hair in braids, gave her the same distant nod as the men outside, she broke into a grin—until Mara punched the chief in the face with a killer right hook.

"Whoa," she said, wincing. "Is there something I should know? Should we all start hoarding food and stocking up on batteries? Cause regime changes can be *vio-lent*."

Mara turned and smiled at her, but the chief glowered. "Mara is not challenging me for leadership of the pack. I've decided, after recent events, that some of our more talented females need to be trained alongside their brothers."

He turned to the girls. "That's because they are just as strong, just as fast, and just as capable as any man—and we don't know when or where the next danger will strike. We must all be prepared to defend our pack."

It wasn't so much the words, as the weight he gave them, that made Logan want to clap by the time he was done. A few of the kids *did* cheer, but stopped immediately when the chief gave them his alpha stare. They resumed their practice poses before Mara dismissed them to freestyle.

Logan joined the chief and Mara as they walked outside. "It's about time you started training the girls," she said. "If you like, I can show them a few things too when I have time."

"Are you trained in combat?" he asked a touch sarcastically. "Don't you just throw things at people or blow them down?"

Logan crossed her arms. "My tiger mom had me in judo the minute I could walk. These days, I'm considered an expert in over a dozen styles of martial arts," she informed him. "Gia trained me herself in krav maga and pencak silat."

Douglas stopped walking and turned to her in open-mouthed shock. "Pencak silat?" He coughed. "Well, if you have time..."

Time, shit. She was wasting it. "Oh yeah, speaking of, I actually had something to run by you about your scaly situation. Is Sammy around?"

"Yes," Mara said. "He's upstairs with Salome. He and Yogi have been bunking here for the last couple of weeks. Sal's still at school, but on the weekends, she stays here too."

That makes sense. Logan couldn't blame them for not wanting to stay at home with all those memories of their father. And she was glad the chief was embracing them, making sure they weren't ostracized from their community.

"Well, I have some news about his condition. Or lack of news..." she amended.

Mara and the chief exchanged glances. "I take it you don't have a solution?"

"Not the kind you wanted—and I put our best book nerd on it. Alec hasn't found anything that can change Sammy back into a wolf. Not yet anyway, and he's gone through most of our records. So far, he's got a big fat nada in the way of fixes. So my sister Serin suggested something."

She broke off and looked up. "And there's that something now."

High overhead, a telltale shimmering ripple approached at Mach speed. It vaguely reminded Logan of the see-through camouflage the Predator used in the movie, but in this case, it was *much* bigger.

"You may want to stand over here," she warned, hugging the wall of the barn. "We need to give him a little more room."

"Him? Him who?" Mara asked with a frown.

There was a second—much louder—thump next to them. The invisibility glamour dropped away, revealing a green-and-gold dragon roughly the size of a small cottage.

Douglas swore under his breath, and the teenagers inside the barn poured outside with shouts and exclamations. All the noise and bustle alerted the people in the house. Soon, Salome and Sammy came running outside.

"He's right there," Logan called out, pointing to Sammy.

The dragon nodded once and shifted with a small swishing sound. In its place was a much smaller bespeckled blond man with a ponytail. Fortunately for the mixed company, he was fully dressed. Unlike the wolves, dragon shifters could fashion clothing from some of their scales when in human form.

Douglas looked askance at the man's long hair and Birkenstocks as the man approached Sammy and Sal with a friendly wave. He bent down to speak to Sammy. When nothing else exciting happened, Mara ushered the other kids back into the barn with a stern command to get back to work. However, their attention wasn't on practicing their kicks and strikes. All eyes were on the two dragons who were, for some reason, practicing an intricate handshake now.

"Let me guess," the chief drawled. "His name is Draco or Drake."

Logan's lip curled. It was a fair assumption on Douglas' part. Most dragon shifters had ultra-cool names and tattoos to match. This dragon shifter was an exception. "Actually, his name is Ed."

"Ed the dragon?" Douglas asked sardonically.

Mara swallowed a laugh. "Oh. Is that short for Edward?"

Logan giggled, her sense of humor getting the better of her. "It's Edmund actually. We call him Eddie sometimes, but usually, it's just...Ed."

This time, Mara did laugh. "Okay, then."

Logan shrugged. "Until a fix is found—if one exists—Serin thought you could benefit from a mentorship of sorts. Most of the dragon shifters we know are kind of...odd, but Ed's okay. He collects novelty cookie jars."

"Cookie jars?" Douglas asked, his nose wrinkled.

Logan opened her hands. "Well, they all hoard *something*. Most have tons of money in jewels and coins tucked away, but Ed's refreshingly non-materialistic—although I'm sure his 401K is rock solid. Financial acumen is a dragon thing."

"Is it really?" Mara looked briefly intrigued, and then she humphed. "You learn something new every day."

"He'll be helpful," Logan assured them. She couldn't go out on a limb and assure them Ed was harmless. He was a dragon shifter after all, but Serin vouched for him, and Logan trusted the Water Elemental's judgement—even with what was going on with her still-missing mate.

She explained that Ed was prepared to share his experience as a dragon shifter with Sammy, including a few tricks to avoid setting things on fire when he was annoyed. The offer was accepted with typical grudging grace.

Logan turned to watch Sammy and Ed get to know each other. They were walking toward the clearing at the border of the woods, presumably to practice something dragony.

High up on the hill, she spotted some new construction. Someone was building a house overlooking the compound. Logan was about to ask if the pack had decided to give the Kane family a new house when Sammy shifted for Ed. Smiling, Ed pointed to his feet while saying something.

"I suppose this is the best solution we could have asked for," Douglas admitted. "Considering the circumstances," he qualified.

"Personally, I'm just glad Sammy can still shift," Mara said with a philosophical head bob. "He's young enough that he's the envy of all his friends. It might not stay that way when he gets older, but for now, he's still pack to everyone."

Logan acknowledged that, and then asked the question she had been dying to ask since landing. "So...where's Connell?"

"Oh, after a few days, we couldn't keep him in bed anymore," Mara informed her with a twinkle in her eye. "He said you were taking too long and decided to go after you."

"He left?" She had busted her ass to get back here, and he was *gone*?

"Yes, but he's been in touch. Mostly to complain," Douglas said with his trademark deadpan expression. "Apparently, you haven't stayed in one place long enough for him to catch up with you. He said to tell you he found the damn island by the way—his words— but you had already left."

Logan's mouth dropped open.

Mara grinned at her. "What he actually said was that he was going to nail your little butt to the floor when he caught up with you."

"My butt is *not little*," Logan grumbled. "People have got to stop saying that. I told him there was no way to get to T'Kairie without me. I can't believe he found it. But no, I wasn't there this whole time. I had to travel a lot because I was helping my sisters investigate the missing artifacts."

Once Serin had arrived and all the Elementals had gathered at the archives, the shit had hit the fan. No one had come right out and accused Jordan of stealing from them—especially since he hadn't been there to defend himself, but he was her prime suspect.

Not everyone agreed. Serin's parents and Jordan's uncle were particularly loud in their defense of him. And even Diana admitted that she hadn't picked up on any lies or anxiety from him during the little time she'd spent in his company.

Despite that, Logan was still suspicious. Either Jordan had something to do with the theft of the artifacts, or he knew something about it. It was the reason he had disappeared.

If he'd betrayed them, he was hiding. But if Jordan had stumbled on some knowledge of the robbery, then he was probably dead.

Whatever the truth was, she felt terrible for Serin. Her sister's brittle silence on the whole matter of her mate had been painful to witness. Logan suspected she was in the first stages of grief, but Serin hadn't wanted to talk about it.

Though the Mother's rules dictated they couldn't all be in the same room at the same time, she and her sisters had divided into teams to look over all the evidence. Alec had been amused by the game of musical rooms—up until Diana had punched him in the arm with a fist like a hammer. Then the quips had stopped, and he'd helped them decide which clues should be a priority. After that, they had split up and left the island, each pursuing their own lead. But hers had dried up, and she'd decided it was time to do what she could for Sammy...and to get back to Connell.

Lost in thought, she was surprised when Douglas spoke to her again. "Riley told us about the man she saw Bishop with. She said you were looking into it. Did you find anything out?"

Oh, that. She didn't have good news to share. "I'm afraid the car was a rental, and the name on the reservation an alias. To make matters worse, the rental place was a dive with no cameras."

"So it was a dead end?" Mara asked

"For now," she conceded. "Gia and my sister Serin are still running down some leads, so we may still find Bishop's supplier and the witch who has Malcolm's wolf."

She paused, unsure what else to say. Deciding it was better not to make any promises she might not be able to keep, she asked about her furry idiot instead. "I don't suppose Connell mentioned where he was the last time he called?"

Douglas almost smiled. "He said he was tired of chasing his tail, so he decided to wait for you at your home."

What the hell? "Home? I don't have a home," she said, starting to get a headache.

Logan lived on the road, in a manner of speaking. Her home was the nearest safe house. Crap, was she going to have to go all the way back to Provence to find Connell? Was that where he thought she lived?

For some reason, the two Weres in front of her were smirking. "When he called, he mentioned that he'd eaten all of your cake— twice. Your mother said if you weren't going to show up for your own birthday celebration, your aunt wasn't going to make you anymore from now on."

"*My mother?*" He was with her mother? Logan groaned. If he had tracked her mom and Aunt Mai back to their house in San Diego, she was in deep shit.

She had intended on having that serious discussion with Connell about their relationship. Yes, he was her mate, and yes, they were together. However, Logan wasn't going to give up her job for him. She doubted he would ask that of her, but she had no idea what his expectations were.

Knowing Aunt Mai, she was already planning the wedding. "I gotta go," she said, sick to her stomach.

She was airborne in the next second—although why she was hurrying to deal with the hot mess waiting in California was beyond her.

From the ground, the wolves' laughter carried an unnaturally long distance after her.

ogan did a few circuits around the block before she went through the kitchen skylight of the Li family home, a two-story bungalow not far from Balboa Park. Her mom and aunt always left the skylight open for her in good weather, and the weather was mostly good in San Diego.

All looked normal in the kitchen. There were several pots cooking on the stove, and rows of dumplings lay out on the counter ready to be steamed. Grabbing an egg tart, she munched while taking a good look around.

Logan snagged another tart and went out to the living room. It was quiet. Everything seemed in order...or at least in the normal amount of disorder.

Books were stacked in piles halfway up the walls at random intervals. They would be stacked higher, except California was earthquake country. Years ago, Logan had put her foot down and painted a line all the way around the room. It marked the maximum height her mom and aunt were allowed to stack books. There were also notepads, pens, brushes, paints, and the occasional musical instrument scattered all over the place. Her mom and aunt liked to dabble.

"Mom?" she called out in Mandarin. No answer...from anyone. *Maybe Connell left*, she thought cheerfully.

Hopping down the two stairs to the den that doubled as her mother's office, she found her distracted parent bent over her computer, typing quickly with two fingers.

"Hi, Mom." *Nothing.* She walked over and waved in her mother's face. "Mom. I'm home."

Hope finally looked up. "Oh, hello, *Baobei*. When did you get in?"

"Just now," she said, hugging her mother tightly. She leaned away and grimaced. "So I heard you've had company for a little while. I'm really sorry about that."

"Don't worry about that, *Qingaide*. Connell is a nice boy. Mai and I have agreed to give him our approval to be your mate."

Logan's mouth dropped open. "*You did?*"

"Yes." Her mother waved, a little distractedly. "He made a good case."

She sat down on her mother's desk with an audible thump. *Her mother approved of Connell.*

"What did he say?" she asked, her eyes so wide they hurt.

Her mother reached up to fix her hair and seemed surprised to find a pen tucked behind her ear. "He told us once you are officially his mate, you would be pack. It seems like a sound proposition given your work, darling. And I will sleep better knowing that big man is at your back."

She stared at her mother as if she'd grown an antennae and a tail. "Who are you and what have you done with my mother? Because that does not sound like you at all. Was it not you that told me men are nice but fundamentally unnecessary?"

That was something she had heard many times from both her mom and aunt.

Her mother shrugged philosophically. "It's one thing to be a feminist, but it's another to be stupid," Hope said reasonably. "You're an Elemental now. You have many enemies. Allies are a sound strategy. Although if Connell is going to be visiting much longer, we'll need to increase our visits to the grocery store. I had no idea how much those wolves could put away."

"Oh...sorry," Logan said weakly.

She was hard enough to feed as an Elemental. Add a wolf to that and the grocery bills would be astronomical.

"It's about time you got home," Aunt Mai clucked, bustling in with a spoon in hand. "That dog has been eating us out of house and home."

Mai's diaphanous batwing shirt floated around her like an elegant butterfly as she moved in to give her a kiss.

"Hi, Aunt Mai. I apologize for the extra houseguest."

"What you should be sorry about is missing your own birthday party. I made Nian Gao twice. Since you couldn't be bothered to come home to eat it, I suppose it was good there was a hungry dog around to eat the leftovers." She sniffed.

"Sorry about that too," Logan said, trying to look appropriately chastised. "Things have been a little crazy at work."

Her aunt softened and hugged her again. "Of course they have. You know we are very proud of you. How could we not be? You are upholding the proud legacy of Feng Po Po. Why don't you tell us all about the latest news?"

"Um, maybe later?' Logan asked hopefully. She had to talk her mate. "Did Connell leave?"

Her aunt huffed. "You didn't see him crawling around in the backyard?"

"Oh my God! Is he wolfed-out back there?" Logan asked in a panic.

She ran to the kitchen to peek out the window. Her aunt and mother followed. "If the neighbors see him, they'll call animal control," she said, craning her head to check the whole backyard.

Where was he? A wolf his size should have been glaringly obvious. It was a small backyard.

"I said *crawling*. He's practicing his other forms," Mai said, sounding grudgingly impressed.

Logan's head whipped back to her. "His other forms?" She ran outside and spotted the big snake lying in the grass. It wasn't quite a python, but it was pretty damn close.

"Holy shit!"

There was a shimmer. Suddenly, there was a very naked Connell in front of her. Blushing madly, she looked behind her, but thankfully, her parental units hadn't followed her outside.

Connell hugged her close. Frantically, she pushed him away. "Get some pants on before you do that! They're probably watching out the window."

"So what?" he said with a grin and moved in to hug her again. At least, she thought that was what he was going to do... up until he grabbed her and bit her at the base of her neck—hard.

"Hey," she protested, putting a hand to the bite.

Connell held up his hands in a victorious V. "It's official. We're mated. Let's celebrate."

That was it? Seriously? No ritual or anything like that?

"It is *not* official until you put on some pants," she hissed. "The neighbors are going to think we're nudists."

Laughing, he walked over to one of the lawn chairs on the deck and slipped on his pants. "I don't think the nudity bothers your mother or aunt. At least, it didn't when my dad shifted in front of them."

"*Your dad*? When did they see your dad shift?"

"He was here last weekend—you know, when you were supposed to be home to celebrate your birthday? Happy birthday, by the way."

"Thank you," she said dryly. "So he visited. Why did he shift in front of them?"

He paused and cocked his head. "Honestly, I've forgotten his excuse. But I think he was just showing off."

Her head was starting to spin. "Are you being serious right now?" Douglas didn't strike her as the type for that kind of display.

"Yes, because—and you'll never believe this—he likes your mom. She's a lot younger than I thought by the way. She looks, well, I can't tell how old she is, but she's in great shape."

Connell put his hand on his hips and smiled, temporarily

blinding her with his toothy white grin. "And the chief definitely
noticed," he continued. "He keeps calling her now. They spent over
two hours on the phone last night. I think he's planning to invite her
out to Colorado for a visit. Mara thinks he's smitten."

Logan lowered her head and looked at him from beneath her
lashes "He's *smitten*?"

"Mara's choice of words. Apparently, he even got a haircut. That
can only mean one thing. He's interested."

"Ugh," Logan said, tempted to cover her ears before she heard any
more disturbing news. She had thought Douglas' hair had seemed a
bit shorter and neater at the neck. "I don't want to hear more."

She rounded on him and held up a finger. "Wait, yes I do, but not
about all that grossness. Why is Aunt Mai so annoyed with you? I
thought she'd be measuring me for a wedding dress as soon as I
landed."

Connell avoided her eyes. "I may have accidentally eaten the last
pork bun at dinner last night..."

Logan was aghast. "You ate the last pork bun? Oh my God, you are
dead to her!" She waved a hand dramatically in the air. "You are never
coming back from this."

"I'll win her back," he said with lazy confidence. "I always do..."

She hated that he was probably right. What woman could resist
his charm?

Connell nudged her with his hip. "So what does your mother do
for a living? I've been here for a week and a half, and I haven't been
able to figure it out."

Logan rolled her eyes. "She's a college professor."

"When does she teach? Cause she's around the house a lot."

"She's on sabbatical this semester writing her latest book."

"What's it about?"

"War," Logan said gleefully.

"*War*?"

"Of course. It's her subject matter. She teaches history on the
world's greatest tacticians. It's a very popular series. Active military
personnel fight to audit her course."

Connell's chin drew up. "That...makes a lot of sense once you stop to think about it. It certainly explains a lot about you," he said musingly. "And Aunt Mai? Is she a chef?"

"No, she just likes to cook. She's an executive at a Fortune 500 company."

He stopped short. "Really?"

Logan resisted the urge to kick the sexist alpha male out of him. "Stop acting surprised or I'm going to punch you in the nuts."

He grinned. "But you need those."

Logan blushed like the devil. "*Hey!* Do not say anything remotely dirty like that in front of my mom."

Connell grinned, refusing to agree in order to torture her. He threw an arm over her shoulder. "So did you see our house?"

"Our *what*?"

He gave her an exasperated look. "Well, we can't live at my dad's house. We'd never have any privacy."

She stopped moving. It felt like her feet were nailed down to the floor. "Wait...is that house being constructed on the hills supposed to be ours?"

"Don't worry," he said, patting her back. "It will have lots of windows and skylights."

After a minute, she realized her mouth was open. "Look, Connell, I do want to be with you...but I'm not going to give up my job."

She waited, stomach in knots, for the bomb to drop.

Connell's brow raised, and the corner of his mouth lifted up. "That's not what I'm asking. I know how important being an Elemental is to you. Believe me, I get it. And your mom and aunt took turns lecturing me to make sure I would support you."

He leaned against the deck railing. "They didn't have to say anything. I always planned on having your back. You and I belong together. Only a few tiny things have to change. Like having a home base. It should be in Colorado—with me. And when you need to go off and do your business, go ahead and do it."

That was exactly what she wanted—what she had been afraid he was going to deny her.

Connell put his big hands on her shoulders. "I do want to come with you sometimes. If you have a particularly big job, I want in. Especially if it has anything to do with tracking down the witches that sold Bishop all that magic crap."

This was the hard part. "What about *your* job? You're the chief's second, an enforcer. And what does your father have to say about all this? What does he want? Aside from getting into my mom's pants, that is," she added with a scowl.

"Dad and I worked it out. Mara will serve as enforcer when I'm away—provisionally anyway. She's thrilled to do it, and my dad has promised to give her a fair shot."

"Wow." That was staggering news. "But Connell, think about it. Do you really want to spend your life zipping all over the world?"

Wolves tended to be homebodies. Except Connell was nodding enthusiastically. *Well, maybe not this one...*

"Except for the army, I haven't gotten much of a chance to travel. My duties at home always took precedent."

She shook her head at him. "Connell, we're not going to be sightseeing. We can't just stop at the Eiffel Tower or the Roman Colosseum whenever we want."

He shook his head at her sadly as if he couldn't believe how obtuse she was being. "As long as we're together, I don't care. If you're heading into the middle of buttfuck nowhere, I want to be with you. Now...do we have a deal?"

He held out his hand. Logan stared at it for a long time. She hadn't considered how dramatically her life would change when she knocked a werewolf on his ass outside the safe house in Provence.

Logan was used to calling the shots. She answered only to herself, her family, and the Mother. Fitting a massive werewolf into her life was going to require some dramatic changes.

"*Logan.*"

Her eyes snapped up to his. He was watching her with an expression of benign frustration.

"I love you," she blurted out.

"I know." He cocked his head at her, a little confused. "I love you too."

He kept staring at her like she was acting crazy...and then it dawned on her that to him, she was.

"You never doubted that this was going to work out in your favor, did you?"

"Nope." He laughed. "Well, okay. Maybe once or twice, I wondered, but it was only a passing thought. I knew you'd come around." He squeezed her against him before herding her to the back door.

Logan shook her head. God, he was arrogant. But it probably took someone with that kind of self-confidence to mate with an Elemental.

They walked inside. Her mom and aunt were setting the third Nian Gao cake on the table. She and Connell sat down at the table while her mom started adding candles to the top of it.

"I was relieved to find out you just turned twenty-one," he said, leaning over and nudging her. "Mara kept making jailbait jokes."

Logan frowned at him. "Who told you I was twenty-one?"

"The candles. There are twenty-one of them."

Her mother cleared her throat. "Connell, in China, you are one year old when you are born. In American years, Logan turned twenty."

Connell paled dramatically beneath his tan. "You mean, you were *nineteen* when we met?" he asked, twisting to face her.

She shrugged, wondering what was wrong with him. "We met the day before my birthday, so technically, yes."

He sat frozen. "How long have you been in the Mother's service?" he asked.

Logan helped her mother hand out the dessert plates. "Since my seventeenth birthday."

Connell groaned and put his face in his hands.

"What's wrong?" her mother asked.

"My sister was right. I'm a cradle robber."

Aunt Mai tsked dismissively. Giving Connell's distress the attention it deserved, Logan blew out her candles and happily accepted a piece of cake.

"Aren't you even going to ask me how old I am?" he eventually asked in irritation.

"You're about fifty-two," she said cheerfully.

"Give or take a few months," her mother added helpfully.

"*You know*?" he asked in shock, looking at each of them in turn.

"Of course we do. It's not a problem," Aunt Mai said.

"It's not?"

"Do you want to know how big the age difference is between Diana and Alec? Cause they've got us beat by a few centuries," Logan informed him, taking a bite of her dessert.

Connell still looked a little green, so she rubbed his back in soothing circles. "It's different for Supes," she reminded him.

"I guess that's true," he said thoughtfully. His color started to come back. He tapped his fingers on the table. "In a few centuries, the age gap won't make a difference."

"That's the spirit." Logan laughed.

He sat there silently eating his portion for a few minutes. And then another. After a third, he was back to normal. "Hey, did you see my snake form?" he asked eagerly, setting his fork aside as her mom and aunt started clearing everything away.

By the Mother, she had! "Sorry! These totally distracted me," she said, waving at his ten-pack abs. "Congratulations on leveling up."

How could she have forgotten about that? It was a huge achievement for a shifter to gain a second form—one she would have thought impossible just a few weeks ago.

I knew I should have made him put a shirt back on. Those abs were a killer distraction.

Then she remembered something and smiled wickedly. "Acquiring a second form is an amazing feat. Even if it wasn't what you were going for..."

Connell narrowed his eyes at her, and she elbowed him in the ribs. "C'mon, admit it. You were trying for a dragon," she teased.

He didn't bother to deny it. His smile turned cocky. "I'll get there."

"I know you will, babe. I know you will."

The End

Continue the Award-Winning Elementals Series with Water, A Readers' Favorite Bronze Medal winner!

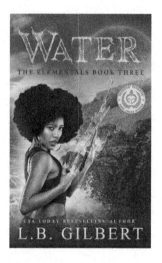

As a high-ranking elemental in ass-kicking stilettos, Serin takes no prisoners as she explores the truth.

Hellbent on seeking justice and answers for her mate's mysterious disappearance, Serin takes no prisoners as she explores the truth. As a high-ranking elemental in ass-kicking stilettos, she embarks upon a perilous quest for vengeance.

In her manhunt, Serin encounters DEA agent Daniel Romero, who's strangely connected to her bonded mate's vanishing. Teaming up with the officer forces Serin to accept the truth. Daniel just may be her destiny. And with time running out, Serin knows that she must protect her sisters and ignore the pull she has for Daniel. Come Hell or high water, Serin will put her life on the line to protect everyone-- and everything she loves.

Free on Kindle Unlimited

AFTERWORD

Thank you for reading Air! You can listen and download L'exode by blob, Logan's favorite composer, here:
http://www.elementalauthor.com/lexode-un-voyage-mystique-a-travers-les-plaines/

If you like it, comment on Soundcloud!
https://soundcloud.com/beublo/lexode-un-voyage-mystique-a-travers-les-plaines

Also reviews are an author's bread and butter. If you liked the story please consider leaving a review.

Subscribe to the L.B. Gilbert Newsletter for a *free* full-length novel!
http://www.elementalauthor.com/newsletter/

ABOUT THE AUTHOR

USA Today bestselling author L.B. Gilbert spent years getting degrees from the most prestigious universities in America, including a PhD that she is not using at all. She moved to France for work and found love. She's married now and living in Toulouse with one adorable half-French baby.

She has always enjoyed reading books as far from her reality as possible, but eventually the voices in her head told her to write her own. And, so far, the voices are enjoying them. You can check out the geeky things she likes on twitter or Facebook.

And if you like a little more steam with your Fire, check out the author's romance erotica titles under her married name Lucy Leroux...

www.elementalauthor.com

or

http://www.authorlucyleroux.com

Made in the USA
Middletown, DE
30 May 2020